Gathering In

Lela Markham

Published by Breakwater Harbor Books

A Word from Lela Markham

Thank you for reading my book. If you enjoyed it, please take a moment to leave me a review at your favorite retailer. Only with your help can independent writers like me reach more readers. I appreciate it!

Transformation Project is at root a polemic against our rigged system of elites telling all of us "lessers" what to do while failing miserably on so many levels in their attempt to centrally manage the society. The political winds of change currently sweeping our nation have not altered my opinion that we're headed in a wrong direction and that the danger to all of comes from those who would be our "leaders". Some of them mean well, but the belief that they are more qualified than ordinary people to "lead" us is the primary problem. Ultimately, I don't think politics will be what saves us, so you'll notice my characters don't really talk about partisan politics much. You know Rob is a "libertarian" elected to a non-partisan mayoral position. You can surmise Katharine Sullivan is a Democrat, but you'll notice she's become a Second Amendment babe in *Day's End* since reality has now set in. You might have noticed that the Army didn't care at all about Ren Sullivan's politics when they needed him to be in charge.

I don't believe politics – choosing who will be in charge this year or next – will save us. If there is any salvation coming our way, it will be from the actions of ordinary people living their everyday lives – milking cows and harvesting apples, inventing the next world-changing technology. I know the propaganda machines of today insist politics is the center of all power, but it's really just swapping one crazy train for another at periodic intervals. Until we start doing something differently, we cannot expect different results.

Power corrupts and absolute power corrupts absolutely. The White House is as close to absolute power as you will ever find. Remember that as we head into the 2020 Presidential election. Look at all who are running and ask yourself – are any of these people "incorruptible"? Then why would you want to make him or her ruler over you?

Lela Markham

Thanks!

This book is dedicated to my daughter Ivyl, a gypsy musician who lives life by her own terms, often utterly baffling her mother. I am so blessed to know this young person. She lights up the world with her presence and she is seemingly unafraid to face new challenges every day. Use your powers well, kiddo.

No book is the work of a single individual. The author gets all the glory but standing behind every published writer is a host of support personnel. Thank you to my church's community group for all the Biblical "debates" that have given me such lovely conversations for the Delaneys to have with their spiritual black sheep.

Table of Contents

"[T]he normal and the everyday are often amazingly unstoppable, and what is unimaginable is the cessation of them. The world is resilient, and, no matter what interruptions occur, people so badly want to return to their lives and get on with them. A veneer of civilization descends quickly, like a shining rain. Dust is settled."

— Lorrie Moore

Gathering In

Book 5

Transformation Project

Prologue

It's funny how your perspective on who is your neighbor can change when resources become scarce. Emmaus lucked out compared to most places after the Pulse. We were surrounded by corn. When we harvested all that belonged to us or the corporations abandoned, we had enough food to last until December or January. Or to feed half the five thousand residents who lived in the area until spring, when hopefully things might change for the better. Some families had more. The farmers had more. Most of them wanted something in return for sharing, which meant that shopkeepers, mayors and school teachers had to find something they could trade. Without electricity and with a

1

lot of engines permanently stalled by the Pulse that most often meant labor.

Passersby, running from the cold northern winter that loomed – well, they weren't welcome at all. Day after day, they pushed past our borders, now secured by electrified barbed wire and men and women carrying AR15s. It felt so wrong and yet there was no arguing with the fact those migrants represented starvation for us. It wasn't our fault they hadn't prepared for terrorist attacks. We hadn't expected to either, but we'd grown the food so it was ours. We either secured our borders so we who were inside could live – maybe – or we didn't, and we all starved.

In a world that had spun out of control, there were no good answers for how to live our increasingly fragile lives. Some reached out, others turned in, and some would make decisions with devastating results. And none of them were evil – not the migrants, not the townspeople -- maybe the USDA.

JT Delaney

Fried

Seattle - Night of the Pulse

The night of the pulse, Geo Tully and Wes Marcus were in the basement of Wes' aunt's home that had become their safehouse.

Wes, a wiry com tech barely old enough to shave regularly, held up a photo album that showed a man standing in front of the post-World War 2 bungalow with a shovel. The front door stood behind him, but not the view of the house that Geo recognized. The articulated arm of a backhoe could be seen on the edge of the frame.

"The porch is an addition," Geo acknowledged.

A Navy Seal from Kansas, Geo towered over his Seattle-raised compatriot. They'd thrown in together when Bunnell & Wilson's Knights Industry division seized control of the city by murdering military personnel. Wes' uncle Fred had been an urban survivalist before he died a few years ago and

3

his aunt Connie had died in Portland's bomb attack. Their house had been a safe haven for two fugitives, so far.

"And look at how deep the hole is behind him."

Geo turned to the front wall of the basement. The shelves had kept him from investigating here. They appeared to be attached to the wall, but when he ran his hand along the back edge of the shelving unit, he found a throw-bolt. He pulled it down and tugged on the shelves, swinging them out away from the wall. Hinged on the far side, they glided on hidden casters. Behind the shelves an open space stretched the length of the porch. Geo tried the light on the ceiling, but it didn't turn on. He used the flashlight on his phone to illuminate the small room. A ham radio sat at one end, covered with plastic, while storage boxes filled the other end.

"I knew that tower had to still have a use." Wes squatted down to look under the table the radio sat on. As an Army communication tech, he knew radios. "He left it disconnected. It'll take me a moment."

The light bulb in the main basement flared and popped off. Wes smacked his head on the underside of the table. Geo's phone light went out.

"What's that smell?" Wes stood, sniffing.

"My phone just fried, I think."

They fumbled around in the dark to find the stairs and make their way to the kitchen. Duke, the Labrador retriever, stood in the living room, staring at the window and whining.

Geo peeked out the curtains as the neighbors came out on their porch, staring around.

"You smell that?" Wes asked. "I'm going to go check for fire."

"Do you *hear* that?"

Duke whined louder. Raucous voices filtered in through the glass. Geo watched as the neighbors ran off their porch. Wes swept the front door open.

"What the hell?" Geo growled.

"They need help." Wes ran into the street.

"Stay, Duke," Geo ordered and followed his stupid partner into the street, where the neighbors could get a full view of their high-and-tights. They'd agreed they wouldn't do that, but Wes had forced them all in. A municipal bus sat at the corner, smoke pouring out of its windows as the people inside tried to get out, screaming, kicking, punching at the glass, but when one window shattered, it just fed the fire that doomed them.

Wes ran to the rear passenger door and tried to pull it open, convulsing and chewing his tongue, smoke rising from his body.

The neighbors screamed as a man leaped from the burst side window, his clothes and hair on fire. Someone smothered the flames with a heavy blanket. A woman lowered herself to the ground and convulsed, unable to let go of the bus and now acting as a conduit for the electricity. Someone flung their preschooler in Geo's general direction and instinct alone caused him to catch her. Geo handed the wailing child off to a woman and

5

turned, expecting to rescue more people, but the fire erupted fully then and engulfed everyone on board.

Wes's eyes turned to goo. Gagging, Geo made his way into the house, muttering under his breath about the stupidity of Army pukes, signaling for Duke to follow him. Donning a headlamp so he could see in the dark basement, he carried the guns into the radio room, stowed what non-perishable food and water they had in there and packed a kit to get ready to leave on a moment's notice. Somewhere along the line, he turned off the spaghetti sauce Wes had been making and then he went up to the craft room which offered him the best view of the street. Duke followed him, putting his glossy black head on his thigh.

"Sorry, boy. You're alone in the world now. Even I'm going to have to abandon you."

Geo would have to leave sooner rather than later. Wes's body would be part of an investigation and that investigation would lead to the house, which would lead to him and he had no intentions of just sitting around waiting for his life to end.

The timing was a pity. Wes could have used that radio equipment to listen in to Bunnell & Wilson and devise an escape plan out of the city. Having to move now missed an opportunity. Survival scored a high priority, but accomplishing the mission was paramount. Without a line of command, Geo pursued the mission most obvious -- determine what B&W had planned and what had happened to the military in Seattle.

The stench of burning bodies worked its way in through the closed windows and Duke occasionally whined with concern. Eventually, a B&W truck pulled up. On a whim, Geo turned on Wes's hand-held walkie and played with the bands until he picked up the conversation.

"...twenty-three. Only one survivor – a four-year-old child. Over." A female Knight spoke with her supervisor, also a female, while men in rubber suits and masks began to load burned bodies in the bed of the truck.

"Do you have contact information? Over."

"She knows her first and last name and her address. Over."

The two on the radio exchanged information.

"Who is she staying with? Over."

"Neighbors, but they don't feel they have resources to keep her. Over."

"Not our problem. I'll forward the information to the crew over in that area, see if a relative comes forward. If not, it's not our problem. Over."

"Ma'am, all due respect, but if we want the public's cooperation, don't you think this needs to be our problem? Over."

"You're preaching to the choir, but I'm not in charge and until this crisis is stowed, we need to stay focused. I suggest you offer your thoughts on the situation via the employee portal. B&W has always been willing to listen to the thoughts of employees to improve customer service. Over."

A long painful silence ensued and then the Knight spoke.

"About these bodies, ma'am? Over."

"Gather what ID you can. The pulse fracked the government databases, so all we can do is try to identify these people. Transport them to Evergreen Crematorium on Aurora. We can't leave bodies for personal identification. The risk of disease is too high. Over."

"Roger that, ma'am. I'll relay to my team. Over and out."

No discussion of door-to-door searches or even interviews. A muni bus catches fire during an electrical surge and they deal with the crisis without suspecting the people who live along the bus lines. That seemed unlikely, so Geo took no chances. He created a sleeping area just outside the radio room. If a breach at the front door occurred, he could roll inside and lock himself in and hopefully survive the encounter. Geo admired Fred, though he'd never met the far-thinking man who had included a battery bank as part of this radio room. The blackout extended to the entire city, but the charge levels on the batteries looked good.

Around midnight, Geo powered up the radio and played with the gauges until he brought in a conversation.

"Sunset Hills. All's quiet here. Over."

He adjusted a dial a bit more.

"Headquarters, this is Appleton at Seattle Seaport Terminal. I need a high-ranking officer here immediately to debrief on intelligence to do with this afternoon's electrical surge. Over."

They talked back and forth and then someone at Headquarters said, "There's not been enough time for someone from the launch ship to have made it to Puget Sound. Over."

"Sir, we really shouldn't discuss this over open coms. Please, send someone immediately. You're going to want to hear this. Over."

"Dispatching Hess, Malcolm, to your location. Over and out."

Though tempted to stay up all night and listen, Geo couldn't afford to drain the batteries listening to radio silence. He would investigate the generator in the shed come morning and Wes had mentioned a bike charging station for when the fuel ran out.

Geo still slept in the basement, just in case.

Tunnel Access

Emmaus, Kansas - Four Days Later

Shane Delaney stayed low as he worked his way through the woods to the stone wall that graced the edge of the Shack's circular driveway. The home of Emmaus' richest resident, the three-story clapboard house with imposing stone chimneys and matching verandas didn't look different from any of the other times Shane came up the driveway, except for the dead body lying in the bushes.

Shane wished his Kevlar weren't locked up in the Jericho Hotel, held captive by a security system rendered mad by the Pulse. Had that really been less than a week ago? So much had happened in such a short amount of time that it felt like months rather than days.

Joe Kelly, Emmaus' squeaky-new police chief, looked incredibly uncomfortable in his bulletproof vest. Shane knelt between him and Jos, the teenager who had discovered the situation. A USDA cargo truck sat in the driveway along with one of their pickups. Flies buzzed around a body dumped

11

in the bushes. Jos used binoculars to view the body.

"I don't know. It could be the groom like you said."

"What's going on?" Shane startled as his father Mayor Rob Delaney seemingly materialized right at his shoulder. "You need to give me lessons in that," he muttered. "After."

"What's the situation?" Rob asked. A split second later, a bullet ricocheted off a stone on top of the wall. Jos and Joe flinched. Rob scarcely seemed to notice. Shane paid attention to the attic window it had come from.

"Three shooters." Joe might be green-as-grass in his new role, but he'd been a cop for five years and had graduated from the Police Academy with top marks. Of course, a cop in Emmaus didn't usually deal with shootouts and kidnappings. A new era dawned following the September bombings. "One high and to the right, one on the second floor and to the left. The one on the ground floor is mobile. There's no way to approach the house without exposing us to fire."

"Any sign of Allison Sullivan?" Rob still had a human soul that cared about the people he represented. Shane had completely forgotten about Ren Sullivan's granddaughter.

"Not so far," Jos reported. Grandson of the local market owner, he'd been sent to check on Allison Sullivan, the only member of the family currently in Emmaus. Most kids would have run from someone shooting at them. Jos had gotten help and come back with Joe to complete the mission. "That body's been there awhile - days." Trained to hunt by his grandfather, the kid hardly blinked at blood and death, a good attribute when surrounded by it. "I can't remember seeing Allison since before the Pulse."

"That was an adult male, about Jos' size, so probably Melvin Kirsch." Rob had done three tours in Vietnam, so nobody questioned his ability to make forensic observations even at a distance. "This house has a panic room, so she might be just fine. Either way, we have to neutralize this threat. Anyone else showing up, son?"

"I don't have the manpower." Shane hadn't even tried to gather a posse. "If the crowds passing by decide to push it, what I've got won't hold, but we need the visual, so they won't push it."

Rob nodded, scanning the three-story façade of the mansion. He didn't really care about Shane's manpower problems – not until the current crisis passed.

"Assuming the roster was correct, four against three isn't bad odds, but they have the high ground. Joe, you are now the Police Chief, in case you hadn't already guessed. You need to get on the bullhorn, see if you can negotiate a surrender. Shane, besides kick-boxing, how's your hand-to-hand?"

Better than Mike's, not as good as Chavez's, but neither of them are an option right now.

13

"I didn't fight in the jungles. The insurgents in Miristan are mostly armed with guns, so up close and personal wasn't an everyday thing. But yeah, I've done some close fighting. How bloody do you want me to get?"

"Let's see if we can negotiate before we have to kill people," Joe muttered. He'd prepped the bullhorn and now he mouthed "Chief Kelly" three times before he put it to his mouth.

"This is Chief Joseph Kelly of the Emmaus Police Department. Stand down immediately."

This shot came from the ground floor.

"Go away. You have no jurisdiction here," a man called back. "We're USDA, federal agents, involved in a lawful operation. Interference with our operation is grounds for armed response."

"As if the dozen shots they've fired at us already didn't make that clear," Jos muttered, still scanning the facade of the building with his rifle scope. "I have an almost clear shot at the guy on the second floor." The kid had shown he would make a good sniper – good eyes, calm nerves. Shane knew there was something wrong with evaluating a 15-year-old as a sniper, but times were changing, and he needed to adapt to them.

"Hang loose," Shane encouraged. "Once we start shooting, negotiation becomes less possible."

"Your agents fired at a community member checking on the homeowners," Joe countered at Rob's suggestion.

"Your community executed three USDA agents for doing their jobs. We don't trust any of you."

Keying the bullhorn off, Joe gave Rob a slightly annoyed look, muttering "Speaking of actions we can't take back."

"Nor would I." Shane knew his father hadn't wanted to make that decision, but the City Council had insisted and there really weren't any other options.

"I think we're wasting our time here," Shane said.

"I agree," Rob replied. "Joe, keep them entertained. Ask them questions. See if you can ascertain if Allison is still alive and if they have any hostages, including her. Shane, with me."

Shane held up his radio.

"Probably going to go radio silence, but once we're inside, I'll key it once and if we want you to open fire on the house, I'll key it twice."

Joe gave him a thumbs-up and Shane followed Rob. Behind him, he heard Joe deepen his friendly tone.

"I know how you feel about tight spaces, but there's a revenuer's tunnel from the stable to the main house and it's the only way I can think of to get there without getting shot," Rob explained.

They went up the driveway far enough to be out of view of the Shack and crossed to the stables. Six saddle horses stood despondently in their stalls, nosing empty buckets. Another shot made them blow and stomp nervously.

A small cellar resided under one part of the stable and Rob and Shane filled it with their height and shoulders. A set of shelves against one wall pivoted on hinges to allow access to an earthen tunnel choked with cobwebs and dead tree roots. Shane muttered a swear word at the dead air that wafted into his face.

"You going to be able to do this?" Rob asked.

Shane climbed the ladder a bit so he could take a deep breath before looking down the tunnel again.

"Yeah. I control it, it doesn't control me."

"We can't afford a panic attack in there."

"I was five, Dad."

"And nine."

"And almost 20 years later." He thumbed his chest.

"You spelunk now, son?"

"No, but I toured Carlsbad and managed just fine." To himself, Shane admitted he'd drank three beers before they'd gotten there, hiked the Natural Entrance Trail first and been so mellow after that he'd only started to feel antsy toward the end of the tour of the caves. But Rob didn't need to know what happened inside his head. All thoughts are allowed, actions and reactions are limited.

"And I drove the Belly of the Beast in Shalimar Province."

Rob raised an eyebrow. Shane had assumed the identity of a half-Miristani and gone in as a contractor. The tunnels of Shalimar were quite extensive and big enough to drive a truck through. This tunnel held a lot more to daunt the carbon-dioxide sensitive.

Rob handed him a flashlight from the shelves that was solid enough to use as a weapon. The beam shined strongly.

"So, I'm going to go first since I've been here before. That should clean out the cobwebs and the worst of the tree roots."

"How do you know it's open at the other end?"

"I know Ren. He'd have told me if he sealed it. If Joseph had had any sisters your age, you'd know all about it. Cai did." Rob looked down at Shane's sturdy boots. "Good, we're ready if we encounter snakes."

"Never had an issue with snakes – or spiders. Just the enclosed spaces they hang out in. So, I'm going to be hanging back as far as I can to give myself breathing space. If I don't follow you, come and drag me through, but it probably won't be necessary."

"That's hardly a ringing endorsement for a commando raid, but you're all I've got, so let's get this done." With that, Rob entered the tunnel, using his broad shoulders to break off dried roots and sweep away cobwebs.

Shane did not have an issue with spiders, snakes or mice, but he also knew he didn't need any additional stimuli going through any tunnel. While Rob cleared the trail, he took advantage of the ladder to get a little bit more air. He settled his

AR-15 across his back, checked the mag in his 9 mm and launched into the tunnel.

Rob's light bounced off the wall ahead. He'd turned a corner, moving out of sight. Shane preferred to go quickly, so not to have to breathe in the tunnel, but the tunnel proved longer than he'd thought it would be and he immediately regretted not risking covering his face with a bandana as the smell of dirt and cobwebs filled his nostrils. The beams were old-growth oak dunnage, probably strong as iron, so Shane didn't fear being buried alive, but plenty of dust floated in the air from Rob's passage. At the bend, Shane realized Rob wasn't through the other side yet and he paused, trying not to breathe deeply. His heartbeat increased, sweat coated his underarms and wetted his shirt and his vision started to darken around the edges. He backed up to go back to the stable, knowing that if he had to wait even a minute or two longer for fresh air, he'd be no use to Rob at the other end.

He overestimated the distance to the wall, brushing the dirt, which sifted down onto him, clogging the air. Hands reached out to grab him and *she* stared into his eyes from over her silk hijab. *No, not now! I can't afford this now.*

***

They'd been told to expect a friendly village, an increasingly elusive concept in the Mirage these days, so they'd all opted to carry for their own safety. A young boy of about ten met them at the town entrance and jabbered away in a patois

18

mixture of the local dialect, the Miragan central tongue and English. Although it seemed impossible for foreigners to master Miragan, Shane's grasp of Arabic and the months spent with Sera meant he understood enough of the boy's chatter that they could at least communicate rudimentarily.

"What's he saying?" Commander Roth asked Shane.

"The levees came through about a week ago, but they haven't been back. They took his older brother despite being younger than draft age. They took his father last year. He's hoping for some food aid as he's feeding three younger siblings by himself."

"Do you believe that?" Logan demanded.

"I do. Take a look. You see any adult males around here?"

"Not on the ground, but I'll bet there's plenty squirreled away in the attics."

"Where's the headman's hut?" Roth asked.

The boy seemed eager to cooperate and they moved deeper into the village's narrow lanes, leaving squads behind as they went, until only Mike, Killgore, Roth and Shane continued. One moment it seemed friendly, and the next an icy finger ran down Shane's back. He turned his head toward the left to see the barely perceived danger. A woman in a dark cotton hijab materialized in a doorway. Shane opened his mouth to call a warning and several shots to his chest slammed him back into a stone wall.

Another Life to Save

Cai Delaney tried to decide who was tougher – mercenary Mike Sanchez or his wife, physician Marnie Callahan. Mike shook violently as Cai held him down so Marnie could remove the rudimentary stitches that had stopped him from bleeding to death yesterday. Sweat poured off Mike as he cursed and swore. Cai had never really wondered about the expression "burning up" before, but Mike's bronze skin felt hot enough to melt something near. The skin to either side of the stitches was red and inflamed. Blood and pus leaked as Marnie snipped.

"Get it cleaned up," Marnie told nurse Lila. "Cai, I need to speak with you in the other room, please."

Mike twisted out of Cai's grip and hurled over the edge of the gurney.

"He'll bring something to clean it up," Marnie told Lila as she led Cai out of the room.

She dumped her gloves in a waste basket in the corridor.

"Who is he?"

"Mike Sanchez."

"Who?"

Cai had only known Mike for a few days and didn't know much, so focusing on the salient facts wasn't hard.

"Works for Knight Industries. He was Shane's partner for the last half-decade. He rescued me from captivity in Hutchinson and got me halfway here before I had to rescue him."

"You did the stitches?"

"No, a farmer's wife. She warned us that she didn't have the means or the skill to properly clean his wound."

"Probably got dirty cloth too deep in, hence the infection. While I am personally glad you're not still in Hutchinson, I need a reason to waste antibiotics and blood products on a stranger."

"What the farmer's wife said too, and so the infection." Marnie mocked him, but still waited for his rationale. "I owe him my life and Shane values him more highly than I do, plus he just dragged in a truckload of food for the town."

"He's AB positive. I've got one unit of AB and I don't know when I'll get another. I'm not wasting it on someone with sepsis."

"So, you're just going to let him die?"

Marnie sighed.

"No. We'll clean out the wound, install a drain and hit him with Cipro, but unless we get more blood, he's going to take a long time to heal – if he makes it. And, I can't afford the painkillers, so you had better master the art of holding someone down to the table."

"Yes, ma'am."

She laid a hard kiss on his mouth and then indicated a door marked "janitorial." Telling him to clean up the vomit, she turned to rescrub.

Safe House

Amisi Ceylon thought she'd driven through some quintessentially American small towns, but she'd not been inside one of their cordons. What a genius idea to control entry, forcing everyone to come in under the overpass. People appeared to be going about their lives inside the wire, although here and there, she saw signs reminding people not to touch the fences.

"Wow, they've cordoned farms," Javier Chavez whispered.

"Did any of the other towns do that?"

"No, not that I saw. It's ambitious."

"The guy that let us in … he's one of yours?"

"Contractor. He's not a guy you want to sneak up on in an alley."

"Neither are you."

"No, I am not. It's a genius idea to electrify the fences. It means they have to cover the intersections only."

"That means we're safe from the crowds we saw on the roads?"

"Safer. I don't guarantee electrified barbed wire is going to keep a truly determined group out if they're prepared to breach the wire. And, it could be a problem for us if we want to get out. Turn right here. It'll be the first left."

"Have you ever been here?"

"No, but I studied maps before I decided on my destination. Look, they know we're coming, but we're not in yet. They're going to want to question us – most especially you. Don't lie. Grant Rigby is a highly trained operative and he will know if you're lying. And if you lie, we're out on the road and I haven't got the resources to keep us alive out there. But you can secure your place here by being honest, telling them what you need and being giving with your medical skills."

"If I weren't with you …."

"I won't let them turn you out on the road alone."

"Javi, you need this place. You can't heal without a safe place to rest."

"I didn't expect to get out of this life alive, Ami, but I do need my eyes to do what I do. I have got an ever-loving headache right now."

"It rests on my trusting these people?"

"No, not trusting *them*. Trusting *me*."

She pulled up to the gate. The safe house advertised as a bed and breakfast, but the tall fence seemed off-putting, though what she could see of the house looked pleasant enough.

"Don't look now, but you're on Candid Camera." She wouldn't have recognized the camera hidden in the gate light if he hadn't pointed it out.

"What do people mean by that?" she asked. "I asked my aunt once and she didn't know."

"I think it was an old TV show. Ask someone who had a normal American childhood. I didn't."

"We are a pair."

"Are we? I'm not used to women like you."

"Like me? Am I different from other women?"

"Different than the ones I've known. I'm intrigued by that, if it means anything. And we want to sell that as well."

"With them?"

He nodded just as the gate opened. A young man in jeans and a sweatshirt waved them in, directing them to park under a tarp carport. A middle aged man in jeans and a plaid shirt stepped out of the shadows beside a motorhome. Javi got out of the car and let the man pat him down. Ami assumed the older man was Grant Rigby. After he checked Javi's gun, he gave it back to him and they stood there talking for a moment. The young man had closed and bolted the gate. While the fence looked like wood plank on the outside, metal plating lined it. The house looked ordinary – white with green trim and fake Doric columns supporting a gracious front porch. The house and the fence did not go together.

The younger man came to her door and indicated she should step out. He patted her down, very professionally and not intrusively, checked her gun and gave it back to her and then indicated she should join the other two on the other side of the car.

"Amisi Ceylon, Grant Rigby," Javi identified. "And, this is ...?"

"Dylan," the younger man said.

"Let's go in and talk," Grant suggested. It sounded like a suggestion, but Ami knew it wasn't. If either of them refused, she feared they'd die. These people or people like them had trained Javi. The knowledge that they were killers held a terrifying comfort because while they could kill Ami, they also could protect her.

They entered the motorhome. Javi took the outside of their side of the table. Grant slid into the opposite seat. Dylan stayed standing, leaning against the counter, casual like a big cat ready to pounce, but not wishing to reveal its intentions. Ami had noted the same stance from Javi on more than one occasion. Trained behavior? Dylan didn't draw a gun as Javi would. He queued up a tablet computer.

"Javi says we can trust you and that we won't regret the extra mouth to feed. Convince me that Javi knows what he's talking about."

"I'll answer your questions."

"Who are you?"

"Amisi Ceylon, born Cairo, April 24, 27 years ago. Naturalized American citizen at 18. Graduated John Hopkins Medical School, interned at University of Maryland. Until the bombs, I was a resident at Northwestern Memorial in Chicago in internal medicine and virology."

"You worked the Emergency Room at UMB," Dylan said, looking at his tablet.

"Could be useful." Grant looked like an accountant. Ami had heard or read that a lot of FBI agents were accountants. Dylan looked like a college student getting a computer science degree.

"We also brought medical supplies with us," Javi said. "You can have them to pay for our food."

"Thinking ahead. Is there some frosting to this cake?" Grant directed his question to Ami.

Now to sell herself and somehow convince people she didn't know that she trusted them when she didn't.

"A colleague who worked for the Institute of Human Virology gave me a thumb drive and some vials. I don't know for certain, but I believe they have something to do with this." She indicated the larger situation. "We heard rumors of a breach at a CDC lab in upstate New York and some viruses were missing.

Grant and Dylan exchanged glances. She'd heard those rumors from her colleagues at the virology conference when news of the bombs had come in. She supposed Samira might have sown the rumors while she was looking for Ami, but that subtle exchange of gaze suggested they'd heard the news too.

Meanwhile, Javi fiddled with his sunglasses. He had that look that said the headache had reached a point where he needed darkness. She could see him blinking, a sign his eyes were burning. He needed to be here.

"I need a password breaker and I don't know what else to access the thumb drive and then access to a lab for the vials."

"If we let you stay, Chavez, you're going to have to watch yourself." Grant's eyes took a hard cast. "My children are here."

"Of course," Javi said. "I'm not going to cause any trouble. I already got warned by – what's his name here – Shane? I knew he was from Emmaus, but I wasn't expecting him to be here."

Ami blocked Javi's hand from rubbing his eye.

"He came home for a visit when the bombs hit, and the town is benefiting from his skills."

"He hated it here. When the winter closes in, he's going to go stir crazy." Javi's last words came out choked. He put his hands on either side of his forehead and squeezed his eyes shut.

"What happened?" Grant asked.

Javi's full lips squeezed into a flat line and he swallowed tightly.

"His eyes were open during the Pulse, looking right at the sky. He's got all the symptoms of flash blindness. His eyes are getting better, but he needs a place to rest where it's dark and I now have medication to more appropriately treat it. But he needs rest now."

"We're going to let you stay and Dylan has the computer equipment for this thumb drive. One room or two?"

"Do you have one with two beds?" Javi asked. Despite his discomfort, he cast an admiring look Ami's way, selling that they were lovers.

"Yeah," Dylan said, suppressing a smile.

"Let's get the car unpacked," Javi told Ami.

"You're going to lie down. I'll unload the car." She stood and looked at Dylan, somehow knowing he was in charge of room arrangements. "The room needs to be dark."

"I'll let your mom know," Grant said. 'Help with unloading the car. Come with me, Javi."

Following them out of the motorhome, Ami paused just as she stepped onto the ground. She didn't trust this. Javi needed to be here and she needed their computer equipment, but whoever these people were, she was not part of their in-group and she knew enough to keep her deep suspicion to herself.

Getting Bloody

Shane struggled to get his mouth free of the large hand across it, but it held firm, cutting off his air and muffling any protests he might make.

"I'll let you go when you calm down. Tap my arm three times when you can control yourself. Take a deep breath. Breathe in, breathe out. Better now?"

Shane recognized Rob held him in a headlock, but not in the tunnel. The tunnel did not have flocked wallpaper or a tin ceiling. They were supposed to be rescuing Allison Sullivan from the last of the USDA agents. He did not have time for a panic attack right now. He tapped Rob's forearm. The pressure on his windpipe eased and blessed basement-fresh air flowed back into his lungs.

"What the hell happened?" Rob whispered.

Shane shook his head, concentrating on breathing without hyperventilating. Scared to attempt speaking he signed, *"I scream?"*

"You silently curled up into a ball. You get bit by a snake or what?"

Somewhere above them, a rifle reported.

"Can you do this?" Rob asked. Shane's heart pounded a conga line as the extra oxygen infusing his cells sharpened his awareness.

"If the alternative is to go back through the tunnel – yes, absolutely. This is the legendary speakeasy, isn't it?"

"It is." One end of the room held an ornate bar with mirrored shelves behind, currently unadorned. A line of booths was pushed up against one wall, but the majority of the space was a hardwood dance floor and a raised stage for a band. A hundred people could party in close quarters here - - Shane's idea of socializing hell, barely tolerable with a lot of alcohol. "That tunnel used to come up through the mines in the 1920s, back when the speakeasy was the only structure on this ridge."

"Good to know." Shane recognized Rob's attempt to distract him, but he'd moved beyond those techniques a long time ago. He pulled out his radio and keyed the mic once. "I think we might be on camera," he noted, pointing to a live camera up in the corner of the room. He suppressed his hands from shaking with adrenaline as he silenced the radio and clipped it to his belt again.

"If it's the USDA we're dead already. If it's Allison, she knows we're here."

Shane doubted the girl still lived, but it didn't matter because they couldn't let the USDA run free inside the wire. He didn't think he'd have recognized Allison. She'd been in elementary school the last time he saw her. In some ways that was good – one less face to haunt his nightmares.

"Our plan?"

"The stairs to the kitchen are right outside that door. That's at the left end of the house toward the back. We go upstairs. If it's clear, we continue to the second and third floor to take out the shooters. You sure you can hold it together after what just happened?"

"The incident that slayed me back in the tunnel – I got up off the ground with two fractured ribs and a cracked collarbone and did my job, carried one of my dying coworkers a half-click back to the truck and then drove through a mortar attack to get out of there. So, yeah, got a black belt in pulling it together after trauma. Let's go."

The camera swiveled as they moved toward the door.

"Whoever is operating that doesn't realize we can see it moving," Shane remarked.

"See it? I can hear the servo motors. We go silent now."

Shane signed *"yes"* and they continued forward.

At the top of the stairs, the sunny kitchen sat empty.

"Where we?" Shane signed, mouthing to assure his father understood what he meant. Most people in Emmaus had a passing knowledge of ASL since some of the local farmers were Deaf, but Shane actually knew how to sign because he'd been best

friends with the hearing son of one of those families since kindergarten. Rob wasn't nearly as proficient as his son.

"This is the back of the house." Rob spoke so softly, Shane essentially read his lips. "In the front is a parlor-dining room. Then a full-length formal dining room there and a formal entryway, then a formal living room." He showed the outline of the rooms with gestures. "This is the old house, so creaky staircases. We need that distraction." Shane keyed the radio twice, prompting Joe and Jos to start firing at the front of the building. The USDA returned fire.

Above, first one rifle fired, then a second one. Using hand signals, Rob indicated the first shot came from the second floor, almost above their heads while the second one came from the third floor at the far end of the house. Shane indicated he'd take the attic. Rob nodded and indicated he'd take the second floor. Shane nodded and headed toward the next flight of stairs, startling when a voice rang out from the table. The firefight outside died down.

"Nester, stop wasting ammunition. Find a better angle to shoot from."

"Yes, ma'am. They're just staying close to the fence. I'm moving to the end of the hall."

Shane held up three fingers and then indicated the far end of the house. Rob nodded. Shane climbed the stairs.

He'd never been in this house – well, the entryway for Halloween. Ren's wife had always dressed up as the Wicked Witch. Ren always hosted the town's 4th of July picnic at Beulah Park. Funny the things that flitted through your mind as you moved into position to kill someone. On the second floor, Shane keyed the radio twice, then froze on the stairs waiting for the shooter on that floor to return fire. Rob waited below him. During that barrage of sound, Shane made his way to the next flight of stairs and continued upward. Now, for the tricky part, making it all the way down a corridor without alerting the USDA. He listened intently and started forward. There were 10 smaller rooms up on this floor – probably meant to be servant quarters back before the advent of electric everything. At the rate they were going, Ren would need a staff this large once more. Shane waited outside the occupied room, listening. He was still not certain of his strategy when a bullet came up through the floor about five feet behind him. The shooter here turned to rush into the hallway and tripped over Shane's outstretched leg. Shane immediately relieved him of his rifle.

Although most of the cow cops had seemed to be bureaucrats who had never drawn a weapon before, this one scrambled for his sidearm. Shane kicked him in the ribs, then twisted, grabbing the pistol and pulling it from its holster. Before he could turn it on the agent, a sharp pain seared through his shoulder, exploding in rage in his head. Shane whirled and drove his fist into the man's

Adam's apple. The USDA agent dropped his knife, scrabbling at his throat, eyes wide with terror. Shane knew from the satisfying crunch sound he'd heard on impact that the cow cop needed a tracheostomy, or he would die today. While blood darkened his jacket sleeve, Shane scrambled around the attic bedroom, finding it devoid of furniture, pens, straws, syringes. The guy suffocated before Shane found anything useful. Out at the front of the house, a woman screamed. Shane looked out the window to see Joe and Jos handcuffing her. He heard the floor outside the door creak and as the door opened fully, Shane leveled the USDA gun, held in his left hand, right at Rob's head.

"Sorry," he muttered, pointing the gun at the ceiling.

"You okay?"

"Better than him."

"He choked to death?"

"My own personal nightmare of a way to go. Kind of ironic. What happened on your shift?" Shane indicated the blood sprayed across Rob's face. He'd always known a Vietnam vet had killed people decades ago, but he'd never given serious thought to what Rob was capable of when necessary. His father being a killer didn't shock him. It just cast the man in a different light – a familiar light.

"Knife to the juggler makes a mess, but it was him or me."

"Yeah, that's why this one's dead. I think that's what he was trying to do." Shane indicated his jacket sleeve.

"You're bleeding."

"Yeah. I might need stitches. Where's that safe room?"

"Basement."

They walked through the house, making their way toward the basement. They spied a lot of Sullivan valuables in the USDA truck, originally loaded with food that had spoiled during the days they'd hidden here. Mission creep, perhaps? Shane stopped in the kitchen to appropriate a dishtowel to staunch the blood flow, then preceded Rob down the stairs.

Shane flinched and drew his weapon as a wall at the end of a hallway began to wriggle and then swung open. Allison Sullivan swung out of the door, looking shaky on her crutches, but otherwise healthy. She'd grown up pretty. Shane guessed her around high school age, pretty much an adult under the circumstances. While Rob asked her how she had survived days in the safe room, Shane swept the room behind her. Ren Sullivan had a far-seeing nature, calculating a two-year supply of food for four or five people. By Shane's math, that meant less than one meal for every person in Emmaus. How sad!

Hiding in the Bushes

Newport, Pennsylvania

Days of wandering the Pennsylvania backcountry roads to avoid roadblocks brought Perry Carmichael's group north of Harrisburg where a nice woman informed them, they didn't want to go.

"Complete martial law," she explained as she sold them some loaves of bread for a gallon of gas. "They'll arrest you and confiscate your vehicle. They're enslaving people there."

Forewarned, they'd gone north, following the Juniata River. Newport had apparently been deserted and Perry didn't know why. If they didn't need gasoline, he would continue right on. These days, an abandoned town suggested radiation exposure. Unfortunately, the tolls local militia charged in gasoline meant they needed to find fuel here.

"We'll go this way." Joseph Sullivan indicated south. He and his wife Katharine started down the sidewalk. Julian Raines, the youngest member of their party, looked around at the houses and the street lined with cars. He was slender, medium height, dark hair with eyes that could twinkle with laughter, but were often mistrustful.

"Where the hell is everyone?" he wondered aloud.

"When we still had radio, they were talking about temporarily evacing towns in the path of radiation clouds. Maybe this was one of those and then the Pulse kept them from getting back here."

"Wish we had a Geiger counter, find out what our dose is."

"We'll get to SullCorp in Columbus and requisition one. Where you headed?"

"That way, I guess." He pointed west. "You?"

"Checking belts and fluids. I know I seem obsessive, but this is the only thing standing between us and walking."

"I'm not arguing. Watch your back, man."

Julian headed off in the direction he'd indicated, carrying two gas cans, the wrecking bar he used for self-defense trailing out the back of his coat like a metal tail, his feet crunching dried leaves.

The empty street of clapboard houses and neat hedges on narrow sidewalks gave Perry the creeps. It felt like one of those horror movies where you find a deserted town and then the zombies climb out of the cellars. He popped the hood and methodically worked his way through the fluids – oil, transmission, brake, steering, and radiator. The truck's age made windshield wiper fluid unnecessary. They needed to find a gas station with a working air hose. That back left tire looked a little squishy. They needed to get more trade goods. Perry had always been an honest man and it didn't come naturally to think about stealing, but there might be stuff in these houses they could exchange for what they needed. Joseph had enormous resources that he couldn't access in the current circumstances, but surely Ren Sullivan's fortune didn't go poof when the electrical grid fried. He'd have to talk to Joseph when he and Katharine came back.

He heard a scrape of a sole on pavement a split second before he felt the barrel of a gun in his right kidney.

"Don't move! Hand over your keys."

Perry got his hands up to shoulder level. The man behind him was taller than him and probably wider. Perry wasn't a young buck anymore, but his military training had included lots of hand-to-hand. He might be able to take him. Except he saw a second rifle barrel visible in a nearby hedge. From the size of the hand holding it, Perry surmised a woman wielded it. He could try to grab the guy's gun, but he'd probably get shot by the woman. The truck wasn't completely out of fuel, but they wouldn't get more than a mile before it ran out. Perry and his group might be able to reclaim it then.

"Easy, fellow. The keys are in my inside pocket."

Perry doubted this guy knew he had a gun. If he got his gun free, he could drop behind the truck and be safe from the rifle and then he'd just have to deal with the man. He reached slowly toward where his gun cozied under his arm, but just as his fingers closed around the grip, the woman shrieked, and he felt the gun swivel away from him. He drew and stepped back behind the truck, pointing his gun right at the man's face.

"Drop your weapon." Julian had one hand wrapped in the woman's hair as he eased her into view while keeping himself mostly in the hedge.

"D-d-don't hurt her," the man demanded. Middle-aged, he looked like he'd lost 20 pounds in a month and not slept in nearly as long. He tried to cover Julian while Perry's gun pointed at his face.

Father and daughter, Perry thought. She couldn't be more than high school-aged, hair-colored hair hanging in a dirty mess from a school-spirit stocking cap.

"I don't want to hurt anyone," Julian insisted. "But you need to turn the gun over to my friend or I might." The girl squeaked as he prodded her lower back. Perry didn't know how he bluffed, but he knew it wasn't with a gun since Julian didn't have one.

"If I give up my gun, you'll hurt her anyway."

"Whoa," Perry cajoled. He made a show of putting his gun on the truck roof. "Nobody wants to hurt anyone, but you were the ones who pointed guns at me, so – yeah. Put the gun down and we can talk, and Julian will let her go. Come on."

The guy wobbled his gun back and forth between Perry and Julian while the girl wept and whispered "Daddy." Finally, the man set the gun down on the ground.

"Kick it over this way," Julian ordered. The guy obeyed and Julian let go of the girl's hair to sweep the gun off the ground. The rifle clattered to the pavement as the girl ran to her father. A 22 semi-auto, the breech for the magazine was empty. "This is at least loaded. Most dumb-assed stickup I ever heard of."

"Please don't hurt us," the man begged, hugging his crying daughter.

"I was just checking my oil," Perry said, holstering his pistol. "Julian, you can put it away."

The younger man's jaw tightened, but he thumbed on the safety and made a show of his finger being outside the trigger guard.

"Do you live here in Newport?" Perry asked.

"No, we're just passing through." Perry waited for more. "We've been trying to get to Breezewood and … I'm sorry. I'm just desperate. My wife and other daughter are alone there."

"You could have *asked* for a ride," Julian offered.

That made the girl weep louder.

"We've met some very bad people along this road."

"Well, we're not bad people. I'm Perry Carmichael, this is Julian Raines. And like you, we're just trying to get home. That's Kansas for me, Seattle for Julian. I think we're headed right by Breezewood, so we could give you a ride, if you give us a reason to trust you."

The guy spoke into his daughter's ear; she whispered back.

"I'm Randy and this is my daughter Cindy. We've been walking for days."

"Someone steal your car?" Julian asked. He had shown that sharpness before. Perry didn't know enough about him and that sometimes concerned him.

"No. It fried in the Pulse. We were in Newark when the bombs went off. We were quarantined there for days and then we started west. Cindy got sick and we had to stop at Hardwick and then the car wouldn't start, and all the lights went out. We caught a ride with someone who did horrible things and stole everything from us and we've been walking ever since. We got here yesterday, and we found those guns in a car. When I saw you – a working vehicle – I'm sorry."

Did horrible things? Perry doubted he wanted to know. Katharine and Joseph came around the corner carrying their gas cans.

"We need to get our gas tank and cans filled. If you help us with that, we'll give you a ride. You've been here since yesterday? Seen any food sources?"

"We found a house a few blocks over. There was food in a pantry. We couldn't carry much of it."

"Julian, go with them. Take the gun to assure they don't take off with our gas cans. After we get loaded up, we'll go over to that house, see what we can find."

Julian indicated Randy and Cindy should lead the way. Perry explained what had happened to the Sullivans.

"Not the best way to get a ride from someone." Joseph's understatement almost caused Perry to laugh.

"I say leave them here," Katharine added.

"They know where there's food and I'm hoping maybe we'll find more gas cans or – I don't know. Supplies. Things we can use as trade goods. We need to find a way to finance getting as far as Columbus."

"But you can't trust them."

"I'm not, Katharine, but we need to use the resources that come our way. Besides, I think the guy is just desperate to get home and went about it in an utterly stupid way. The rifle wasn't even loaded. You gotta hand it to the kid, though. He sold a willingness to shoot the girl in the back when he had no weapon. *I* almost believed him."

"Good actor," Katharine whispered. She knew Julian better than the others did because he helped her escape New York City, and Perry knew his boss's wife was nobody's fool. She might have gotten used to wearing silk blouses and calf-skin boots, but she'd grown up working class and she knew which end of the dog would bite. "Let's get the cans into the tank and then we'll take the truck to the source. We want to be ready to head out when they get back."

First Aid

Emmaus, Kansas

The medical center needed more personnel, Cai thought, as Shane eased off his blood-soaked jacket and shirt to reveal a deep slice across his upper right bicep. He'd shoved a cloth between his clothes and the wound as a field bandage, so the bleeding had slowed a lot, but with the bandage gone, blood began to run again. Cai grabbed a wad of gauze to staunch the flow. Shane grimaced, his hard torso shimmering with sweat.

"I'm going to need you to stitch this up." Shane swallowed convulsively.

"Me? I'm not a doctor or nurse."

"You took the same EMT course I took. I can't afford to lose any more blood and Marnie and her nurses are busy. Mom's working with Allison. Dad's dealing with our new prisoner. If this were anywhere but my right bicep, I'd do it myself, but my left hand is not good enough for stitches in the absence of painkillers."

Cai's hands shook as he prepared the sutures. Shane remained rational, reminding him of the various steps of the process.

"You are remarkably calm about allowing me to put the hurt on you."

"I don't want sepsis like Mike. Cai, calm down. The sooner this is sewn up, the less blood I lose, the better I feel over the next few days. Seriously, take a couple of deep breaths and get this done."

"Marnie didn't offer any painkillers. I think Bart had a bottle in his office."

"I'm not waiting for you to go get it. Clean it out, stitch it up and bandage it. I'll seek prophylactic pain relief at Maggie's if I need it."

While Cai worked, Shane caught him up on events in town since he'd been gone. The USDA raid surprised a lot people around Emmaus, but Shane somehow knew about future threats, so had prepared Emmaus. That ability intrigued Cai, even as he knew his younger brother would tell him to stay out of his business.

"I thought it felt like I'd been gone a lot longer than a few days, but I didn't expect Dad to kill federal agents while I was gone."

"You're not going to lecture me on morality?"

Cai focused on threading the silk through the suture.

"You sure about this?" he asked. "I could maybe pull this together with Steri-Strips."

"Just do it, Cai. The pain doesn't get easier with anticipation."

Cai admitted his feelings about federal agents had changed over the last couple of weeks. His best legal advice – don't hang federal agents -- but the morality of the situation no longer seemed clear to him.

"I was in my own mess that resulted in stuff I couldn't have predicted, so …."

Explaining Hutchinson to his family proved easy with Shane. While Cai talked, he pulled the two edges of the wound together with one hand and slid the needle through to pull it together. Shane grimaced and his left hand clearly clamped the edge of the table, but he barely hissed.

"You need a minute?" Cai asked.

"No. Let's get it done. How'd you end up arrested?"

"It's a long story. Not sure I even remember all the details."

"Doesn't matter. You're distracting me from what you're about to do next."

Cai explained that military command in Hutchinson had gotten out of control. That got them through two more stitches.

"You need one more, I think."

"Just give me a moment. Starting to regret not letting you go for the bottle. Surprised Dad let Bart get away with that."

"He maybe didn't know about it. Bart would pour me a shot late at night." Shane scowled, probably surprised that Cai enjoyed an occasional social drink. "Of course, Dad does that libertarian thing where he doesn't think some things are his business."

"Unless it's my business and then he's all up in it." Cai took the last stitch while Shane joked. Shane finally swore. "That better be the last one. I don't think I can hold still for anymore."

"Yup. Tying off now."

"You need to hurry because I need to put my head between my knees."

"Lie down." Shane didn't resist as Cai lifted his legs onto the table and settled him on his good shoulder. "We probably should have done this from the beginning. So Betadine and bandage, right?"

"There's some xylocaine spray in that cabinet. After the Betadine, hit it with the xylocaine and then bandage. I'm just going to lie here and try not to puke."

Cai grabbed a bowl off the examination counter. He'd already cleaned up enough puke today. Shane hissed at the xylocaine's initial burn, but then settled down and let Cai bandage the stitches.

"Well, thank you for this fun brotherly time," Shane murmured. "You'll have to get us all caught up at whatever group meal has been designated for that."

"You okay or do you need me to stay?"

"I'm fine. Come back in about 15 minutes and whether I'm up or not, make me."

Cai headed out the door then but paused and looked back at his brother. Shane had rolled onto his back and lay with his knees bent and his good arm across his eyes. As Cai watched, a single gleaming sparkle rolled down his cheek and hovered on the edge of his ear. Cai knew he wouldn't get candor if he asked if Shane needed to talk, so he eased the door closed behind him.

Walking

For six long months, Allison Sullivan had used crutches and bore no weight on her left leg and the change felt glorious. Not really. She couldn't feel a lot of her leg and the part she could feel burned with the effort of moving. Still, standing upright without crutches reminded her she'd been able to do that once and she'd be able to do it again. Jill Delaney suggested she use the medical center's main corridor to test out her leg.

"Don't be in a rush," she told her. "It'll take time to rebuild strength and you'll hurt yourself if you go too fast. Without a physical therapist, we can only just use our heads, right?"

Allison stared down the hallway that stretched a mile. Jill had other patients to care for, so allowed Allison to test it on her own.

The nerve root in her hip had been damaged when her leg was ripped from the socket as the horse dragged her. Those types of nerves could regenerate themselves over time, but for now Allison had only limited function. She used her crutches like outriggers and tried to move her leg forward. Nothing. She didn't know how much time passed as her leg failed to move, but she finally decided to try to put weight on her braced leg. Half-expecting to smack face first on the linoleum, taking a step forward surprised her. Her left leg still refused to move, so she used her torso to drag it forward and then took another step. In all, she managed 10 steps using this method before needing to sit down, so she pushed into one of the exam rooms and dragged herself to a chair. She'd already sat down before she realized a boy lay in the bed.

"I'm sorry. I didn't mean to disturb you," she said. He blinked at the ceiling. Slowly, his gaze drifted in her general direction. They'd just made eye contact when a tall willowy woman with gray-shot dark hair and vaguely Wyandot features pushed into the room, carrying a bowl in one hand.

"Oh," she grunted. "Are you ... hi. Are you a friend of David's?"

David Vance. Right. They met a few times when she'd been allowed to do community activities. She didn't recognize him with his head bandaged and looking confused.

"Allison," she greeted, shifting her crutch so she could shake hands with Trish Vance. "I didn't know he'd been hurt."

"USDA. I guess we got the last of them."

"Yeah, I hope so." Allison thought briefly of Melvin. He died giving her time to get to the safe room. She owed him or the universe or someone for that. "So how is David?"

"Still paralyzed. Still not talking."

He stared at them, lips twitching, drool spilling. Allison hadn't heard because she'd been in the safe room, but she wasn't entirely isolated from life growing up.

"So it was a head injury?"

"Yes. They don't know what's going on inside his skull, but it left him unable to do things for himself."

They didn't really know each other before his injury but this spring, when she came back from the hospital in Denver, he said 'hi' to her at the store and asked about her leg. He complimented her riding, apparently having seen her at dressage in Longview and Salina. At the time, she believed she'd ride again, not having been told of the nerve damage her leg suffered and been impressed he actually attended a dressage show. Unfortunately, her mother whisked her away from the "inappropriate" flirting.

"My grandmother had a stroke and for a long time, it seemed like she was just never going to walk or talk again, but she was listening, and she slowly got better." Allison spoke directly to David, though his eyes said he didn't understand. She patted him on the arm. "It'll take time. But you'll get it."

"Thank you," Trish said. "He hasn't had any visitors his own age. It's good to see some."

"I'll try to visit again." Trish moved to a seat on the far side of the bed and spooned up some mushed food from the bowl. David blinked, but didn't open his mouth when she offered him the spoon. Allison gathered her crutches. "I should go."

"He'll be going home soon. There's just no way to keep him here."

Allison's grandmother went to a rehabilitation center and then had therapists and nurses at home. Without those things, would David get better? Allison still smiled and patted his arm again. He turned his gaze toward her once more. She'd touched his left side. His right hand fisted and drew up into his stomach.

"When my grandmother first came home, they told me to always sit on her good side. She could see and understand better that way."

David grabbed her wrist, his face contorted, breathing heavily. Allison put her hand on top of his, speaking slowly, soothingly.

"It's okay. I know it's hard to talk right now. Hard to move. I bet you have a headache too. You'll heal and it'll get easier."

"I'm sorry," Trish said. "I don't know why he gets so agitated sometimes." A bruise darkened her cheek. David had gotten upset before.

"It's okay," Allison said. "He'll let go when he's ready." She kept her tone light and gentle. His grip on her wrist hurt, but she doubted he could control his actions. Her grandmother would get more agitated if you overreacted. David's breathing slowed, his face relaxed and he let go, eyes closing. "It's fine. I'll try to visit again – here or at your house. It's got to be really frustrating for him right now. Maybe he'll get used to seeing the same face."

Allison pivoted on her crutches and swung toward the door. David put everything in perspective for her. She wanted to whine and be depressed about her leg, but truthfully, she still had her hands and her mind.

Who Is Our Neighbor?

Breezewood, Pennsylvania

The sun hovered in the treetops to the west when Perry pulled into Breezewood, the quintessential tourist trap town. Like many of the towns they passed, this one seemed deserted, even the gas stations and motels along the turnpike shuttered, though Julian knew there could be people hiding behind blinds and locked doors. Here and there, family homes showed the marks of fire – charred timbers, smoke rimmed windows, collapsed roofs. Randy's house no longer smoldered as he stared in shock.

"Marsha." His voice echoed off the silence. Julian followed him around the back of the house while Cindy cried. Katharine held the girl, though she looked annoyed. She wanted to be the other side of Greensborough by now but cleaning out that pantry and packing it in the truck took longer than they planned. They found two coolers and more gas cans. Now they could keep full cans in the bed of the pickup and a couple on the roof rack for when they encountered an inevitable roadblock.

"Marsha! Melanie!" Nothing. A wind sighed through the trees and coiled around the house, raising the stink of char. Randy rushed to the detached garage and tried the side door. It wouldn't budge. Julian put his face to the window beside the door.

"There's no car in there."

"That means – what does that mean?" Randy pushed him aside to look.

"That maybe your wife took your daughter somewhere safe. Look, bodies – when they burn – they tend to leave a bad smell and I don't smell that. So, I don't think they were in the house when it burned."

His first year in prison, a rival gang decided to make a statement about a guy on Julian's dorm. They set him on fire, producing a smell like burning pig fat he would never forget, and he didn't smell it today. As he thought this, he heard a dog bark and Randy dropped to his knees to embrace a black-and-white shepherd.

"Jonesy," Cindy cried and joined her dad in greeting what must be the family dog. Randy said his wife's name a few times, but Jonesy just smiled at him.

"I'll get Jonesy's key," Randy said. He climbed halfway into the doghouse and produced a set of keys, one of which worked on the garage. Even after spending time in prison, Julian wouldn't think to look in the dog's house for the keys. It seemed like a really good way to get your face bit off. "The camping equipment is gone." Randy worked on opening the gun safe and then stared at the single rifle and handgun that were there. "This had to be Marsha."

"Dad," Cindy said, holding up a letter. His wife explained they'd been headed back from quarantine when the surge happened and come home to find the house in flames. Jonesy had run away in terror and they'd waited, but she'd finally taken "your dad's old Buick" and headed north to her father's hunting cabin. "I took the hunting rifles and a side arm each for us and left you this so you'd not be disarmed on the way. Keep Cindy safe! The world's gone crazy." She hoped they'd find Jonesy before they headed their way.

"That's 40 miles out of our way. We can't --," Katharine said.

"No, of course not. You need to get back to your daughter. My motorbike will get us there." Randy pointed to a classic softtail with a sidecar that sat in a corner of the garage.

"We can leave you some of the food," Joseph said.

"And fill your tank," Perry added.

Katharine really wasn't a nice person. She hid her anger at these suggestions from everyone but Julian, whose life once depended on reading people's eyes. Katharine sought what served Katharine best. Consider it lucky if it served you too. When Perry suggested they stay the night, she threw a fit.

"We cannot keep stopping every 10 minutes. My god, do you not feel the cold at night? It's winter right around the corner and without snow plows, there's not moving after that."

"She's right. We should keep going." Joseph acted deferential to Perry most of the time, but he definitely wanted to keep Katharine happy.

"We risk getting ambushed in the dark," Perry reasoned. "It's better to sleep the night here and drive on when we can see."

Julian didn't care. As long as they moved forward, he wasn't arguing either way. If nothing else, prison had taught him patience and he'd seen no good reason to change that attitude now.

Perry being the defacto leader meant they settled for starting out at dawn.

Off Bubble

Emmaus

The family gathered at the Delaney home just at sunset. One of the oldest houses in Emmaus, it had a huge dining room from the days when the Delaney family was a dozen strong. Cai hadn't slept well in days and his left shoulder ached with bruising from the night before, so though whatever Jill made for dinner smelled lovely, he really just wanted to lie in bed and sleep until he woke up, preferably to discover this had all been a bizarre fever dream.

"What did you cook?" Marnie asked as she took her seat.

"It's Freezer Surprise. Whatever is thawing is what's for dinner." Jill tried to sound breezy and unconcerned, but Cai knew his mother was worried.

"Jazz and I are starting to smoke meat tomorrow," Jacob announced.

"We'll start with the brine and then the smoke," Jazz Tully explained. Cai surmised she'd become a family member during his absence. Everyone seemed comfortable with her presence, even Marnie who usually felt competitive toward any female of breeding age.

"Whatever we need to save the food," Jill said.

"Where's Shane?" Rob asked, coming from the living room.

"Outside with Glister," Jill replied. "He's in a mood."

"Imagine that," Rob cracked as if he wished he could be in a mood, but had opted to be a grownup tonight. He tapped on the kitchen window. "I'm hoping we can all hear Cai's story at one time."

"What's going on with him?" Jill asked.

"It got bloody." Rob's flat tone caused Cai to wonder how many people died. "And now I have to decide what to do about the remaining USDA officer."

"Put her on the next truck leaving town," Jacob suggested. The back door opened, and Glister ran through headed to the front room. The yellow Lab knew mealtime rules and had a very nice bed there. Shane took a seat, not even bothering to conceal the 9 mm in its back holster.

"I at least left mine in the living room," Rob chided. Shane replied with an obscenity and they just passed the food. Cai wondered if anyone else noticed Shane taking a single spoonful of potatoes and nothing else.

"Cai, we don't get together much these days. We're all very busy," Jill explained. "So, tell us what's been going on with you."

"The last we knew, you weren't able to get to the airfield in Wichita because of a traffic jam," Jacob prompted.

"There were surveillance drones chasing me."

"That was sort of my fault." Shane looked embarrassed. "It never occurred to me to ask my handler to scrub your image from Kanorado. As soon as I told them to do it, they got it done pretty quickly."

"Whatever they did worked because they arrested me for simple vagrancy, not shooting soldiers."

"Shooting soldiers?" Jill echoed.

Shane explained he'd taken aggressive action to get Cai out of the quarantine zone the night of the bombs.

"And, I didn't kill any soldiers. I merely hit their Kevlar."

"Couldn't you kill someone that way?" Jazz asked.

"The whole point of body armor is to protect the wearer from bullets. I took a couple of shots to the chest once. It hurts, a lot, but I got on my feet within minutes."

Silence descended over the group gathered at the table. Rob and Jacob had both served in the Army, Jill was once an Army nurse, and Jazz had two brothers in the military. Having spent days as a slave of a rogue Army unit in Hutchinson, Cai no longer felt certain of his own feelings about Shane's casual attitude toward shooting Army personnel. Shane had shot to stun. Cai had a soldier's blood on his hands.

"Go on, Cai," Jacob prompted.

Cai swam the Kansas River and spent the night in a culvert after the drones mysteriously stopped looking for him. The Army personnel who arrested him seemed not to know about Kanorado and he'd kept his mouth shut for self-preservation. His family didn't take kindly to people being arrested for walking their dog after curfew and refusing to let soldiers search their houses. Those were not crimes by any normal standard. And, yet, Cai ended up in Hutchinson where he and his fellow slaves worked in a shipping and receiving center, organizing all the food the USDA stripped from the outlying towns.

"So, you've been warehousing?" Marnie grinned at him. Cai had worked for Walmart all through college and law school. Thus, her school debt doubled his. Did they still have school debt or did that go away with the Internet in the EMP?

"I know. It started out feeling kind of normal, but I was basically enslaved. I wasn't free to leave. They worked us with little food, not enough sleep, in the hot sun without adequate water." He indicated the reddened and peeling skin above his collar. "We were essentially slaves."

"How'd you get free?" Jazz asked.

"Mike showed up with a squad of Knights and they didn't like what they saw."

FEMA was supposedly in charge at Hutchinson, but a rogue military outfit enslaved even FEMA. The Knights were hired by Ren Sullivan to get a truckload of food to Emmaus and pick Cai up on the way. Mike's Knights unit removed the Army rogues from power. Shane asked how Mike had been hurt.

"We were headed home when we were attacked, and he got stabbed. Mr. Beach helped us get here."

"He's a brave man," Jazz said. "Anders McAuliff is rewarding him with salt."

"We made a fair trade with him, but if Anders wants to increase the reward, I'm not going to argue. We couldn't have made it here without him and it's getting dangerous out there. So what's been going on here while I was gone? I don't know that killing USDA agents was a particularly politic move."

"You weren't here. We had to act quickly," Jacob protested.

"And this is martial law," Rob explained. "As the highest-ranking officer in the township, it was my decision to make, but we made sure we had a coroner's inquest to assure we had our facts straight."

"The facts won't matter if the military ever gets here."

69

"We had to make a decision and we made it, and there's no way to unmake it now."

"I thought you weren't going to lecture me on the morality," Shane muttered.

"This isn't about morality. This is about what's smart. Those USDA officers are going to head to their headquarters and report what you did and that's going to bring the Army down on the town."

"Yeah, in the old world, probably, but I'm betting the US Army is so broken they'll never get back to us. There's no chain of command anymore. It's all just rogue units. In the meantime, there's a crowd of migrants pushing up against the northern border. I need to go check on my crews." Shane pushed back from the table, having not eaten a bite of food.

"Whoa," Jill said. "You just took stitches and you can't pretend to eat and then skate out of here as though everything is fine."

Shane's eyebrows drew together, his full lips compressed into a straight line.

"Everything's not fine, Mom. I'm just choosing to take my lousy mood somewhere else. It's not that I'm not happy you're home safe, Cai. It's that I'm not fit company for people right now and so I'm going to go make war and then check on Mike, who will absolutely understand this mood."

Shane grabbed his blood-stained jacket from a hook by the door and moved toward the door.

"Take mine, son," Rob ordered. "Give your mother a chance to clean and mend yours."

Shane stared at him like he spoke a foreign language, then dropped the jacket on the counter and grabbed the one from the next hook. Wordlessly, he left.

"Is he okay?" Cai asked.

The family who had been here all along, including Jazz, exchanged knowing looks and Marnie took it upon herself to answer for the group.

"He's ahead of the curve adapting to this new world."

"Which means he's less likely to be surprised by the insanity," Rob added.

"But more likely to eat the barrel of a gun," Jacob finished.

"And we let him have one?" Cai demanded.

Nobody said anything in reply, which Cai interpreted as meaning they hadn't figured out how to relieve him of his weapons and still make use of his skills. He stared at the food on his plate, singularly unhungry.

"I'm going to bed, I think," he announced. "Is there hot water for a shower?"

"Make it quick," Rob said. "I'd like to get the blood out of my beard before I go to bed tonight."

"Yes, sir." Not bothering to ask why Rob had blood in his beard, Cai moved to stand up and Marnie caught his wrist, pulling him down so she could whisper in his ear.

"I'll see you up there."

71

He nodded. He paused at the door to look back at them as they exchanged information over a meal. He wondered if Shane felt as if he didn't really inhabit this space. He floated three degrees off bubble, and they were the bubble. He'd left a new husband and City attorney and come back a former slave and murderer. Would it take time to feel ordinary again or must he adjust his reality to this new normal?

Night

Mike slept, but Lila expressed her gratitude to be able to go home when Shane relieved her.

"You know David is still here? And two of the National Guardsmen. If something comes up, you'll need to call me on the radio."

"I will. I wouldn't know what to do with David Vance if he got agitated, but the others – those are battlefield injuries. I know those."

Lila leaned in and gave him a hug, which set off proximity alerts for him and she saw that immediately.

"You're okay, right?" She still insisted upon patting him on the shoulder and pulling away would look paranoid.

"Yeah." Even he knew he lied, so he tried for a half-truth. "I'm just not ready to go to sleep."

"Abigail will be here around 4:00 am. You sure you can stick it out until then?"

"I'll call you if I can't, but yeah. Still an insomniac."

Saying that to Vin's wife reminded him of a time when sleep wasn't so elusive. He sometimes wondered, did the insomnia come before he learned to lull himself to sleep with marijuana or after he'd stopped smoking it? He really didn't know. Jason's crew had some. On nights like this it tempted him, but he'd never act on that thought. The situation relied on his sharpness and, if lack of sleep dulled his edge a bit, being high made it blunt.

The medical center held the priority for fuel, so had lights, kept low to save electricity. The patients all slept. Shane went into the room where Mike slumbered under a heavy dose of sedatives. His temperature still ran high. Shane looked at the blood-tinged pus in the bag hanging beside the bed. The yellow-green color didn't bode well for his friend's survival.

God, we could use your help here.

Where did that come from? Driving through a mortar barrage, he found a rudimentary belief in the god he'd so long denied. Shane found it convenient to blame the eternal crap bag for all the evil in the world, but he didn't expect him to be a cosmic sugar daddy. That kind of delusion belonged to people who thought the meddlesome old man in the long white beard *loved* them. He knew *if* his parents' god was real, he'd lose no love on a monster like Shane. God's love of monsters stood in the way of Shane even believing in him. Men like

King David, with hundreds of deaths on their hands, didn't deserve heaven.

I deserve death.

Did Mike? Probably a card-carrying member of the asshole in arms did, yeah. Did Alicia deserve to be alone, pregnant and unprotected in a world now spun out of control? All of morality pivoted there for Shane. He knew *he* deserved death by painful torture, but he also *knew* that would hurt his parents deeply and the knowledge kept his 9mm in its back holster and not in his mouth. He had to do his best to not hurt himself while they still needed his skills.

Mike stirred and opened blurry eyes.

"Hey," Shane whispered.

Mike focused on him with effort, swallowing noisily. Shane checked his chart and got him some water. Marnie's handwriting deteriorated significantly in the years since they wrote notes to one another, but he still had enough familiarity to figure it out. Mike shivered as Shane settled him back on the bed.

"We're in Emmaus, right?"

"Yeah."

"Cai good?" They really seem to have become friends over the last few days. Shane marveled, but the world wasn't exactly normal these days. Dogs mating with cats might be next and he wouldn't be shocked.

"He is. Sunburned and a little disillusioned with the world, I think."

Mike grinned, then winced in pain.

"He did good out there." He licked dry lips. Shane gave him another sip of water. "I screwed up and he ... it was like he channeled you."

"We were raised by the same people." Shane frankly thought Mike delusional. Cai channeling Shane? Impossible!

"You always said he wasn't realistic." Shane nodded. Cai Delaney embodied a goody-two-shoes who thought himself better than Shane. "He's seen the rough side of life now."

Okay. Maybe a peek into the real world could wake up even his older brother.

"Yeah, I kind of caught a whiff of that from him. The chart says I can give you another valium."

"You'll need to soon, but I just want to talk a minute." Shane nodded. "Alicia's alone in Santa Fe. She's with her mom, but you know what I mean. If I don't survive this, I need you to step up."

Shane didn't waste time on platitudes. Sepsis could end you and Mike knew it.

"How do I find her? What's her mother's address?"

"Address? I'm n-not – Didn't think I'd need it. I know how to get there."

"Street names?" Shane could see the confusion in Mike's brown eyes. He probably could see exactly how to get there, but Shane knew from experience that he didn't pay attention to street names or house numbers. That's not how Mike found his way around. "How about her mother's name?"

"Magdala Esquibel." Shane whipped out his phone and typed it in. "But how you going to google that with no internet?"

Mike didn't know Shane still had access to geosync satellites and Rigby could help too if he would. His Central Security Agency handler seemed pretty determined to keep Shane in Emmaus – willing to even let Cai stay in slavery to make it happen. When he went, he'd have to make sure Rigby and his dad remained mostly in the dark about it. Neither trusted him to leave and come back. Rigby ought to know better. How many times had Shane gone off script and come back to provide the rewrite? And, Rob – that man needed to stop thinking of Shane as twelve. He's been around the world, in four war zones – five if you counted Emmaus now – and he still lived. He sometimes wished he didn't, but clearly he had the ability to survive firefights. Peace and quiet and time inside his own head might kill him. War – not so likely.

"Wow, this really hurts." Sudden sweat coated Mike's forehead.

"You need to take your antibiotic and then back to sleep for you. Alicia is a smart *chica* and her mother sounds well-prepared, so don't worry. Just heal and we'll go when you can ... unless you remember how to get there."

"But if I die --."

"Yeah, you know I will. You don't even have to ask."

After Shane gave him his meds, Mike's lids grew heavy and he fell asleep soon after. Shane rolled an office chair into the hallway and sat down. If he dozed off, he'd wake himself up by falling out of the chair. He trusted his hypervigilance to keep him posted on any noise in the building. He spent the night alternating between wide awake staring at the opposite wall and a light doze in which he made strangers choke to death. He heard when one of the National Guardsmen woke up to use the bathroom, but the guy went back to bed without asking for assistance. Shane unlocked the door for Abigail in the dark before dawn and went home tired enough to get four hours of sleep before he returned to the barricades once more.

Objects in View

Emmaus, Kansas – Next Day

Jazz rode shotgun as Rob steered around stalled cars on the interstate. USDA agent Reyes sat in the back seat looking exhausted and scared. Jazz knew they sent her to her death, but somehow that seemed less objectionable than hanging her on the courthouse roof. She had a chance for survival, if she used her head and luck fell her way. She might find a town willing to take her in or a working vehicle so she could get home to Albuquerque. She couldn't stay in Emmaus. No USDA agent could, especially not one who killed Melvin Kirsch and terrorized a 15-year-old girl, not to mention wasting days of food. What hadn't mattered a month ago now stood as a killing offense and Reyes was lucky they were giving her a chance to survive.

"This is probably far enough out." Maybe two miles east of Emmaus, Rob put the truck in park and unbuckled to get Reyes out. Jazz slid out and stood at the ready, hand near but not on her 9mm in its modified shoulder-back holster. Maybe 30, not unattractive, Reyes had short dark hair and big blue eyes.

"Where am I supposed to go?" Jill insisted they provide a decent set of clothes, good walking shoes, hat and gloves. Her hands secured with zip ties, Reyes used her elbows to pull her USDA jacket around her slender frame.

"Anywhere but Emmaus." Rob looked around as if to orient himself. "Don't go that way." He pointed west. "And as soon as you can manage it, I'd get rid of that jacket because folk round here don't have a lot of use for cow cops anymore."

"I was doing my job," she whimpered.

"Melvin was too." Her eyes flickered. She knew they did wrong at the Sullivan house. Jacob counseled her last night and Jazz knew he pushed on the morality of killing a man protecting a young girl. "And, I know, the USDA would have assured we got plenty of food at some later date, if we just cooperated." His voice dripped with contempt. "Of course, they didn't know about the Pulse. They were looking short-term when we were looking long."

"That's right. How could we have known?"

"Ask that question at some other town because here, we don't care, and if we see you at our wire, we'll put a bullet between your eyes. So, go."

Rob cut the zip ties holding her wrists and pointed vaguely south toward New Mexico. The highway led east though. Then he signaled Jazz, who came forward with a child's backpack of food.

"Day's food and water."

"A day? You people are crazy! And when I report this to my superiors, they'll make you pay."

"They might." Rob shrugged. "If they still exist and aren't scrambling hand to mouth same as you. Jazz." He nodded toward the truck and they got in.

"This feels wrong," she admitted as they watched Reyes head east. She could turn south at the next off ramp.

"Yeah. A day's food isn't enough, but we've got people in Emmaus already going hungry, and she did kill a man."

So did you – and so did Shane. Jazz wouldn't speak her thoughts, but truthfully, they all had blood on their hands. She hadn't killed anyone yet, but every meal she ate meant someone else wouldn't. It hurt knowing her existence depended on someone else's death.

Reyes topped a small rise and started dropping into the asphalt, each step taking her away from them. Living meant making hard choices now. Jazz needed to toughen up. Not everyone would live. Sounding like Shane right now should have scared her, but it didn't. It sounded a lot like realism and realism cast harsh shadows that made no one look attractive.

"You thinking about your parents?"

No, but she couldn't tell the truth, so she accepted the change of topic.

"Florida without air conditioning." She shuddered. He looked sad. "My dad had a stroke last year. He was doing pretty good but the heat – and, then Mom would be on her own." She'd stopped crying over those imagined fears. She'd accepted she'd never see her parents again.

"And, your brothers too, right?" His sandy coloring belied his relationship to Shane, but now she saw the similarity in their noses and something around the eyes.

"Shane said Geo logged onto Facebook a while ago and listed himself as safe. He was somewhere in Washington State. Jim was in the Middle East, so he's probably fine." She took a deep breath, chuckling nervously. "Weird that you worry less about someone in a war zone than in the US now." Rob nodded. "Why aren't they bringing those troops back here to help?"

"I don't know. Maybe they are and they're just not here."

"Can't that radio tower broadcast and pick up a long way?"

They both looked at the KERB tower visible just over their left shoulders, high on Mission Ridge. It seemed odd to Jazz not to see its familiar red light, but of course, Click Michaels only operated the tower on generator power when needed. That cost fuel, now in such short supply.

"Supposedly. It was built for that. But Ross Mitchem gave up that long license a long time ago and Click hasn't been able to figure out how to get the old transmitter up and running."

"I just feel so cut off."

"Pa says it feels like the old days."

"How did they stand the isolation?"

"That's not necessarily a bad thing." Jazz cast him a sidelong glance, perplexed. "Whatever is happening out there could affect us, but there's nothing we can do about it, so worrying about it would only take away energy from working on the things that affect us directly."

"Like keeping people out of our wire?"

"And keeping food and medicine flowing in so we can survive."

"The objects in view?" He grinned at her, recognizing a Delaney family saying. Jazz felt she could ask a hard question of this man who currently felt like a father. "Does it bother you that other people might not survive because we do?"

He breathed heavily, in and out, nodding, then giving a long shrug.

"Soldiers learn how to compartmentalize." His tongue caressed his lower lip. "I can't save the whole world and if I don't concentrate on saving my family first and my town second, I won't succeed at saving anyone. That's the unfortunate situation we're in."

Jazz took in a slow deep breath and let it out even slower.

"We're going to pay for that, aren't we?"

Rob shot her a sidelong glance before nodding.

"Compartmentalization comes at a price. You see it with Shane every day."

83

"I don't see it with you."

He fingered his beard. Was he thinking about the blood he'd needed to wash from it just last night?

"I've had decades to learn to decompartmentalize what nearly killed me and sort it to a place where I could live with it. And, I had to if I wanted Jill in my life – and probably my parents and sisters too. If I went the way I was going – Jill was already gone, and my mother wasn't talking to me. When Pa held out that lifeline, there were strings attached and I knew it."

"Did you and Jill have kids yet?"

Rob shook his head. Maybe they were just trying to forget Reyes, but it occurred to Jazz that Shane might never have been born had Rob Delaney not gotten sober.

"We lost a baby – a daughter -- and I used that as an excuse." His gaze shifted into the past, remembering, before smiling in self-mockery. "She didn't. Cai was born a couple of years after we got back together – after she knew I wasn't going to flake out on her again. I was sober ...." He calculated in his head. "Sober 15 months before she let me move in with her again. It was almost another year before we decided to move on with our future. Cai was born one month shy of my third sobriety anniversary."

Jazz knew she shouldn't be nosy, but he seemed willing to talk. Reyes had dropped out of their sight, but he hadn't started the truck. It seemed an invitation to talk.

"Do you ever -- ?" Her cheeks flushed hot at her inappropriate thoughts, asking daughter-in-law questions when she wasn't even dating his son.

"I want it – some days more than others – a lot this last month. But saying 'no' is so much a part of my lifestyle now that I can't imagine saying 'yes.'"

Somehow that calmed her nerves. The town would crash and burn without a few people, she thought, and Rob Delaney played a key role in keeping things together.

"Now you want to tell me why you're asking these questions?"

Her cheeks flushed hot again and she didn't know how to explain herself. Rob grinned at his own thoughts.

"He could do worse than dating you and you could do a whole lot better than dating him."

"We're not." Shane hardly even talked to her these days. Dating required communication, didn't it? He needed a friend, not a lover.

"I know. There's a part of you that wishes it could be more and there's a part of him that wishes it too, but he's running scared and with good reason." He scratched his beard, put his big callused hands on the steering wheel. "You know, I grew up in an era where movies taught us the love of a good woman could save a wayward man whose heart was in the right place." He flashed that self-mocking grin again. "Movies are fiction. Jill couldn't save me. That's why she left. And in leaving, she gave me both an excuse to keep racing toward the cliff and a reason to turn away from it. Pa gave me the means to turn away, but I had to want something more than what he offered ... something more than what she represented." He sighed. "I'd like nothing more than to throw you out there as a bit of bait to draw him in, but ... you don't deserve the harm he could do to you before he's repented."

Jazz dashed away an unexpected tear. Rob put a big hand on her shoulder.

"The good news is that crises make good turning points, and *everything* right now is a crisis. My bride would probably love it if you joined her for morning prayers. He could use more than one praying woman in his corner."

Jazz nodded and wiped her cheeks dry. Rob started the truck and turned around to head back to Emmaus where Jazz hopped out at the gate to take her place on the barricades while he drove toward City Hall.

Therapy

Emmaus – Two weeks later

Sera's hair fell to the middle of her back in luxurious waves of mahogany, uncovered. He rarely saw her so vulnerable in a public place. Shane's hands tangled in her curls as they moved to the music. He caressed the curve of her neck with his lips, breathing in the jasmine scent she wore. She smiled at him and drew him toward the door leading to the stairs.

He wanted so much to dream about what came after, but his psyche wouldn't let him. Increasingly, he struggled to go there even when awake. He remembered the yoke of a plane between his hands, which morphed into a steering wheel, as he stared through the windscreen at the bombed out building.

***

His eyes opened into darkness, feeling like he'd been slammed into the net seats of an inverted C130. Jacob shifted, destroying his hope of not waking him.

"You okay?" the old man asked.

His heart beat so fast it sounded like a waterfall in his ears. Glister the yellow Lab licked his fingers hanging off the edge of the bed.

"Just a dream," he whispered. "Sorry I woke you."

"I'm 96 years old. I've been awake about an hour, trying not to breathe too deeply so you'd stay asleep as long as you ever do. Congratulations, you made it four hours."

"Is that a record?"

"Since you and I have been sharing this bed? Yeah. When was the last time you got a full eight?"

The easy answer rang true.

"Never. Even in high school – six, maybe seven, after I'd gone balls-deep, maybe."

"You saying you need a girlfriend?"

"I wouldn't gift me on someone I cared about."

The bed Jacob shared with his wife for seven decades really didn't fit two tall men, but Shane gave up his bed to Mike when they moved him from the med center. He could share with Jacob or sleep on the too-short couch in the increasingly cold living room. Not that the bedrooms were much warmer. The coal cookstove in the kitchen just didn't get enough heat to the rest of the house, but the days warmed up enough that he couldn't justify stoking the furnace in the basement. Once stoked, the furnace would need to run continuously until spring.

"It's time you talked about it, son," Jacob said.

"There's nothing to talk about, Grandpa. It won't make it better."

"It always feels that way on your side of it. I didn't want to talk about it, but we did on the troop transport home. Started with the funny stories and then the ones that hurt. And, your father – yeah, he thought if he just drowned in the bottom of a bottle, he wouldn't have to talk about it, but he eventually let me in. And EJ - ." Jacob sighed. "Nobody wants to talk about him with you, but you need to think about where that sort of self-hatred leads."

"You ever think maybe he was mentally ill?" Shane sat up, reaching for his clothes. Cold flowed over his legs, testament to last night's freeze.

"You mean schizophrenic or bipolar? Yeah. We didn't know much about that back then, but I've wondered since. And you might be correct, but let's say you're not. Killing people comes back with you and if you don't deal with it, you become a danger to yourself."

Shane hit the lantern on his phone to locate his socks and shoes. Jacob stared at him in the brief period of light.

"I'm not drinking. I'm not doing drugs. I'm not taking unnecessary risks. Hell, I'm safer to myself than I ever was before I went to war."

"That's growing up. Happens after you hit 25. But you're thinking about hurting yourself. I see it in your eyes when you think I'm not looking. And, I know you're still seeing that woman."

Shane sighed. How Jacob knew about his PTSD specter, he didn't know, but Rob had brought it up too. Pretending she didn't exist felt right until he felt her icy hand on his skin. If they ever had their suspicions confirmed, they'd lock him up for his own safety and he absolutely knew that would kill him. He'd hang himself before the first day ended. He couldn't tell them the truth and survive.

"Why are you getting up so early?" Jacob asked when Shane silenced the alarm on his phone.

"Keri needs my help on the farm. Everybody else is sick."

"Flu?"

"Yeah. Her and baby Lisa are the only ones not in bed."

"Do the two of you have any idea what you're doing?"

Shane's sister Keri married Alex Lufgren, who owned the biggest farm in Emmaus, but as far as Shane knew, Keri lacked 4H experience. He could clean stalls and collect eggs. Family didn't turn down family when they asked for help.

"I guess we'll discover the depth of our ignorance as we go along. What are you up to today, old man?"

"Loading bullets."

"Oh, joy! A whole day in the basement. Glad to miss out on all the fun."

"Who would you talk to?"

Shane sighed, seeing his hope of distracting Jacob dissolving in the hot light of sunshine.

"Mike, maybe."

"Then do that. He's on the mend now, right?"

"He is."

"And you're shining me on, so if it comes to it, I'll talk to him myself."

"You do that, Grandpa." His use of the honorific should have put the old man off. "I've got work to do."

"Someone else who needs to talk – Cai. You know what happened to him out there?"

"I'm the last one Cai would talk to."

"And the first one he probably should talk to."

"I've never been enslaved, Grandpa."

"No, but you've killed someone most recently."

Shane bit his tongue to hold back a vile retort and then reason supplied something better.

"I think Dad and I are even on that score. And, what does that have to do with Cai?"

"For a smart man, you are so unobservant."

"You think Cai would kill someone?" Shane meant to scoff, but his words echoed back at him.

"I think he had to and he doesn't want to admit it to anyone."

Shane sat back down on the bed, feeling suddenly exhausted. Weren't his own sins enough to bear?

"I'll try to talk to him when I get a moment. Just – Keri needs me now and then I'm on the barricades this afternoon. So, maybe you should try before I do."

"I have. Boy's been home two weeks and the fact that he's hardly talking is what's giving him away."

"Really?" The last couple of weeks were a blur of activity, doing things by hand that used to be done by electricity or a combustion fuel engine. Shane pushed past all that to Cai and recognized reality. "He's – yeah, not so chatty these days. I like that, so it didn't seem odd to me, but now that you mention it …. I'll find time to talk to him. Just remember, I don't like to talk, so he may not feel all that chatty with me either."

Shane left the room because he didn't want to encourage any more conversation. The bathroom tap ran cold, so Shane brushed his teeth and resolved to take his kit downstairs to the kettle on the coal stove. Shaving made him feel stronger. The few times he tried to grow a beard in the Mirage made him feel scruffy and never quite clean.

"Hey, you got a minute?" Mike whispered from the open door of Shane's room. Trying to get heat into the bedrooms, they blocked doors open. Glister settled heavily onto the rug, like they were inconveniencing him – which they probably were. A dog's bladder could only last so long. Shane turned on the lantern feature on his phone and set it on the nightstand. "God, that makes my eyes throb."

"Strong antibiotics will do that." Shane didn't turn off the lantern but moved it so it didn't directly shine in Mike's face. The tall dark Chicano man hadn't shaved, not his chin or his head, in sometime. Shane now knew he wasn't hiding a bald spot. "What do you need?"

"How much longer?"

"The drain's been running clear for a couple of days now, so maybe tonight when I get home." Marnie had turned Mike's care over to Shane to protect him from exposure to the flu as much as she could.

Mike shifted up against the headboard, holding his side where the drain protruded, a lump under the bandages. He moved more and slept less, but Shane could see how weak he remained. Marnie stubbornly refused a blood transfusion to speed his recovery.

"Do you have any way of getting hold of Alicia? I know you ain't just a Knight merc."

"If I could get a hold of her for you, I would. I've tried. The problem isn't at our end, it's at hers. Probably her cell phone fried in the Pulse. I know she showed up on a sat image a couple of days before you left Hutchinson. She was at an arroyo, so that doesn't tell me anything about how to find her. I'm not wandering around west Santa Fe knocking on random doors and risking getting shot, so you're going to have to come with me. That's another week out at least, which with the progress

I'm making on the plane I want to use is about right."

"You know how I feel about flying, right?"

"You know how many hours on the road to Santa Fe is compared to flying, so …. Besides, you owe me for Carlsbad."

"You had fun."

"I was drunk. So let me see your bandage and then I gotta go." Mike pulled down the covers. "No weeping. I think you're getting that out tonight. Just take it easy today."

"I don't really have a choice. I still get tired just going to the bathroom."

"Keri's paying me in blood pudding, so …." Mike gagged. "Builds the blood, man, and you need it. Never thought we'd be down to draining blood from cattle. I gotta go, *hermano*. Sun's up within an hour. Keep drinking water."

"*Si, si, el jefe*, bossy man, boss."

Shane grinned at the long-standing inside joke. Although they'd technically been equals in the Knight structure, Shane's other mission and Mike's easy-going nature caused Shane to make many of the command decisions in their two-man team. He headed downstairs to the warm kettle and the bathing station Jill created in the mud room. While he shaved, Marnie came into the kitchen to pour coffee into a mug. She put a cup next to his towel. She'd married his brother, but she and Shane had dated all through high school and college. That complication meant they tried not to interact much now, mainly for Cai's sake. Still, awkward as it felt to live in the same house with your former lover, ordinary gestures seemed right among in-laws.

"Thanks. What do you want?" Shane asked. Shaving by lantern light challenged his skills. His inquisitive fingers found a patch he missed and he re-lathered to take care of it.

"Have you talked to Cai lately?" She sipped coffee.

"Um, not really. Why?"

"He didn't sleep with me last night."

"Trouble in paradise?"

"Don't be mean. I wouldn't be with you if I weren't with him."

"Good, because my heart moved on a long time ago." For a moment, he saw Sera's smile, which morphed into Jazz, a bandana covering her hair, coal-dust streaking her cheek.

"I see how you look at Jazz when you think she's not noticing. What's broken inside you that you're not acting on it?"

"Broken, shattered, ground to dust. Not anything to do with you. I sometimes wonder how we lasted as long as we did."

"Me too. Wild spirits make fast friends, but we took different paths sometime in college."

"Yeah." Shane recognized the danger of nostalgia for former lovers who shared his brother's heart in common. He wouldn't go there. "So, no, I haven't talked to Cai. Let me guess – I should."

"Something's wrong, Shane." *Besides the apocalypse?* What wasn't wrong about this situation?

"He talk with you about Hutchinson?"

"No and that's why he left the room last night."

Hutchinson could be Cai's Ramah. Mike would know.

Shane rinsed his razor in the bowl of water and put his kit away. Two more blades and he'd have to learn to use a straight razor. That instrument so close to his jugular didn't bode well for his survival. He needed to assert to Jason Breen the importance of replenishing his blade supply.

"Jacob already asked me to talk to him and I'll try sometime today. I need to head to Alex's now. Keri's the last one standing and needs my help."

"Wash your hands and keep them away from your face." She sounded so much like a doctor he had to laugh.

"Does that really help?"

"Considering you've been inoculated against Third World diseases, maybe. You get a flu shot last year?"

"Nope."

"Then your immune response is probably normal. It's the rest of us flabby modern livers who might be in trouble. Fortunately, so far, this seems to be a relatively mild virus. You feel like crap for about 10 days, but nobody's died so far."

"I'll try to skip the whole 10-day crapshow. Gotta go. Turn out the lantern when you leave."

"Yeah. Thanks for being willing to talk to Cai. I know you two don't get along, but maybe he'll listen to you."

"Doubt it, but he's still my brother, even if he's suspicious of me."

Shane stepped out the door, whistled for Glister and headed for the garage where they moved the horses last week. With gasoline a diminishing commodity, horses were back in style as the transportation of choice. It meant more time getting from one point to another, but they needed to save the fuel for when they wanted to travel outside the cordon. Shane saddled Rocket in the predawn coolness. A return to the 1880s loomed. Cars, generators – these things ran on fuel. Yeah, you could recharge stuff with them, but when the fuel ran out ... Some of the farmers experimented with making biodiesel. Alex was working on that when he got sick. What Shane didn't know about creating fuel from corn would fit in a large stadium and probably overflow to a second one. He made a good assistant, but until someone wanted to redesign an airfoil or something, his skills really lay in knowing when to shoot someone, an undoubtedly sad commentary on his adult life. Truth be told, he jumped at the chance to do productive labor this morning because it proved in his own heart of hearts that he wasn't entirely a monster completely devoid of value.

"Come on, Glister. Let's get going."

He swung up into the saddle and posted a brisk trot before he reached the end of the driveway. Rocket liked this new world order where horses were ridden every day and she rewarded him with a ground-eating pace he thoroughly enjoyed, riding through the still dark town, headed west along Old 24.

Detour to Danger

Pittsburgh, Pennsylvania

Cars clogged the road ahead of them into Pittsburg. Joseph stirred in the passenger seat.

"That doesn't look good," he remarked. He consulted the map. "There's a tollbooth ahead. Probably a lot of cars clogging it. Maybe Pittsburg wasn't such a great idea."

Joseph and Katharine advocated for Pittsburg after the group spent days in a tiny town finding and installing a fuel pump after theirs suddenly died. Folks in the town were real helpful about the fuel pump and gave them rides to the area junkyards, but they were less giving with their food. They ran out of everything they liberated from a pantry days before and they needed food and gasoline, again. They seemed destined to hit roadblocks and delays at every curve of this journey. Someone had pushed the cars out of the way and removed the toll bar to create one open lane at the station.

"There's grocery stores along Freeport Road," Katharine reiterated.

"There were." Perry avoided stating the obvious. The Burger King to their right looked looted. A stripped semi sat in front of the Denny's. All of Wendy's windows were broken. Cars and a FEMA tent choked the Target parking lot. Perry took the second exit into the lot.

"We'll probably find gasoline in some of these cars."

Julian sat up when Joseph tapped on the window to the back, blinking and rubbing his unshaven jaw.

"We're looking for fuel and food."

"Of course, we are," he mumbled, scratching a hand through his wild hair. He pulled on a watch cap and crawled toward the tailgate. Night guard duty meant sleeping in the back while they traveled.

"I thought we were going around Pittsburgh," he said as Perry and he armed themselves.

"We voted. They won."

"I'm not sure this should be a democracy."

Julian spied movement in the parking lot and stepped up on a bumper to get a better view.

"This place has an *Escape from New York* vibe to it."

"It's the first big city we've been in since Newark. You thinking about Harrisburg?"

"I'm thinking about Snake Plissken."

"Are you old enough to remember that movie?"

"Not when it was new, but my dad loves those movies. And what's not to love about a movie where the inmates are in charge."

"I guess that would appeal to you."

Julian told him about his felony while they were pulling the fuel pump. Apparently, Katharine knew but they agreed Joseph didn't need to. Although he faced a lot of jail time if caught with a weapon, Julian opted to be armed. The odds of FEMA, or anyone else, having a working database to call him into account didn't come close to the risks of being unarmed these days.

The FEMA tent proved stripped of anything useful. People camped in there judging by fires at various places on the pavement floor, but it looked like they moved on days ago. They continued to the store.

The store's windows lay shattered on the floor just inside the threshold. They stepped in, the glass squares crunching beneath their boots. Not much remained on the shelves.

"What do you think?"

"Looting is pretty standard during blackouts." Perry grabbed whatever he could find to stuff in his backpack. Crackers, cocktail onions, all contained calories.

"Seems like --." Julian cut off as Perry stuffed two jars of cocktail onions into his bag. When he didn't continue speaking, Perry's ears perked up.

"You okay?"

"You ought to come see this." Julian's voice sounded curiously flat.

Perry rounded the shelves where Julian went. Two dead bodies lay near the empty liquor cases. One of the bloated bodies wore a Target uniform.

"We should go." Perry plucked at Julian's jacket sleeve. "There's nothing here."

Julian startled, glanced around.

"There's an aisle of automotive stuff."

Right, prison – the kid knew how to compartmentalize. Perry filled a cart full of oil, antifreeze and brake fluid.

"I say we just roll this to the next store. Nobody's going to care if we take it." Julian's suggestion made sense, unfortunately. A month ago Perry's morality would have rejected the suggestion.

The GetGo station next door was looted too, but not deserted. The woman apparently didn't hear them coming, so she startled and reached into her coat.

"We don't want trouble," Julian assured her. "We're just looking for food, same as you."

"Do you know what's further into the city?" Perry scanned the area around them, looking for threats.

"You don't want to go there." She sounded younger than she looked and looked like she slept wherever she could and hadn't showered in a while. "Everybody good left shortly after the Pulse and just the gangs stayed."

"And you?" Julian asked.

She shrugged, swallowed tightly. Perry guessed her about 20. Maybe a little young for Julian who said he was 29. He might be telling the truth. He acted older, but he had a rough few years, so that made sense.

"I should have, but now I'd just get stuck out on the road when winter comes. There's no working cars. I've been looking for days."

"Yeah. I hear you."

"You're not from around here?"

"We came off the road. Headed west."

"You got a vehicle? I'll pay you to take me south."

"We're headed west."

She made a dismissive face. She needed a shower and her nose glowed red with cold, but there'd been a pretty girl there only a few weeks ago.

"Not directly you're not. You can't drive through the city. The roads are clogged with broken down vehicles and the gangs will kill you for your vehicle, your food or whatever you have. Hell, they'll kill you just because they can."

"We're trying to get to Columbus. We need fuel and food."

Perry considered kicking Julian, but the kid read people well and it was too late anyway.

"There's not a lot of food left here. I wouldn't be this far out if there were. That's why I want to leave. I didn't expect it to get so bad so quickly."

Julian's eyes narrowed.

"So bad? What are you talking about?"

"There's no food. There's rumors."

"Rumors?" They all moved outside where they could see around. Cars choked Freeport Road, stopped where they stood on the day of the Pulse. Perry's military training warned this might be a con job, else they'd just stumbled into the most dangerous place in the world.

"Mostly in the central city." Her addition helped ease Perry's fear marginally. "Please, Mister. I'll do whatever I have to if you'll just get me out of this town. South is better than west, but west is better than here."

Julian glanced at Perry, but before he could ask his question or Perry could answer, movement behind a group of cars caught his attention.

"Dogs," the woman said. "They're hungry."

"They're hunting people?" Julian asked.

"Not yet, but – another reason to leave."

"Anything left in that store?" Perry drew his weapon to be on the safe side, nodding toward the grocery store he could see on the next block.

"I found tampons, duct tape and Sailor Boy crackers. I'll share – well, not the tampons."

Nails on the pavement alerted Julian who turned as a German shepherd launched himself at him, bearing him to the ground. Perry fired over its head. It kiyayed and scrambled away into the cityscape. The woman held her gun now too.

"I guess I just haven't met the dogs who started hunting humans...until now."

"Nor do we want to." Julian scrambled to his feet, drawing his own gun. "What do you think, Perry?"

"You been bit?"

"He got my coat sleeve." He pushed up the sleeve. He's probably bruise, but no skin was broken. "What's our plan?"

"I think we need to get out of here. Cities are a bad idea these days."

"But we're still trying to get to Columbus? Isn't that a city?"

"We have people there who might be able to help us. Let's sweep through this mall area before heading out."

"Mister --."

They heard the first shot.

"That's small," Perry said. "Kate. Follow me with the cart."

He turned and ran back toward the truck, hearing a larger weapon fire two shots before he got there. Joseph lay under a man whose body Katharine tugged on.

"What happened?"

"Two men chased us." Joseph rolled the body off him and stood, staring at the blood on his hands and jacket. "Katherine shot this one, but he didn't stop until I shot him too."

"Where are the gas cans?"

"We had to leave them to get away." Katharine loved to find excuses. Why not just shoot the two men and keep the gas cans?

"We'll go get them after we're all here. How much gas did you get?"

"Tank's half full. We got another 10 gallons where we left them."

Julian and the girl came into view, pushing the cart.

"Who is she?" Katharine had a feline light in her eyes.

"We were asking her for information. I wasn't aware we invited her to come with us." Perry said that for Julian's benefit.

"Anyone want to explain the dead man?" Julian apparently assessed the girl useful. She now scanned the parking lot, looking for threats.

"There's packs of dogs roaming the city. I guess even family pets will turn on humans if they get hungry enough. I'm Andi, by the way. And, I mean it. I have jewelry, money … my body. Whatever it takes to get the hell out of this city."

Julian looked at Perry while Joseph opted to wash his hands in a mud puddle, a long way from the scion of a billionaire family he'd been at the start of this journey. That dead man represented his first kill and he seemed hardly to care.

"If you help us, we'll give you a ride." Perry didn't like it, but the thought of leaving a young woman alone didn't set well with him either. "You guys get this loaded. Joseph, let's get those gas cans."

Weaving through the parking lot, Perry now scanned high for humans and low for dogs.

"Those gunshots might attract the wrong kind of attention. We need to find those cans and get out of here."

Somewhere down the block to their right, a cat fight echoed. A woman stared at them from a partially boarded-up window in the bank they passed. They retrieved the gas cans and headed back. Andi and Julian handed items to Katharine to organize inside the truck.

"You didn't find any food?" Joseph didn't complain about his lack of luxuries, but he'd asked Perry to consider the number of calories they needed to survive.

"Crackers and cocktail onions."

"I guess that's better than nothing." Virtually nothing, but their lives measured in small increments these days and Perry only hoped it got better in Columbus.

"To some in the city, that guy there is food." Andi nodded toward the dead body.

Joseph's forehead wrinkled while Katharine's eyes widened, then narrowed in thought.

"Okay -- Andi. Do you know this area? How do we get around Pittsburgh to head west to Columbus?"

"Um, well, I'm a city gal. I've only been out of town a few times, but – go back to Monroeville and we're going to take Pike Express north to bypass the town."

Julian snorted. Slowly, Perry joined him in the chuckle, followed by Joseph. They discussed going around Pittsburgh via Pike Express before deciding to check out the city.

"Yeah, this is what comes with not following our first instincts." Perry scanned the area, reassessing the whole democracy aspect of this group. Movement came from the west. "Let's mount up. That looks like it could be trouble."

"Trouble?" Andi looked where he indicated. "Yeah. Let's get out of here." She climbed in the passenger seat. Perry got into the driver's seat and the other three climbed into the bed of the truck. "Thank you," Andi said.

"That group back there looking for you?" He eased the truck into Drive.

"They think they are. You do what you have to do, you know? A woman alone."

Perry said nothing because he didn't know what to say. He just headed east again, skirting the broken down vehicles to get back to Monroeville and head north and then west...he hoped.

Family & Friends

Emmaus, Kansas

Keri Lufgren married a farmer less than six months ago and he believed he'd married a teacher, so she only recently learned how to work the milking theater and seemed disappointed Shane had no idea how to use the pasteurizer. He accidently figured out how to use the chiller. Since the EMP, they were lucky any of these things worked. Her husband Alex preferred to spend money only where he had to, so had few electronic gadgets and could run the barn off windmill power. Of all the farmers in Emmaus, Alex prepared best for the apocalypse, mainly by not modernizing.

By mid-morning, Shane cleaned all the stalls and moved the heavy milk containers into the truck for Keri, but she admittedly hoped he knew more because she felt badly waking Poppy to ask her questions. Alex's teenage sister was on the mend, though she joked that sore throats didn't prevent the Deaf from speaking in American Sign Language. Alex still puked at regular intervals and the

Ramirez family were miserable. Toddler Lisa just wanted her mommy, making Shane and Keri's lives difficult. When Keri came to check on Shane, he wrapped the girl in a fresh diaper.

"You're doing a great job there," Keri noted. "Where'd you learn how to change a diaper?"

"They don't use Velcro-closure covers there, but the Miristani use a similar setup. I changed a few diapers when I was in the Shalimar province."

"That's not women's work there?"

"Paderesh is different from a lot of Muslim areas – maybe because they aren't Muslims. They're Christians … sort of. Whoever was available – most often the mother or an older sister – changed the diaper. They thought it a little weird that a *ganha* would do it, but I changed Poppy's a few times, so it didn't look that hard and just seemed the least I could do for their hospitality. At least they didn't make me wash the diapers. They're still pounding laundry with rocks there. And, should I be concerned about what I found in her diaper?"

Ordinarily not a talker, Shane felt comfortable in Keri's presence. She knew the reality of a man's blood on her hands and neither of them wanted to talk about their trauma.

"It's probably fine. Babies' digestive systems don't work the same as humans."

They grinned at each other and then the radio crackled to life.

"Maverick, this is Click. You got ears on? Over."

Former Chicago reporter Click Michaels came off a commuter plane that landed in Emmaus during the original crisis a month ago. He needed something to do and the owner of the radio station KERB was out of town when the bombs hit, so Click stepped in. His job mostly consisted of relaying messages over Mission Ridge between the different parts of Emmaus and Mara Wells because their hand-held radios couldn't reach.

"Click. Hey, this is Maverick, over." Lisa stuck her hand down Shane's shirt, her little fingers curling around one of his nipples. He made a funny face at her.

"They need you on the northeastern border. There's a mob trying to break through. Over."

"I'm at Lufgren's Crossing and on horseback, so I won't be there immediately. Um, is Murphy on site? Over."

"He's headed that way now. Cai is supervising currently. Over."

Shane saw Keri frown. His thought exactly, but the flu ravished their defenses. Shane welcomed anyone who could still show up on the barricades -- lawyers, barbers, farmers. Soon as Baby Lisa could talk, Shane would teach her to fire a gun.

"Headed that way now. Tell them to fire over the crowd first and then take out the front line if they don't get the message. Over."

"Shane!" Keri gasped.

"We gotta do what we gotta do, Keri. And I gotta go." He handed Lisa to her. "Good luck. Maybe Cai

111

can help you tomorrow and I can go be Death on the barricades. He probably doesn't know anything more than I do, but I'm a lot better at security than I am at milking cows."

By the time Shane got to the hot spot, the crowd had dispersed, discouraged by the two dead bodies lying on the other side of the school-bus gate Emmaus used. Rob just got there as Shane rode up. He left the reins over Rocket's saddle so she'd feel free to move away from danger if shooting resumed.

"What happened?" the mayor demanded. "We're not trying to kill people."

"Not trying to, sir," Murphy said. About Shane's age, he'd done a couple of tours in Iraq as a National Guardsman before his unit won a Pyrrhic victory against the Army and the USDA, leaving only four survivors, who now worked with Shane to keep the migrant hordes at bay. Shane could use about six more like them but made do with what he had. "But sometimes it can't be helped."

"Did you authorize this?" Rob demanded of Shane.

"More or less. Any day the mob gets inside the wire is a bad day, so whatever it takes to keep them on that side of the barricades is an acceptable solution." Shane watched as Cai made his way off the roof of the bus. "Do we know who had the unpleasant task of killing two people?"

"Nobody's admitting to it," Cai said. "I shot over their heads."

Shane looked at Murphy.

"I wasn't here yet. You know I would do it – but I'd also admit to it."

Shane looked up at Jos Osimowicz on the bus's roof. He shook his head. At 15, he proved a good worker and soldier, but he so far managed not to kill anyone. One of the older Bennett kids stood with him. He didn't look like he popped his cherry today. A couple of older farmers stood behind the barbed wire farther down the line. They weren't looking Shane's way. It wasn't Shane's job to worry about their psyches. He'd worry for Cai or Jos or the Bennett kid, but grown men old enough to be his father weren't his concern.

"If it worries you, Dad, walk down the picket and ask. I think people are just scared enough of starvation that they no longer worry about killing strangers."

Rob cocked his head like a Labrador trying to understand calculus before he sighed.

"We need to assign someone to take care of the bodies."

"Yeah, that's – Murphy, you got a couple of guys willing to go outside the wire and post those bodies at the next intersection?"

Now Murphy blinked at him. Shane would do it himself if Murphy declined.

"Yeah," he said reluctantly. National Guard proved less willing to kill American citizens than the Army. Different training, Shane supposed.

"What are you doing?" Rob asked.

"We're going to post the bodies with a sign trying to detour them away from us. Hopefully, the evidence of us being willing to kill people will get the pressure off our border."

"Have you lost your mind?" Cai demanded.

"Yeah, kind of." No use arguing. He wasn't sane by the standards of August, but October was a different era altogether. "But it's the only way I can see for us to save lives. Those people are dead. Let their deaths mean something."

"By desecrating their bodies?" Rob had never scowled so deeply, not even when Police Chief Bart Rawlson called him to City Hall to deal with Shane during his wild youth.

"They won't miss them. If their people come back for them, they can take them, but I think they'll be more use to us posted out there than buried in the ground."

Rob sighed.

"Your heart gets any colder and it's going to stop beating."

"My icy heart is why you asked me to do this job, because I can ignore my conscience to do what is necessary. Jos, you okay with plying your graffiti skills?"

"Yeah." The idea didn't set well with the kid either, but he at least understood the chain of command here. Shane would do it whether they helped him or not.

A half hour later, Jos spray painted DETOUR, DO NOT END UP LIKE THIS on a square of plywood while Shane and Cai set a post in the ground. Two of Murphy's men stood with their M16s at the ready.

"A month ago, I never would have thought I'd be doing this," Cai admitted. "You?"

"I first saw this in the Mirage like three years ago. Wasn't my idea that time, but you know – live and learn."

When they finished, Shane asked Cai to walk back with him and sent Jos with the two guards.

"People are worried about you," he explained. "I haven't asked Mike to tell me what happened out there, but I'm hoping you'll tell me instead."

Cai stopped walking. Sometime during his outside adventures, he learned how to hold an AR15 at the ready rather than just strapped across his back. His gaze dwelled on the horizon but he cut a quick glance at Shane before answering.

"You ever run across any slavery in the Middle East?"

"A bit."

"Ever been held prisoner?"

"No. Well, except by American cops who didn't like me selling marijuana to the locals, but no – not really." He was never officially arrested. The sheriff was amenable to the stupid-kid argument and willing to allow Rob or Jacob to mete out punishment. That worked until college.

"Yeah, well, I've been there now. And, while I get why you are the way you are, I don't want my

115

heart to get hardened and cold like yours is. But I don't know how you quit feeling guilty when you've got blood on your hands."

"You had to kill someone?"

"It was an accident, but yeah."

"An accident? There's how you keep your heart from dying, man. My first time – no accident. I wanted the guy dead and I accomplished it."

"Yeah, but this morning – when some of them didn't disburse after I fired over their heads, I thought about firing into the crowd. Then someone else did it before I did."

Shane nodded.

"I know it stinks, but there's no shame in killing to protect those you care about. If they get in the wire, we all starve this winter. That reality sucks more than the reality we're living through right now."

Cai nodded, turned toward the Emmaus barricades. Shane eyed a truck driving toward them on the county road from the east. He dragged the AR over his shoulder to point in that general direction. The truck stopped and a man got out, hands held high in the air.

"Brian?" Cai muttered and started walking in that direction. Shane whistled to get Glister away from the bodies and then followed Cai, who embraced this newcomer.

"Brian Halloran, this is my brother Shane. How'd you get here?"

"I remembered what you said about Emmaus." With skin like light brown sugar and dark hair no curlier than Shane's, he reminded Shane of several men he knew in the Knights, except he didn't have a feral cast in his blue eyes. Pretty much everyone now scanned the horizon for threats.

"Cai," Shane started to warn.

"He's a physical therapist and you can't tell me there aren't folks who could use his help."

"Yeah," Shane agreed after a moment's thought. He didn't think Brian came to offer his professional services.

"I found April."

"That's great, man. You got her somewhere safe?"

Brian's gaze dropped to the ground.

"She's at the medical warehouse they were going to. The Army guys have a half-dozen women there. They've pimped them out and I think they must have a supply of something because when I bought my way in to talk with her, she was tweaked on something."

"Damn," Cai muttered.

"Medical warehouse – so, pharma?" Shane asked.

"Yeah. According to her, they don't seem to have sold it."

"Where is this?" Brian hesitated. He didn't know Shane and distrust was commonplace now.

"Hays," Cai said, then looked at Brian for confirmation. He nodded. In the services, Shane found the multi-racial guys more practical on some issues, so he didn't hold back.

"Jason told me they tried there and got rebuffed. They weren't interested in selling for corn or salt. They asked for diamonds, which – yeah. Wow! Jason said some of his guys wanted to hit the place, but the crew there are trained military and Jason didn't want to risk his crew."

Shane calculated how many volunteers he could gather.

"You get a good look around?" he asked Brian.

"She drew me a floor plan. It's in the truck."

"Get in your truck and follow us. We'll all sit down and discuss this. Does your wife have any useful skills?"

"She's a speech therapist."

"So you both have a little bit of medical training?"

"She worked as a phlebotomist to put herself through school."

"Good. We only accept people who have skills and Cai's wife is the town doctor, so you'll have to convince her of your usefulness. But, a warehouse full of pharma doesn't hurt. And, I think Mike was there, so he can probably give us some security details."

"Dad's going to lose his mind," Cai predicted.

"Not if they have antibiotics, he won't." Shane whistled for Glister again and started striding toward the barricades.

Professional

Shane hadn't been to Jericho Springs in two weeks and hadn't heard from Grant Rigby since he sent Javier Chavez to the Jericho B&B. He needed Chavez's help, but there were risks in letting Rigby know what he had planned. Rigby thought Shane should stay in Emmaus and not use his skills outside of town.

Since almost all of his clothes and everything else he owned remained in the Jericho Hotel, Shane stopped there first to verify the security system still wouldn't let him in. The computerized module controlling the system fried in the Pulse, sealing the locks on every window and door in the refurbished building. He didn't get in and the keypad gave him a good shock. Sooner or later, he might need to do something drastic because he stored Alex's seed corn in the basement, but for now, he admitted defeat and turned toward the B&B.

Nobody answered his text or acknowledged when he banged on the gate, so he eventually scaled the fence. A distinct possibility existed of one of the Rigbys shooting him while performing this maneuver, but a guy had to do what a guy had to do.

Chavez answered his knock on the front door.

"Hey," the CSA deep cover agent said, easing his gun into its back holster. "Hope you don't need anything high-level because everybody but me is sick – well, and the two little girls. If you can believe it, I'm actually making Jello." He shook his head in self-mockery. "And, I didn't poison them with mac-and-cheese."

"The flu?"

"Yeah. I think Ami and I brought it. I got sick first."

"That sucks, but it probably wasn't you. Half the town has it and I interacted with you pretty much before anyone else and I haven't been sick. Anyway, you feeling okay?"

"It sucked for a week or so, but I'm mostly on the mend. What do you need?"

Shane told him about the pharmacy warehouse.

"I can't afford to pull the National Guardsmen off the barricades. I've got a couple of ex-cons and my brother. I'd like to have at least one other professional on board."

"I need to know more than what you've told me."

"Of course." Shane pulled out Brian's floor plan sketch. After he told Chavez what he had planned and received a couple of good suggestions, he restated his request.

"Yeah. I'm bored out of my mind here. Love to shoot up a building and liberate some ladies. You should know, though – my eyes were open during the Pulse and I was blind for a few days after. I can see now, but they're not quite right."

"Can you tell friend from foe?"

"I can. It's just blurry in some places and they don't adjust to changes in light like they should."

"Blind, you're better than Cai."

"That's your brother?"

"Yeah. But we need the meds and Cai's going off with his friend Brian to rescue the guy's wife and they'll both get themselves killed."

"I don't really care. I'll take a five percent cut of whatever we get."

As far as Shane knew, Chavez was born a CSA operative. During his training, Shane noted Chavez didn't connect with people on assignments. If the op called for watching a child raped or puppies drowned, Chavez would dispassionately perform the op. Shane didn't think he qualified as an actual sociopath. He just kept the larger goal in mind far better than Shane did. Maybe he had more practice at it.

"Everybody else is taking a one-sixth share, then donating half to the medical center, but if you want to gyp yourself, okay?"

"I'd get, what, an eight percent share?"

"About. You in?"

"I am. When do we head out?"

"Tomorrow morning at the crack of dawn. Bring whatever weapons you have."

"You need a sniper, you know? And, that can't be me right now."

Shane nodded. He didn't like the choice he had to make on this one, but he knew he couldn't protect Jazz from the world they lived in now. When Shane asked to borrow two of his guys, Jason Breen suggested three potential snipers. His sister Keri was the only functioning member on the farm. Jos Osimowicz had to ask his grandmother's permission and Huffy had categorically rejected the offer. That left Jazz, a fully informed adult who could not only shoot well long distance but had some hand-to-hand skills and comfortably handled a variety of firearms. Petite and athletic, they could use her to get through any tight spots they encountered. And, though Shane felt sexist thinking it, she would be helpful with the captive women after they were freed.

Shared Scar Tissue

West Virginia

Julian threw another stick on the fire as the turkey turned on the spit. While driving down a West Virginia backroad, Perry slammed on the brakes and dashed off into the woods, firing his gun four times and coming back with two wild turkeys. The map identified this abandoned quarry for them. Driving as far as the spiraling road would allow found a broad shelf right above the deep blue water. They could build a fire without being seen from the road.

They would eat one turkey tonight and cock and save the other one so they'd have something to eat tomorrow.

"We could try fishing." Andi suggested. "My grandpa showed me how to make a pole with a little bit of string."

"We have a couple of fishing poles. Maybe you and Julian could take care of that at dawn," Perry encouraged. He would stand guard duty tonight, meaning someone else would drive tomorrow. Even

125

Julian, who never bothered to renew his license after prison, could drive West Virginia back roads.

"Where are Katharine and Joseph?" Andi asked.

"Um, yeah – they're married." Julian gave her a wide-eyed look. At first she looked perplexed, but then she snorted.

"Right."

She turned the spit. He liked her practical manner.

"So how come you didn't leave Pittsburgh when everyone else started heading south?"

She sighed.

"My boyfriend assured me we'd be safer in the city than out on the roads. It wasn't like we could go to Atlanta, where I'm from, so I believed him. But it didn't take long for everything to go to shit. We ran out of food so fast and then he went out and didn't come back. Then these guys showed up and - -."

"You don't have to tell me."

"It wasn't like that. I saw what they wanted so I gave it to them."

"Submitting to it doesn't make it any less wrong that they demanded it."

She stared into the fire.

"I think he pimped me out."

During the long silence that followed Andi's revelation, Julian stared into the fire and appreciated that Perry only growled softly. Andi didn't cry. Her delicate jaw bunched like she was pissed and then she continued.

"We hadn't eaten in three days and he went out early to look and never came back. I waited two days and they showed up. Something one of them said – they knew I was there because someone told them." She shuddered. "I pretended I was down with it so they'd give me some freedom, but I was looking for a way out. Thank you."

"The temptation is to ignore the humanity of strangers," Perry said. "I got shot down once. I was an Air Force pilot. Behind enemy lines in Kosovo, pretty beat up from the landing, couldn't speak Albanian. But this woman and her daughter helped me. They didn't have to. Maybe it ruined their lives to help me. When we got to where we were going, there was finally an interpreter and he said the woman said, ``Just because you are a stranger doesn't mean you're not human.' I always remembered that."

"It's hard to remember that when you're the one being abused," Julian added. A score of prison experiences filtered through his mind. He shared scar tissue with Andi, he thought.

"When the world goes off the rails, it's hard to keep your footing." Andi continued to stare into the fire. "I don't suppose it'll be any different further south."

"It would be warmer." Julian pulled his sleeping bag around his back for emphasis. The quarry had the benefit of being out of the wind, but he could feel winter crouching on the hilltops.

"I'll go with you as far as Columbus. Maybe I can catch a ride south from there."

"These roads are nowhere for a woman alone," Perry murmured.

Nobody argued with him. When Andi pronounced the turkeys ready, Perry cut up one in five more or less even portions and put the other one in the truck to cool. The Sullivans joined them around the campfire and they discussed their plans for tomorrow. Katharine thought they ought to bath and wash clothes while they had a chance which would give Julian and Andi time to fish. They agreed to take the day, try to catch a couple more turkeys and then head out for Columbus.

Perry stood guard that night, so he let Andi have his sleeping bag in the tent with Julian. The two of them lay there in the dark for a long time before she rolled over against him and said, "We could – you know?"

He'd loved Jenna, the woman who jilted him at the altar, but so much happened in the weeks since then that he felt like he hardly remembered her. Yet, he barely knew Andi.

"Maybe another night. I don't do hookups. We kind of got to know each other for at least a few days."

She giggled, not rolling away.

"Yeah, but we can share body heat, right?"

He liked that idea. They fell asleep with their backs to each other, warming the tent with their breath.

Jobs

Emmaus, Kansas

Mike tried to ignore the pain as Shane pulled the drain out of his side, but it clearly hurt. Shane dumped the tube into a biohazard bag and asked Cai to reposition the lantern so he could better see Mike's wound.

"Okay, you're going to need a few stitches to make sure nothing gets infected again."

"Stitches. Good times! One of you better start talking so I won't slug you."

"We're going on a mission," Shane reported as he prepped the wound with a lavage of iodine. "Treating people like you has run the town dangerously low on important meds, so we're going to go knock over a pharmacy warehouse."

"We? I don't think I can help you with that considering I get dizzy getting to the bathroom."

"We are a motley crew of the willing. The thing is, even though I'm taking the best I can scrounge

131

up currently, it's dangerous, so I need you to do me a favor while we're gone – watch over our folks."

"Of course."

"Just don't tear your stitches while you're doing it. Go up and down the stairs on your butt and don't do that more than once a day."

"Okay. I'm starting to get bored. Got anything for me to do that I can pretty much do sitting down?"

"Clean guns, grind corn," Cai suggested.

"Jacob will bring you what you need and set up a table in the hall. You don't have to do the stairs."

"How old is your grandfather?"

"Ninety-six, but he's spry, so you don't have to worry about asking him to do stuff. He claims you get old when you stop moving, so he's revisiting ADHD."

"Is that where you get it from?"

"Could be. Okay, last stitch. When I get back, hopefully you'll be on the mend and we'll start planning Santa Fe."

"I've got Nehemiah Lufgren making a batch of aviation fuel for you," Cai announced.

"Seriously? When did you start that?" Not that fuel production was his job, but Shane hadn't expected Cai to even realize what he had planned.

"A week ago. Grandpa said we're getting low."

"Yeah. It's amazing what farmers can put their hands to when they have to. Tying off now."

Mike let out a pent-up breath.

"Oh, good. I can pick my nails out of my palms now."

Shane smeared around the stitches with triple antibiotic ointment and rebandaged Mike's wound.

"So when are you leaving?"

"First light tomorrow morning. You probably won't even be awake."

"And you're going too?" Mike asked Cai.

"Yeah. April's my friend and I need to do what I can for her."

"You know he's dangerous, right?" Mike nodded his head in Shane's direction. Shane smirked. "He knows what he's doing, but guys like him and me – we deal death."

"I know that."

"And you're prepared to get bloody?"

"He's identifying drugs for us," Shane protested. "He only needs to get bloody if something goes wrong ... just like with you on the trip here. You rest and go easy on the sit ups. We'll see you in a couple of days. Come on, Cai, you and I need to get some sleep."

Shane jerked his head at Cai to have him follow to Jazz's room. Funny how a couple of weeks had changed it from Keri's bedroom to Jazz's. Getting used to that took less time than adapting to the mood lighting of lanterns.

"We're leaving at dawn," Shane informed her and Brian, who gave Glister a rub in the hall. Labs were such pet sluts. "Jason's providing a truck and a blocking vehicle just in case. You're clear on your roles, right?"

"I'm taking out the front window and hanging back unless you tell me otherwise," Jazz said.

"I'm shattering the glass of this side door as a distraction, then waiting outside until the shooting is over," Brian said. "If any men try to escape that way, I can kneecap them if I want, from behind the dumpster."

"I'm protecting her back until you signal me to come identify meds," Cai reiterated. "What if something goes wrong?"

"Get the hell out of there. Don't give the brothel another slave." Cai grimaced. Jazz rolled her eyes. Her gun and self-defense skills *were* better than Cai's. "Frank and Josh spent years of their lives responding to situations that were volatile and unpredictable. Ditto Chavez and me. You're a lawyer, a physical therapist, and a school teacher. Dad's not happy I'm bringing any of you."

"Since when do you care when you annoy Dad?"

"I grew up, Cai. This is the adult version of me. I wasn't born that way like you."

Jazz snorted and even Brian chuckled. Shane turned toward Jacob's room just as Marnie topped the stairs.

"What is this?" Her blue eyes snapped sparks at Cai. "I have to find out from your mother that you're leaving?"

"I'll be back." He sounded confident and looked scared.

"And, you! I asked you to *talk* to him, not convince him to go out and risk his life."

Shane recognized Marnie intimidated Cai, but Shane never worried about pissing her off.

"He's a grown man, Marnie. I'm going to bed. You two need to take this where you're not waking the entire household --." Marnie slapped him across the face hard enough to momentarily scramble his vision.

"You're risking Cai. You're risking Josh *again*. You're self-destructive and that's fine when it's just you, but you don't have the right to take other people with you."

Her words rang off the walls, followed by absolute silence. She turned and slammed into Cai's bedroom as Glister hid behind Jazz on the bed. Cai turned to follow Marnie, but she had locked the door. Shane's cheek burned, but he walked to the door as Mike came to the door of his room. Even injured, he had Shane's back and probably Cai's as well.

"Move," Shane told Cai, holding up his lockpick set. These were old solid doors with single throw lever-locks, so it took only a moment to unlock it. He could imagine Marnie's stunned expression as she discovered her childish maneuver didn't work. "You might want to let her know that if she ever hits me again, I will hit back." He said it loudly enough to be heard on the other side of the door. He turned on his heel and came to Jazz's door.

"Let's go, Glister." The dog shook in fear. Shane met eyes with Jazz. "Yeah, fear might be the appropriate response right now. Sorry if he urinates on your pillow." He strode to Jacob's room, leaving everyone to sort out their stuff without him.

Dawn Excursion

Headed Toward Hays – Next Day

Shane's mottled cheek begged discussion, but his green eyes told Jazz not to go there. Cai joining them this morning surprised her. He must have gotten some sleep because he didn't look more exhausted than usual. She also knew Jacob and Shane spoke for all of about five minutes and then no sound from their room until Shane's alarm woke at 4:30 am. Glister slept on her bed last night but got up at the alarm to make up with his human. Shane hadn't bothered to shave this morning. Jazz wondered if he conceded to the swelling or if he always skipped shaving before he went commando. Cai tried to say something while they were getting ready and was rebuffed with "Don't worry about it." From the fierce whispers from their room last night, Jazz surmised Cai and Marnie hadn't come to an agreement.

Jazz's mother always said brothers were meant for adversity and the three Tully brothers argued plenty. The Delaney brothers had a complicated set of adversities to overcome. Any lingering doubts she had about Shane's feelings for Marnie were obliterated last night. While everyone else watched Marnie storm to her room, Jazz looked at Shane's face and saw a resigned sort of calm with just a bit of spicy anger. He didn't let others hurt him. She learned in town security training that he had skills that could be deadly when pushed. That blow angered him, but mostly it seemed to remind him of something he long ago accepted. Whatever ended his relationship with Marnie, killed it root and branch.

The sky blushed with pearlescent pastels as they drove eastward, losing altitude as they went.

"So, who are you to the Delaneys?" Josh Callahan rode with Jazz on the sleeper seat of the semi. Cai drove the secondary vehicle with Brian directing the way and Shane's new friend Chavez riding shot gun. Frank Giffin drove this older truck with Shane riding shotgun. All she knew about Josh was he was Marnie's brother and had spent five years in prison with the McAuliff militia. A month ago, that history would have made her nervous. Now it exuded competence. Weird.

"I'm Keri's friend, but Jacob offered to let me stay with them when the furnace fried at my apartment."

"And you're from Mara Wells?"

"I am. How do you know that?"

"Paul Osimowicz thinks you're all that." Factoring that he'd been in prison for the five years since Shane left town, Jazz figured he was the youngest on this expedition. "You two dated in high school?"

"Paul's a creep and I don't want anything to do with him."

Something flickered behind his blue eyes. His features resembled Marnie's except his nose had been broken at least once.

"I'm cool with that. My sister and mother are strong women, so I don't have a problem with women who won't let guys push them around. Hey, Shane."

Shane turned so he could look at Josh, revealing his reddened cheek. His neutral expression masked something that made Jazz's gut tightened.

"Thank you for letting me prove myself."

"Jason picked you. I just didn't object."

"Yeah, but you swapped out Paul."

"I need Jazz's long-gun skills and Paul gives her the creeps, so …. You know your role, right?"

"When Jazz takes out the front glass, I follow Chavez in on the right flank, sweeping for the prosties, while you and Frank go left for the warehouse."

"Sounds like you listen. Good. Remember, they're likely to shoot back, It won't be like prison guards coming at you with batons and tasers. Just work your way in. Don't shoot the women unless they shoot at you and don't question Chavez. If he tells you to do a handstand, don't hesitate."

The dark Hispanic man who joined them scared Jazz on some deep visceral level. A feral cast to his eyes warned not to trifle with this man. Josh and Shane had bits of that look too, but the depths of cold in Chavez' eyes went to the earth's core. Frank, on the other hand, grinned and asked her about her day. Not all felons were violent criminals and she supposed not all mercenaries were dangerous. Or, er, yes, they were dangerous, but not to people they liked.

"Why aren't we hitting them at dawn?" Frank asked. "Groggy guards are easier than wide awake ones." Okay, maybe he wasn't such a nice guy after all.

"My intel says things don't get started there until around noon, which makes sense. Maggie rolls out of bed at 10 am because she's up until two. Flesh peddling is another late-night enterprise, so hopefully we'll get them before they've had coffee, but when we can see what we're doing."

"Are we minimizing casualties or is this a free-for-all?" Frank asked.

"You can decide how much blood you want on your hands, Frank. I personally shoot to kill because I don't want live threats at my back."

"That's why the kid is partnered with Chavez, right?"

Silence settled over the cab of the truck. Jazz knew the rumors – Shane somehow sent Josh and the McAuliff militia to prison. Shane surprised her by grinning at Josh and addressing the issue directly.

"You angry enough at me to shoot me in the back and blow the op, kid?"

"I'm angry, but Dad only took me in because I said I could produce for him, so blowing the op for revenge isn't going to happen. I need my cut too much."

"Just so you know. Chavez will put you down if anything happens to me during the op."

Josh looked stunned before he grinned. Mercenaries and felons had similar standards that didn't make sense to school teachers, Jazz supposed.

They took the interstate so they wouldn't have to deal with town cordons, though it meant dealing with crowds of pedestrians and occasional broken vehicles blocking the path. Shane didn't shy from showing off his AR15, so the pedestrians gave them a wide berth.

When they got to the Hays off ramp to the warehouse, they stopped to coordinate with one another and don their National Guard body armor. Since most of Murphy's squad died, they didn't need it any longer.

"We came by here a couple weeks ago," Frank explained to the whole group as they reviewed the map. The warehouse occupied a secluded corner of a suburb of Hays. "They seemed utterly uninterested in corn or salt, which might mean they already offloaded most of the drugs. Hays is just right there, right?"

"Not according to April," Brian said. "And her pupils said they were drugging her."

"Oxy and meth have a value," Josh pointed out.

"Yeah, but what we *need* is antibiotics," Cai corrected.

"We've been trying to purchase it for weeks now and nobody is trading," Frank explained.

Jazz tugged on the Kevlar vest Shane handed her. She watched him as he adjusted the straps on his and finally got hers situated. Frank frowned when Shane handed one to him.

"Problem?" Chavez asked.

"Owning body armor - totally against the law for me September 25. Didn't really want any. I honestly never planned to rob another place ever again."

Josh clapped him on the shoulder, grinning like a fiend.

"I'm liking this whole avoiding the ex-con thing."

"You're too young to be sensible."

"Enough," Shane said. "Far as I'm concerned, you're mercenaries following me into a potential firefight. I don't care about your pasts. You don't have to kill anyone, Frank. You just need to back me up. Chavez and I are going ahead on foot to scope out the ground. Stay in the trucks and be ready to bugout in case something goes wrong."

"What if the Hays security forces come check us out?" Cai asked.

"They won't," Brian insisted. "I watched this place for days. Hays set its borders and aren't trying to control this area."

"But what if?"

"Tell them you're on a trading mission and you're just taking a break while your principal is trying to negotiate with the warehouse," Frank offered. "Or let me do the talking."

"Just stay cool," Shane said. He jerked his head for Chavez and Brian to follow and they disappeared into the trees beside the road. Jazz studied her copy of the floor plan and considered where she should be to get the best shot without risking hitting innocent bystanders.

Raid

Hayes

At 9:38 am, Jazz Tully propped Cai's Savage 111 on the hood of the smaller panel van and sent a .338 Federal cartridge 400 yards into the top of the plate glass window that fronted the pharmacy warehouse's reception area. The glass shattered into a million pieces and a heartbeat later, Shane and Chavez rolled flash-bangs into the interior, followed by Josh and Frank tossing teargas canisters into the wings. Brian fired a shot into the top of the side door, shattering its glass. Women screamed in surprise and men bellowed.

Cai watched anxiously through field glasses as Javier Chavez shot two men immediately and then Shane shot one. They passed out of his sight, but he heard three more shots from three different guns. Jazz scanned the building with the scope, lips pressed into a tight line.

"Brian's got one on the side," she reported. Cai nodded, hearing what sounded like Shane's voice giving orders. Frank emerged from the front window, peeled off his gas mask and gestured the all-clear. Cai did another visual sweep of the building's exterior and Jazz slid behind the wheel of the panel van to move it closer to the building.

"All clear?" Cai asked Frank.

"That Chavez guy is a stone-cold killer," he reported. "Killed four. But Josh caught one he missed."

The soldier Brian caught struggled and begged for his life. Younger than any of his captors, he seemed less terrified of Brian than Frank.

"Stop it. I'll speak for you, man, but you can't annoy these guys."

Frank frowned at Brian. The teargas cleared for the most part, but Cai could feel it in his nose, threatening to make his eyes water.

"He's the one who let me in to see April. He knew I was her husband."

"I didn't want to do this," the kid begged. "I couldn't stop them, but I tried to do right by those women."

"I need to find April," Brian said to Cai. "Can you handle him?"

His hands were tied behind his back with a belt. Cai had a pocket of zip-tie cuffs. When he offered a set to Frank to use, the ex-con shook his head.

"I ain't a cop and I ain't using those on another human being. Won't stop you from doing it though." Frank walked down the corridor to the warehouse, leaving Cai to cuff the soldier on his own. That accomplished, he glanced through an open office door and saw scantily-clad women huddled in the corner, crying, cringing in terror as Brian entered and approached a blonde woman. Jazz flinched when April began to flail and try to run from her husband.

"Jazz, see if you can get those women calmed down," Shane ordered. "Brian, back off a minute. She's not rational. Just let Jazz talk to them."

Brian looked like he might cry. Shane zipped the soldier to a shelving unit and asked Cai to come with him to where Frank tried to figure out how to get into the warehouse.

"Now we know why they didn't try to off-load most of the meds." Frank pointed to a keypad on the wall. "The security door's fried. The Schedule Ones were in that room over there. We're going to need a ram. Kid, come with me."

Frank and Josh headed outside to back the panel truck up to the front entrance for easier and to get the ram they brought with them just in case.

"What should we do about the bodies?" Cai asked as Shane came back to the central corridor.

"Strip them of their weapons and anything else of value. They won't be needing it."

"Are you still human?" Cai asked.

"That's the seared conscience, Cai. I'll feel it later, but now – there's a job to be done."

As if to illustrate the point, Chavez flung a blood-splattered tactical vest in their direction.

"Idiots thought they were safe," he muttered. "They posted one guard and he ran out the door to be arrested by a physical therapist. Disoriented by the flashbang, I guess."

"I told you, I didn't want to do this." They ignored the protests.

"Don't forget jewelry," Shane told Cai. "Even the gold in their wedding rings has a value."

"Why don't I just start pulling their fillings?"

"If you've got that skill, go for it."

When Cai gave Shane an incredulous look, Chavez laughed.

"In Iraq, we had an interpreter who would pull the fillings. Gold's gold, he'd say."

"These were men."

"*Are* slavers men?" Cai blinked at Shane, dumbfounded by the question. "That guy you had to kill in Hutchinson – was he a man or a threat to your life?"

"That was an accident," Brian protested.

"Yeah?" Shane looked at Cai for the answer.

"I'm thinking about it." Cai turned to get to work instead of psychoanalyzing himself.

Frank and Josh came back carrying the ram and Shane went with them to help batter the door open. They shone their flashlights around the warehouse space and took in the shelves filled with supplies. In these circumstances it felt like they'd broken into Ft. Knox.

"I'll work on getting the dock open. Frank, bring the semi around," Shane ordered. Chavez took up a position out front to assure nobody showed up to stop them. The pallet jacks here still worked, so Cai and Brian got to work with Josh to pack the truck, taking virtually anything not nailed down. Shane and Frank returned to stripping the bodies. When they'd gathered all potential valuables, he asked Cai to join Josh in loading the bodies into the panel truck. Jazz came out of the office area.

"How are they?" Cai asked, straightening from his task.

"Terrorized and coming down off the drugs they've been on. For the record, I'm not sorry any of these men are dead." She pointed to the dead body Cai and Josh prepared to lift. "Can't think of anyone who deserved it more." She shook herself, refocusing. "Apparently there's power here. A generator. They were running it for a few hours a day for the clientele, who were paying in food. The freaking apocalypse and men still want to have sex with women they aren't married to." She shook her head angrily. Petite and athletic, her pulled-back hair revealed her roots were a lighter auburn than she normally sported. A sign of the times - women letting their hair go natural. His mom and Keri too. "These ladies would like showers and some food."

"I'll pull Brian off to help you." Shane stared in the direction of the women's sleeping quarters. "Might give April a chance to process what's happened. She's the prettiest of the women, so it makes sense she was the most terrorized."

149

"You sound like a man who has liberated a brothel or two," Chavez said from his post by the front window.

"Or three." Shane always seemed deeply ashamed of his mercenary career, but Cai caught a hint of something that sounded like pride on that account. "Good work, Jazz. I saw some cases of food and a hot plate in that office over there." Shane pointed. "The guys must have bunked in there. We'll take the ladies out the side door so they don't have to see the bodies – unless they want to. I've got extra clips if they want to make sure they're dead."

Jazz grinned at him. Cai never imagined his sister's friend as blood thirsty, but maybe she could handle the man Shane became in these circumstances. The world they now lived in demanded toughness and Cai knew he needed to stop clinging to a life that no longer existed. Apparently, Jazz already had, and Lord knew Shane needed someone to ground him and remind him of his humanity.

"Shane, come see this." Chavez held up a clipboard. "My eyes aren't up for all of this, but it looks like something you might want to know."

Shane flipped through a sheath of diagrams of several other buildings, paying no attention to most of them until one piqued his interest.

"That's Wyandot Lake." Curious, Cai didn't follow Josh back to get the next body. Shane's fingers skimmed over the floorplan. "Supposedly there's a lot of stuff there, all locked up. Ed Greyeyes would find this useful, especially if we can provide some guns." He glanced toward the pile of M16s and 9mm on the counter. "And, it looks like we can do just that."

"How long can you folks make it?" Chavez asked.

"My folks can make it to Christmas with current supplies. Some people like Alex can make it longer."

"Alex?"

"My brother-in-law. He owns a big farm. The one right next to you, actually."

"The deaf people?"

"You noticed that, huh?"

"I want to know my neighbors."

"Just so long as you don't shoot them."

Chavez laughed. Josh came by with the last body flung over his shoulder. Cai didn't feel guilty for not helping his brother-in-law with this gruesome task.

"They haven't done anything worth that … yet. They have goats, right?"

"They do."

"I like goat's cheese. There's a reason not to shoot them."

Cai shuddered. Their gallows humor didn't reassure him. What had Shane's alliances let into their community?

151

"So, what are you doing with your half of your cut?" Chavez asked.

"Giving most of it to the med center, paying Alex for eggs and milk, keeping a little bit in case we need it. You?"

"Giving it to the house. Rigby is well supplied. Why aren't you?"

"I am – if I could get into the hotel." Chavez frowned at him. "I own it – that old hotel across the creek from you. The security system fried in the Pulse and I'm waiting for the batteries to run down so it'll let me in."

"Modern technology, right? Amazing until it goes AI on you."

"Something like that." While they talked, Cai helped them load the military guns on top of the bodies.

"What are we doing with these women?" Chavez asked.

"Whatever they agree to. Jason would be willing to start a cat house, but only if they're willing."

"Jason?"

"Jason Breen. He's a businessman, runs trucks. He's the guy I ran moonshine for in high school. He's also Cai's father-in-law." Chavez's brows shot up toward his dark crew cut. Shane hadn't told Cai much about Chavez which probably meant he wasn't fit for normal human company.

"It wasn't such a white-picket upbringing as I thought." Chavez didn't seem as shocked as most people would.

"Small town middle America – Peyton Place with corn." Chavez laughed at Shane's apt joke, then he sobered.

"How are you getting through the winter?"

"What do you mean?"

"The boredom."

"Oh – yeah – I don't know. You?"

"Sex will help."

"Yeah. I wondered about that. She's pretty. Middle Eastern?"

"Egyptian, but she's been here more than half her life. Her name is Ami."

"And, she's really a doctor?"

"Absolutely."

"She hasn't volunteered her services at the clinic yet."

"She's had the flu. We all have. I'll remind her when she's feeling better."

The way they talked seemed like two casual friends just shooting the breeze, except for the dead bodies being transferred into the van for transport to the local cemetery.

"You sure about this?" Frank asked. "You risk stirring Hays up against Emmaus."

"They were keeping women enslaved here and you can't tell me Hays wanted that to continue.

They can send you away, but the least they can do is bury these assholes.".

After the women had showered and dressed in Army castoffs, Shane gathered them in the larger office and explained the situation to them.

"We rescued you because Brian told us you'd been enslaved, and we needed the pharma. Our obligation to you is cleared. We're willing to swing over to Hutchinson and drop you there. FEMA and Knight Industries are in charge there now, so what happened shouldn't happen again. Shouldn't, but the world isn't normal anymore, so ...." Shane shrugged like it didn't matter to him and maybe it couldn't. "We're willing to drop you along the route to Hutchinson or back toward Emmaus and we have a businessman in Emmaus who would help you build a brothel if you want. We can't take you in unless you have worthwhile skills, but Jason would cover your keep."

"Could we stay here?" one of the women asked. Shane blinked in surprised.

"I think so. There's materials in the warehouse to board up these windows. You'd have to figure out how to heat it. What would you do here?"

"I'd find more women willing to do this – without the drugs – and turn this into something cool. That warehouse space would make a nice club and people pay us in food and fuel."

Another of the women turned to her and it seemed she had a partner. April now let Brian hold her. She seemed kind of out of it, but clearly settling down. A slender blonde with brown eyes, she'd clearly been through a rough time.

"What are you going to do for security?" Frank focused on the practical considerations and also served Jason's interests. "This world is no longer safe."

"Let us have Quincy," the first woman said. "And some of the guns."

"How do you know if you can trust him?"

"He's just a kid," Brian said. "He knew I was April's husband. He kept that from his superiors."

"He argued for more food for us," April whispered. "He tried to make things better." She wept again.

Quincy promised to be good and he was turned over to the two nascent madams. Some of the women wanted to go back to Hutchinson and some of them wanted to stay with the two women at the warehouse. In the end, no one trusted Jason's offer and Cai didn't blame them. The thought of turning women into prostitutes, even if voluntary, didn't set well with him. He hoped that didn't change even as the world turned on its axis.

Country Doctor

Emmaus

Damn, Cai Delaney! Screw Shane! I never thought Cai would just follow Shane into danger like that. What is wrong with him?!!!

Cai acted weird since Marnie told him about her pregnancy. Inconvenient timing for sure, but she also knew Cai would vehemently resist an abortion, even if she could find someone to do it. She assumed he'd be stunned and then adjust, but he started avoiding her and acting standoffish when they were together.

Risking his life for no reason concerned her. Lots of other people were far more qualified than Cai to go on this expedition. Yes, they needed the meds, but not so badly that Cai should risk getting killed. Marnie didn't feel the least bit guilty about hitting Shane last night. The man was a menace. Cai might think he had something to prove with Shane, but why Josh, who ought to have gotten real-world woke-up in prison, would risk his life with him again baffled her. Didn't the first time turn out badly enough?

Marnie knocked on the Vances' back door, surprised when Allison Sullivan opened the door. With her honey-blond hair caught back in a ponytail, she wore an oversized apron over her jeans and shirt that said, "World's Greatest Dad."

"Hey, Dr. Callahan – or is it Delaney?"

"Legally, it's still Callahan because I wasn't married to Cai when I got my license, but I'll answer to either one. Dr. Delaney does sound a little superhero comic book."

"Ooo, I just started reading some of those last night."

"What are you doing here anyway?"

"Being useful – or trying to be anyway. Your mother-in-law said I can't stay at my house any longer. And, she's right. It'll take too much to heat it with fuel and if I'm there without staff I can't haul wood, so --." She shrugged. "I paid Jace Welton a cut of Granddad's pantry to mothball the place and I asked Trish if I could help with David if I brought my own food. So, here we are."

She limped to the back bedroom where David Vance sat in a wheelchair.

"How's he doing?"

"My grandmother was still in the hospital when she was like he is. I get why that can't be now, but I also understand why it was then. He gets really agitated if there's a lot of noise. He takes hours to feed. I don't think he understands what we say to him. He has to be lifted in and out of bed. And, he has to wear diapers."

"How long have you been here?" David focused his gaze on Marnie's moving pen.

"A week. And he is getting better. He's moving that leg a little now. Jonathan almost dropped him this morning and I'd swear he steadied himself, tried to anyway. He points at things he needs now."

His range of vision appeared to be improving as well. He probably bled into his brain, which might still be swollen. At previous examinations, he'd clearly been blind on the right of his visual field, but now he followed the pen a little past midline and then tilted his head to follow it for the rest of the way. Head control improved. Marnie removed the staples from his scalp last week and now checked the shaved area above his left ear, deciding he no longer needed a bandage. His hand wavered up to touch the area, left eye wide and questioning.

"You were injured," she told him. "You hit your head. There was a cut and a skull fracture."

The questioning didn't leave his eye. The right eye gazed straight now and the pupil reacted normally, but the lid still drooped. His arm remained flaccid, resting on a pillow in his lap. When she checked reflexes on his leg, it spasmed and she had to sooth it back onto the footrest. Was this new sign progress or not? Her inexperience yawned.

"How's he eating?"

"Better than when I first got here, but it still takes forever to get a cup of mush into him."

"Hmm, swallow reflex seems to be returning."

"Opening and closing his mouth seems to be the problem and I don't think he can chew or suck."

Marnie sighed. She didn't know what to do for him. Maybe if she'd been on the job for years as a doctor, she would have that knowledge, but in the emergency room in Lawrence, she mainly called specialists.

"David," she said. He focused on her. Definite improvement. "Are you hungry?"

Since he wore his lunch, she kind of thought he would say 'no' and eventually he jerked his head to the left in what she thought was a negative.

"David, raise your arm."

After a long delay, he lifted his left hand from the armrest.

"David, who is Allison?"

Nothing. A few more attempts like that and Marnie concluded not much had changed with the aphasia. He had dodgy comprehension of yes-no questions, but he could follow commands that used simple vocabulary. Meanwhile, questions other than yes-no confused him.

"So, are you reading these comics because things get boring around here?"

"Too much work to get bored. I'm reading them to David. James said he loved those comics and I figure it beats little kid books for trying to get him to relearn speech."

Three weeks since his injury. Marnie doubted David's future functionality.

"How's your leg?" she asked.

"I don't need the crutches anymore, but that's not the leg getting better so much as I'm getting better at using it."

"Well, hopefully when this crisis is all over, there's still doctors who can do nerve transplants. While I'm here, might as well examine you too."

"Can we go to another room? He can't talk, but he can see."

"Of course."

Allison impressed Marnie when she touched David on his good arm and explained she would be back soon. Whether he understood or not, she still treated him like a thinking human being.

Allison and David could both use Brian Halloran's services, but Shane drew him into his chaotic storm the moment he arrived. She needed what Brian had to offer and, damnit, Shane Delaney needed to start making better decisions if he was going to be put in charge of anything.

"You okay?" Allison asked.

"I'm just really tired." Marnie dabbed at her eyes with a handkerchief. "But I have a lot of places to stop, so I should get going."

"Don't worry," Allison said. "I can see David coming back a little every day. Maybe by next week, he'll surprise you."

"Next week? Maybe next month. You don't overdo. Your hip takes a pounding when you can't move the rest of the leg."

"I know. I'm trying to be sensible."

Marnie complimented her on her efforts and headed to her next patient. Kim Randolph had a cast that needed to be removed.

Requiem for an Asshole

Hutchinson, Kansas

Cai's gut twisted as they neared Hutchinson. He hadn't really thought about how it might affect him to come back here after what happened there. He expected to see soldiers around every corner and feel the zap of the taser in his ribs at certain intervals. Was this the PTSD Rob and Jacob said affected Shane's decisions?

They ran late because Shane insisted upon boarding up the huge front window while Frank and Josh took the bodies to Hays. The mid-afternoon sun provided just enough warmth to make the naked trees look out of place.

At Hutchinson, the fairgrounds now had hardened fences and guards in towers with gun mounts, but it didn't seem oppressive, more like defensive. Shane left Josh, Brian, April and Chavez to guard the trucks while the rest of the group made sure the remaining seven women got through the cordon. The Knights recognized Cai immediately and welcomed him back like an old friend. Shane grinned like he gained respect for Cai.

"Not sure I like him, though." The Knight officer cast a dubious expression at Frank.

"Kriczek, don't worry about it. If he acts up, I'll kennel him." Kriczek stared at Shane until something seemed to pass between them.

"Eric Faraday. Thought you were in Thailand or someplace equally better than this."

"I visited family. What can I say? Not clairvoyant."

"Mike kind of always said you were."

"Mike still believes in fairytales. And, he's okay by the way." Kriczek nodded. Cai hadn't thought he and Mike were friends and it didn't really look like Kriczek had wasted any time on worrying about Mike. "So, can we talk to Jacobson?"

"Sure. He's in the Command trailer. Cai knows where that is." He nodded to Cai. It felt odd to get such quiet respect from a Knight.

"They're not taking our weapons?" Frank asked.

"I noticed," Shane replied. "Libertarianism at its finest, baby. Lead the way, big brother."

Merchants and customers crowded the fairground selling their wares. Cai gawked at how quickly the midway was transformed into a bazaar. He kept glancing over his shoulder at the others who followed along like ducklings, Shane with a knowing and weighing expression trained on the crowd.

Jacobson came outside the command trailer to meet them. He asked after M

"It's a little tight in there for so many people and it's lighter out here. So, these are the missing women – some of them anyway."

"Some of them decided to stay in Hays and do what they've been doing for weeks now," Shane explained. The two knew one another, Cai realized, by the way they embraced. Not a hugger, Shane allowed it with some people and he always gave back what he received. Jacobson and Shane's embrace reminded Cai of friendly Dobermans smacking chests in a game of rough and tumble. They were friends now. If the command ever came down, they'd go for each other's throats. Neither Shane nor Jacobson seemed concerned that women choose to be prostitutes.

"Were all you ladies FEMA workers?"

Two were, but the other five hoped to get back home – mostly Wichita. Lana wasn't in this group. Cai wondered if the older woman made it home to Wichita already. It would be too late to bury her dog, but at least she'd be safe there – maybe. Jacobson fingered his mustache thoughtfully as they explained their situation. He opened the door to the trailer and called in for Helen DeWald. She embraced Cai like an old friend. She also embraced the two abducted FEMA workers. Then she looked at the other five women.

"We have a trading convoy going to Wichita day after tomorrow, so we should be able to get you there. Can't guarantee what it will be like. The Knights expelled the Army and absorbed the National Guard there. Cai, aren't you from the same town as Warren Sullivan?"

"I am. He's a good guy."

"He'll be good for trade," Shane added.

"Good, Faraday, but can he hold the city?" Jacobson asked. Helen released the women to go to the showers and find bunks. That left Jazz, who she gave a weighing look at.

"She's with us," Shane explained. Helen gave Jazz an admiring look now. Cai had to admit she'd been an integral part of the team. "I don't know what's going to happen in Wichita. According to Mike, Crispin is the Knight commander there, so yeah, maybe Ren can hold it. But the fact is, we're all flying blind here. There's never been a situation in the US like this, so who knows what's going to happen? I seriously didn't expect *this*." He indicated the fairgrounds.

"What did you expect?" Helen asked.

"A military depot. A UN outpost. Not a freaking *zocalo*."

"I have no command structure." Helen shrugged. "I've tried and tried to get hold of my superiors and nothing has worked." She nodded firmly to herself. "So, this is the best I can do. And it appears to be what people want and need."

"Not saying I disagree with that. I just didn't expect it. Whose idea was it to allow people to remain armed inside the wire?"

"Mine," Jacobson said. "My guys can handle it if it comes to it." He pointed to the one tower visible from their vantage point. "But it just seems like an armed society is a polite society. The Mirage would have been different, better, if everybody was armed instead of just those intent upon harming others?"

"That's right, you grew up in Chicago."

Jacobson laughed at Shane's observation.

"I saw my cousins terrorize our neighbors because my cousins were armed, but the neighbors were law-abiding. My dad, he was armed. He followed almost all the other laws though. He was the black-sheep of a criminal family. He had his own legit business, and nobody terrorized us because they knew my dad would end them if they did. So, yeah. Not going to take your guns – unless you prove you can't handle it and then on the next visit, you'll be disarmed."

"We're all cool." For a man nervous of body armor just a few hours before, Frank seemed quite comfortable with the pistol under his arm.

"So, we've got trade goods – salt and corn. What can we get for it?" Shane asked Helen.

"From us – canned goods. We've already sold a lot of what we had on hand and we have that trade mission going to Wichita. You know Hutchinson is sitting on the biggest salt mine in the US, right?"

"I do know that. And going down the *zocalo*?

"Depends. We don't ask what they're selling – we just want 10 percent."

"You've come a long way in a few weeks," Cai remarked.

"We all felt strongly that we couldn't devolve into what Wilkins tried to create. How badly were those women abused?" Helen directed her question to Jazz.

"They were raped and turned out as prostitutes."

Helen shook her head, looking sad. She breathed a heavy sigh. Cai suspected Wilkins similarly abused her. She came back from it and didn't appear defeated.

"Jazz, Frank, go *together* down to the *zocalo* and see what's available for what we have – not including what we picked up this morning. Helen, Jacobson, let's talk canned goods."

Cai followed Shane into the command trailer and sat down with pencil and paper to see what their corn might buy them. Shane and Cai bought several pallets of canned goods and arranged for one of Jason's trading crews to join the convoy going to Wichita.

While Shane finished with Jacobson, Cai wandered to the shed where he killed Dershowitz. The air had a slight nip of fall in the afternoon sun, but Cai felt sweat break out all over his body. He heard Shane walk up a long time before his normally stealthy brother got to him.

"Jacobson told me this is where it happened."

"Yeah." Cai grunted, wiping sweat off his forehead. "This is where I was enslaved and then forced to kill someone so I could live."

Shane stared at the place where the Vulture died. Someone scrubbed away the blood, but the concrete still had a stain.

"You're not going to say anything?" Cai asked.

"What can I say? It's a more righteous killing than my first one. The guy wasn't physically endangering me when I decided to make him dead."

"Why?"

Shane's gaze drifted into the roof. His mouth twisted in a cynical smile.

"He was on our crew – a serial rapist who beat a girl within inches of her life the night before. I found him in a situation where I wouldn't get caught and I ended him. I don't feel guilty about it – except in my dreams." Shane shook himself like a dog coming out of cold water and put a hand on Cai's shoulder. "If I had to do it over again, I'd still kill him. The authorities weren't going to do anything about him, and he was a monster. But there's a cost to death-dealing and so you want to limit how often you do it. You also want to grieve it better than I did. I committed murder, so I couldn't tell anyone without risking prison. I didn't talk about it with anyone until Mike and I were in the Mirage drunk one night and Mike told me about his first time, so I spilled. The funny thing is, I met Mike the night it happened. I could have told him then and maybe I wouldn't still dream about it, but

I didn't. I let it seep deep into my soul and the stain's never going to come out."

Cai turned from Dershowitz's stain.

"But you've killed people since. That couple who had radiation sickness …."

"Yeah, a mercy killing, which doesn't absolve me of all the people I straight up killed for less altruistic reasons … people who shot at me in the Mirage and Iraq. I think I killed someone in Afghanistan too. Maybe. It all blends after a while. And, you're not getting through the winter without more blood on your hands. I wish that weren't true. I'd like not to have more blood on *my* hands. But that doesn't look like our future. Dad had to put his knife through someone's jugular at Sullivan's."

That news stunned Cai and he blinked. Rob had been a jungle fight. Cai knew that but had never reconciled it with his father. Shane apparently didn't have a problem with that.

"Are you okay?" Shane frowned at his question. "You don't sleep and sometimes – you see stuff, don't you?"

Shane shifted, eyes hiding behind long lashes.

"War always comes back with you, to quote Grandpa. I see the people I've killed and the people who died around me. I didn't kill most of them. They died because the enemy did stuff that resulted in their death, but I still feel guilty."

Cai nodded, tears pressing behind his eyeballs.

"Larry wanted us to demand some dignity. They strung him up in a bag in the hot sun and he died."

"He haunt your dreams?"

"Yeah. And Dershowitz. He'd have killed Brian and probably me, but --." Cai gripped the back of his neck with both hands, making his left shoulder pop ominously. "He was still a human being and I still took his life. How do you live with that?"

"I do it by not entertaining thoughts like that." After chortling nervously, Shane rubbed his eyes, sobering. "I don't recommend that for you. Talk to Dad and Grandpa. Somehow, they came back from that."

"You haven't."

"Far from it. But then I'm still in it, aren't I? I'm Dad's hired gun, tasked with keeping people out of our cordon so we can live at their expense. It's absolutely necessary, but I'm thinking those are a few thousand more nightmares that will haunt me going forward. So, yeah. Sorry I can't give you better advice, but – Dad and Grandpa have been there. And – you know about Keri, right?"

"Keri? What about her?"

Shane toed the floor, clearly uncomfortable sharing this information.

"She had to kill a guy a few weeks ago. Maybe she's who you should talk to. Or your wife? I'm pretty sure she had to decide to stop treatment on people in the last few weeks. It's stuff you don't want to do, but it's the world we live in now. And while I volunteered to sell my soul in purgatory, you guys aren't going to have the choice."

171

Cai mulled over conversations he had with Shane since he came back home.

"When you decided you are a deist now, did you also become a Catholic?"

Shane frowned. Cai gave him a second before realizing Shane really might not understand his point.

"The nightmares I'm having – God didn't do that. *I* did. What's going on right now is not God's fault. Human beings chose to be broken and we continue to choose to be monsters. And, when our consciences bother us -." Cai paused because he sensed a trap Shane would take verbal and intellectual advantage of to take the topic away from a personally uncomfortable conclusion. "God is actually ultimately responsible for our conscience. He made us that way *before* the Fall. But we damaged ourselves by stepping outside His plan and *we* give ourselves nightmares when we do what is against our consciences." Shane heaved an exhausted sigh, no longer brilliant and hostile. Cai wished he could make him feel better.

"But, hey, Shane – you saved a group of women from degradation today."

"Good works don't balance out sin, Cai. Right?"

Cai nodded, recognizing he just walked into a cul de sac of Christian doctrine. It would have sailed over most non-believers' heads, but Shane reluctantly attended Sunday School, and church services. The valedictorian of his high school class hadn't forgotten the lessons he rejected.

"I'm trying to make you see that God isn't going to reject you because of your past."

"You assume I want to be accepted by the cranky old man in the nightshirt."

Cai snorted, then chuckled, surprised to realize Shane's petty insults of the Creator of the Universe no longer irritated him. He recognized diversionary tactics now.

"That cranky old man loves you and you can go to Him with your brokenness, completely bathed in the blood of your victims, and He'll understand and grant you the grace to be forgiven."

Shane shook his head.

"That's the problem I have with your god, Cai. That he would forgive *my* sins – what the fuck is up with that? That's forgiving the unforgivable. And, while it might help you sleep at night because you won't have to answer to him for the guy you shot – yeah, okay, it was you or him and I completely understand that. – But what I've done – not even close. I envy you for finding a way to not wallow in it, but I can't accept a god who would forgive it."

"We're not talking about Dershowitz, are we?" Shane froze, throat working convulsively. "Marie?"

"Nah, I'm as guilty as you are on that," Shane replied. "I just don't understand how forgiveness works. How can God forgive what shouldn't be forgiven?"

"We're broken. He isn't, so He can do what we can't."

"Sounds like magical thinking to me."

"And inconvenient for you if it's true."

Shane heaved a sigh. A still small voice echoed that Cai should back off now.

"Thank you for sharing with me," Cai said. "Not feeling so alone might help."

"I hope it does. It's not been my experience, but – yeah, that might just be me." Shane shook himself again. "I should go check on everyone else. I'm responsible for them and if they screw up, it's entirely possible Jacobson will shoot me in their place."

"Seriously?"

Shane nodded and turned to leave the shed.

"Maybe that's part of your problem. You've bought into the whole group sin fallacy."

"And, maybe we should stop talking about this topic because Christian doctrine doesn't apply here."

"Well, that is Christian, but it's also libertarian and that sure looks like what this new society is sorting itself into."

"You think?"

They were the same height, but his brother's stride seemed longer and faster. Cai had to walk faster to keep up.

"Jacobson kind of got me thinking that way, yeah."

"Are you?"

"What?"

"A libertarian like Dad – an anarchist like Grandpa?"

"Hmm, I'm a registered Republican. I admire a lot of what Dad and Grandpa believe, but I don't – well, I didn't – think it was workable. Now I don't know. I think voter registration no longer exists and maybe their ideas make sense in this new world we're in. You?"

"I build walls to keep strangers out so we can survive the winter. What is that? Totalitarian?"

They reached the transformed midway and Shane paused to look both ways.

"Doesn't look like the OK Corral yet, so maybe I get to live another day. Jazz and Frank are supposed to be working the *zocalo_*. You want to go check on the truck or them?"

"I'll check the truck. This whole Middle Eastern bazaar aspect of this baffles me."

"And it feels normal for me, so yeah. Don't let Josh give you any guff and if Chavez has already killed him, don't object or he might kill you too."

"Who is he?"

"Chavez? The guy who trained me, so if you think I'm a badass – yeah, be afraid."

"He is scary in a way that Mike isn't. I thought you were badass that first night, but the longer I know this new you, the more I worry you're going to end up shattered."

Shane raised his eyebrows, but not in surprise and he didn't argue against Cai's point. He disappeared into the crowd, leaving Cai to pray for his brother alone.

Zocalo

After passing a group of buskers with an impressive collection of food beside their open guitar cases, Shane found Jazz and Frank dickering with a bearded guy surrounded by live chickens in cages. Shane refrained from interrupting them, though he planned to kick Frank all the way back to Emmaus if they were trading corn for chickens. Emmaus had plenty of chickens.

It turned out the guy had a pallet of citric acid for sale for five bags of corn. Jazz haggled him down to two bags of corn by the time they shook hands. Cass reminded Shane of something out of a Cheech and Chong movie – loose natural-fabric clothing, long hair in a braid, a headband across his forehead. A marginal businessman during ordinary times, he flipped to selling something other than pot and Shane suspected he would come out way ahead.

"I'm supposed to meet the guy with the beans in 15 minutes." Frank glanced at the watch he wore. Shane wondered what septuagenarian it had belonged to before the Pulse. His windup was a gift from Jacob when he was 12. "If you want me to handle this too, I can. Shane's here now."

"Thanks, Frank." Jazz refrained from rolling her eyes. She didn't need Shane's protection and she knew it.

"Cai's at the truck too," Shane provided.

He truly admired Jazz always, but the lithe teacher's trade skills impressed him. He's not seen her in merchant mode before. She clearly knew her business.

"How many beans and how much will it cost us?" he asked her after Frank walked away.

"Frank negotiated two pallets for 10 bags of corn. Salt was a waste coming here."

"No real surprise given Hutchinson and Emmaus have competed for half a century. Assuming Vin and Alex's ethanol project works, this trip was worth the fuel. It's not a criticism, but why citric acid?"

"Your family can stave off scurvy with crabapples, but what about the rest of the town?"

"Good thought. I'm pleased with what we accomplished here today. And, I think Frank at least will be welcomed back here." That was really the whole purpose of this trading run to Hutchinson, to vouchsafe some Emmaus folks before the Knights swapped out strangers.

"Jason needs to be careful to send the right people." They stopped at the buskers, now singing a bluegrass-flavored ballad about the bombs. Bluegrass didn't impress Shane, but the lyrics compelled and the female singer's voice commanded attention in any genre.

"Yeah. I'll suggest that." Jason Breen did accept suggestions – on advisement. "Did you talk to the guy over there?"

"We ran out of time."

Shane led the way to a booth with barrels of potatoes where a woman asked what he had to offer in trade. Her potatoes were more precious than corn in over-supplied Kansas, so even with Jazz's help, Shane parted with two pallets of corn for a pallet of potatoes. That tapped their trade corn, so Shane said they'd meet her man at the truck and he and Jazz headed toward the gate.

Cai, Frank and Chavez talked with a man as they approached. Frank shook his hand, which piqued Shane's curiosity. Frank explained they'd been unloading corn for the beans and citric acid when the guy asked about the salt.

"He's got potassium iodine. Apparently, FEMA has plenty, so it was going to be a wasted trip for him. He'll take 10 bags of salt for one dry gallon."

"You're sure it's *potassium* iodine, not sodium iodide?"

"Yeah, I asked, and Chavez checked it. A few weeks ago, I didn't know we needed potassium iodine to protect our thyroids from increased radiation levels. What a horrible way to learn biology!"

Shane opened his mouth to compliment Frank's efforts, but Cai interrupted.

"Meanwhile – Shane, I need to talk to you and Jazz." Cai jerked his head for them to follow him a little way. Shane cast a "sorry about that" expression Frank's way and the ex-con grinned like he totally understood.

"What is it?" Jazz asked when they stopped.

"April's bleeding."

"From?" Shane asked.

Cai stared at Jazz, clearly uncomfortable.

"Vaginally?" she asked. Cai nodded, blushing.

"Could be miscarrying – which isn't a bad thing under the circumstances. We got penicillin on this run, right?" Shane nodded, although he didn't understand the meaning of the question. Wait – penicillin – vagina – *Oh, shit!* "I'll let Marnie make that determination."

A whirlwind of dust and debris emerged from the residential street across from the parking lot, wrapping them in dirt and cold before passing on.

"Feels like winter," Cai remarked.

"Let's hope not. We're nowhere near ready for it," Shane muttered as they headed toward the trucks.

War Stories

Emmaus

Jacob used the edge of the soap dish to flatten the toothpaste tube. He'd looked under the sink to no avail. He'd have to ask Jill if they had more or could get more. He squeezed a tiny amount on his toothbrush. As he left the bathroom, movement in Shane's room drew his attention. Mike cleaned guns half the day, then ran out of steam mid-afternoon and needed a nap. Of course, that meant he couldn't sleep now.

"How are you?" Jacob asked.

"Chillin'. Getting dark out there. When do you think they'll be back?"

"I don't know which I don't like. Shane himself made an order against night trips after one of our convoys was attacked last month. I don't like it when he breaks his own rules."

"I never met anyone better at flipping the script than Ric."

Jacob could barely make out the Hispanic mercenary by the fading light from the windows, but he could sense the smile.

"Why do you call him 'Ric'?"

"He went by Eric Faraday for the whole time I knew him. I knew it wasn't his name. It's practice in the Knights. Nobody uses their real name. I use my real first name. Most of us do. I'm curious why he changed the whole thing."

"Eric is his middle name. Faraday's his mother's maiden. That's all I know. He came back different. Do you know why?"

"You served in World War 2, right?"

"I did. And men do come back from that different, there's no denying. Something else happened."

"The Mirage is a chaotic place. You have to do things that don't necessarily fly in white-bread America. Then you come home, and people complain that you've changed." He sighed. Jacob nodded. "You know that coz you were in France or Germany and it wasn't all parades, but maybe you forgot. And, maybe the American government ought to quit paying companies like Knight Industries to send guys to fight wars that ain't even declared halfway around the world for control of resources and then we won't come home different."

"I agree with you. It doesn't mean I'm not worried about Shane."

"Yeah, and maybe you should be, but he's a strong guy and he needs to be useful."

"I know. That's why I haven't said anything about him working on that old Skywagon. Deke Hanson abandoned that thing a long time ago. Mothballed it nicely and then went to Florida and never came back. So, it's mine because of the storage fees. And, I figure you know what Shane's got in mind."

Mike nodded.

"My wife's in Santa Fe with her mother and they're alone. I want to go get them."

"And, you should – soon as those stitches heal up. Shane's probably got a few more days of work on it. Ought to coincide nicely with you being ready to travel. Just – if there's something I need to know about that boy – don't keep us in the dark."

Mike nodded, but he didn't say anything. Did he have nothing to say or did he not want to give away Shane's secrets? Jacob suspected the latter. He didn't press. Just said goodnight and went to his own room. He awakened when Shane slipped into bed.

"Everything all right?"

"No one on our side dead. Most of the women returned to Hutchinson and the ones who didn't decided what they wanted to do. Here?"

"It's been quiet. Posting those dead bodies got the crowds off our north border."

"Yeah." Shane's voice sounded wistful in the dark.

Jacob concentrated on settling his breath, listening to Shane not do the same. Jacob lay there praying, waiting for his grandson to doze off. Eventually, he did, only to jerk awake every hour or so. Was he haunted by the men he killed today or whatever it was that he'd brought back with him from Miristan?

Why the heck do they call it the Mirage, Lord? The reality of war has deadly consequences. Why do they have to joke about it? Did we teach them this stupidity by only telling the stories we wanted to remember?

Jacob sat up, settling his pillow against the headboard.

"You're going to listen now."

Shane swallowed tightly.

"I need to sleep."

"You do. You aren't. You're listening."

Jacob sent a silent prayer to God that telling this story he had never told before would fall like a seed on fertile ground and bloom in God's good time.

"I know you've seen the movies – *Saving Private Ryan* and what all. And they tell a story. But it's not the story of the guys who were there – not my story.

"We were lucky. We weren't the first company to hit the beach. Able Company took it in the teeth so we could learn from their mistakes. My company was still five thousand yards from the beach when the artillery fire hit us. The shells fell short at first, then Boat No. 2 was hit dead on. Men I knew and trained with drowned. When we hit the shallows, a shell hit Boat 5 and killed a couple of guys. The boat sank, drowning some more.

"There wasn't a wall or a tree or even a pothole to hide in. No cover at all. The mortars were bad enough – pounding your ears, but soon as Able Company hit that beach, machine-gun fire came from both ends. If you were standing, you were ripped apart before you made five yards. If you fell in the water, you'd drown because your pack was overloaded. I jumped into water over my head and the only reason I didn't drown was this Cherokee fella I got to know later – Redfeather -- he was using the surf as cover, standing up to his nose in the red froth. He was *tall* and he cut away my pack so I could flounder to where I could breathe and stand on my feet. I learned later that half the company died before they ever hit dry ground. The surf ran red as the few of us who survived followed Redfeather. He crept forward with the tide, like a crocodile. We hid among the dead bodies of our fellow soldiers, their blood in our mouths."

The scene blossomed in Jacob's mind, as clear as the day it happened.

"There's this rock, up on the beach and Redfeather, me and two other guys make a break for it. All I've got left is my rifle – not even a helmet and my ammo is wet. One of those guys dies before we make it, but then four others follow us. Two of 'em die and I get a helmet out of it. Redfeather sees another hiding spot and we run for it. More follow. Men fall, but more make it to the hiding spots. The smoke from our destroyed boats is providing us cover. Now, that's irony, right? Soon we're at the seawall, which didn't mean we were safe – just meant we might live a little longer. There's these pillboxes up on the brow of the hill and they can see everything. All we can do is crawl through the tall grass, hugging the ground, until we find this shallow gully. We get to within 20 yards and we fling a grenade at the pillbox. Shrapnel peppers the front wall. The next one rolls back at the guy who threw it, injuring him. Redfeather, who is a private and never expected to command his own company, decides this is a bad strategy and we crawl along a drainage ditch to flank the enemy. He takes them out with his rifle.

"Hey, we've seen we can actually kill the enemy. The Germans ain't gods. They're just doing a real good imitation of it. There was no time to grieve for our dead friends, so we moved onto the next town, joined up with a Ranger company and tried to get revenge for what happened out there in the surf. Dealing all the death in the world doesn't bring back those you lost though.

"It's not until I'm on the troop ship home – years later, that I wake up in a cold sweat reliving what happened out there in the surf like it was happening right then. My ears were ringing just like they were that day and I could taste the salt water and blood, feel how the body I used for cover moved up and down in the surf. My friends were having the same nightmares – maybe different parts of the same beach -- and we talked about it and sometimes we cried. We struggled to remember the names of guys we would never forget. And, to sooth our pain after reliving the horror, we told the good stories – the funny stories. And when we got home, we told our wives and sweethearts that we really didn't want to talk about it. When we did talk about it, we talked about heroism rather than the death. We set our boys up to be mangled in Vietnam and they in turn set you up to be mangled in the Middle East."

Shane sniffled in the grey darkness. Jacob dropped a hand on his shoulder and counted it progress that Shane didn't pull away. They lay there, each remembering their own war, for a while before Shane croaked out a story.

"We didn't assault any beaches where the enemy had months to dig in. That was just dumb." Jacob snorted because he'd often privately thought that himself. Shane heaved a deep breath. "I got shot one time – just in the vest. God, that hurts! You can't breathe at first and then when you do – feels like it's gone right through you. But we were in a fire fight, so I didn't have time to indulge the pain. I dragged a buddy out to the trucks, then drove out of their mortar barrage. Bits of the road just turned into dirt fountains, sometimes so close I thought we were dead, but somehow we weren't. And then we got out of range. And sometimes I wake up from that one."

"And all the others? The more you visit them with people who understand, the less they visit you in your sleep."

"You don't dream about it anymore?"

"Every now and then, but no, not so much. We didn't know we were doing it – therapizing each other with those stories. We thought we were just refreshing our memories, mourning our dead. It was a different era. So many of us had come off farms, so we knew about death. We'd seen it. Redfeather – Jason – no, Jim Redfeather -- had killed a man before he ever left the States – a rustler who had killed a man on the reservation. They chased him to ground and he ran right into Redfeather, a 15-year-old kid who didn't want to kill anyone. So, you know – we weren't as sheltered as your father's generation. And we later learned about the Nazi camps, what they were doing to the Jews and that helped. In retrospect, we told ourselves we did the right thing."

"The Mirage isn't the right thing by anyone's standards."

"Yeah and some of the things we did – war is hell and hell isn't lovely even when you wrap it in a patriotic bow. Yeah, we saved a bunch of Jews – good on us. Killed a lot of Germans and not all of them were soldiers. Some of them – most of them – didn't need to die. We just wanted revenge for our buddies. Did you need to kill those yesterday?"

The bed shivered as Shane heaved a sigh.

"I don't know. Maybe we could have negotiated an exchange for the meds, but the women were a renewable resource, so we probably would have just alerted them that we were coming if we'd tried to buy them. It never seems to matter though. My conscience can be consciously clear, but I still dream about other stuff where it's not."

"Set off by the more recent killing?" Shane sighed. He didn't exactly nod, but Jacob knew. "Yeah. I wept over the first deer I shot after I got back. Vi's Dad was with me and he talked about World War 1. I thought he was seriously confused, but then I went and talked to him a few times when the nightmares got bad. That's how I knew how to help your dad."

"Way he tells it, you witnessed to him and he became a Christian."

"Yeah, denial protects us. There was a lot of talking before he accepted Christ – or maybe a lot of talking before he *felt* like he'd accepted Christ. Hard to tell. And, it does help to have that faith relationship."

"How do you know? I mean – it's your default. You've never known anything different."

"Not true. I accepted Christ in a foxhole somewhere in eastern France. The one nightmare I still have is from a time after that, when I acted in revenge instead of self-defense. I want to believe His grace is sufficient to cover it as it covers the other, but it confronts me every now and then."

Shane twisted so his gaze met Jacob's. They locked upside-down gazes

"Did you ever worry you were going to hell?"

"Yes. All the time before – some of the time after. It got easier as my faith grew. And, I believe He doesn't see our sins after we accept His redemption, but I still judge myself because I shouldn't have done it."

"Done what?"

Jacob had never told anyone this story and he wouldn't tell it now except he sensed Shane needed to hear it.

"Killed a kid. We were sweeping a village and he shot at me. He might have been maybe nine or 10. We'd lost two guys to a sniper an hour before. Not him -- too small to hold a rifle that big. I cornered him in a stable and he shot at me with a pistol. I could have just taken the gun away from him, but instead, I unloaded three rounds into his chest. And God's grace may be enough to cover that, but my conscience will never accept it until I stand before Him and hear that I am forgiven."

A long poignant silence fell between them. Jacob saw Shane's mouth open as if to speak and then the sound of gunfire carried on the chill morning air and Shane rolled out of bed to look out the window before his radio crackled to life.

"Maverick, we've got a large crowd of refugees pushing on the south-east entrance at Old 24. What are your orders? Over."

Shane whispered a swear word and reached for his pants, juggling the radio.

"Bullhorn first, warn them, then fire over their heads and then - ." Jacob watched as his shoulders heaved up and down. "And then fire into the crowd. I'll be there in a few minutes. Over and out."

Shane dropped the radio onto the bed and buttoned his jeans as the town's air raid siren filled the morning air. All around them, they could hear screen doors slamming and engines starting. Shane had planned for this. If need be the whole town over about 16 would turn out to stop strangers from getting inside the wire.

"It's never going to end, is it?"

"Never's a long time, son, but the war's at our gates and you can only deal with the objects in view."

Shane swore again, grabbed his shoes, shirt, and a jacket and shot out of the bedroom. Cai looked just as disheveled as he followed Shane down the stairs. Rob and Jazz followed a moment later, Jacob prayed that nobody on either side would have to die today, then got up to dress so he could join Jill at a secondary cordon in case the first one failed. This was their life now.

Fit

The basement computer center never felt warm. Dylan wrapped a blanket around his shoulders before lowering himself into a chair.

"I'm sorry to press this matter," Ami said. "I just really need to get started on the information on this thumb drive."

"I get it." Dylan ran a shaking hand across his face. "Why am I still feeling so shaky when everyone else is better?"

"The flu affects different people different ways. This one has a longer duration than most, but the symptoms really aren't that bad. Besides weak, how are you feeling today? I saw you held down breakfast."

"Mostly just this vague headache behind my eyes and I can't seem to get warm. Yesterday I felt better, but now I'm feeling ick again." He rubbed the right side of his forehead, then plugged in the thumb drive.

"Don't hover," he grumbled. "Sit down. I'll show you what I find."

He typed occasionally, often staring at the screen with a grumpy expression. Grant came in after a while and asked how things were going.

"Password breaker got through the first layer. Whoever set this up was my-level good. Pull it up on Monitor 3, so she can see what I have so far." Dylan rubbed between his eyes. "That's only part of it. There's a whole section that is double encrypted and that'll take me a bit longer to get into. But you have quite a lot there, so maybe I can go get some aspirin and take a nap before I tackle that."

"Yes, of course. I'll review this and you can finish tomorrow."

Dylan clapped a hand over his mouth and scrambled for a garbage can to puke. He took it with him as he headed to the rest of the house.

"Do you want to be alone with this?" Grant asked.

"Until I know what it is, that might be best."

He nodded and followed Dylan out of the room.

The virus, bioengineered at Lakeland CDC facility in New York, used a hybrid virus of common flu and a swine flu variant. Designed as a first-wave tool to knock down resistance during an invasion, patients became contagious within a few hours of exposure. Following a 24- to 72-hour incubation period it caused flu symptoms up to two weeks. The scenarios for infection proposed for the US suggested multiple population centers to disburse the virus more quickly. The analysis estimated the death rate would be very low, mostly among the elderly.

And then Ami opened a vid file and saw Samira's face looking anxiously into the camera.

"You must open the second file now. I've provided a medium for treatment, but I haven't yet discovered all the needed material because I haven't got it. This virus is engineered to target certain DNA and hormones, so the counter measure will be found in DNA, I'm sure. But I don't know that I'll be the one to uncover it and so, I'm asking for your help. The vials represent all of my work thus far. Don't be fooled by the low death rate. There is a second-wave component to this and there is also the potential for mutation. If the swine flu variant does not remain attenuated, it could become as aggressive as the 1918 flu. Details of the second-wave component are found behind another layer of encryption. You know me so well, I'm sure it won't be hard for you to guess my passwords."

Ami sighed. It had taken her an hour to read the file and she didn't know much more than what she knew from having experienced the flu herself. She'd have to wait until Dylan felt better tomorrow. She headed upstairs. Dylan slept on the family room sofa while his parents prepared dinner in the kitchen. Ami gave them a broad overview of what she'd discovered so far.

"The flu. That seems anticlimactic," Grant said.

"Could any of us have mounted a defense in the last couple of weeks?" Ami asked.

Grant shook his head and Emily laughed.

"The girls weren't so sick," she noted. "A Girl Scout troop could have invaded us and none of us could have done anything about it."

"And when it passes you have a population who can get back to work for the invaders," Grant theorized.

"Second wave? What does that mean?" Emily asked.

"Not certain. Perhaps a stealth virus that reactivates symptoms months later. I couldn't go beyond where I was because of the encryption. Samira seems to have thought I'd know how to get into the drive, but I really don't."

"Dylan needs rest. He can try again in the morning."

As if hearing his name, Dylan sat up on the couch and stared at them.

"You all right, son?" Grant asked. Dylan didn't even blink. He stood and moved toward the bathroom, whacking his shin on the coffee table. He fell full-length to the Persian carpet and then started to jerk, his hands fisting, drool running down his chin, eyes rolling back in his head.

Busting the Wire

Rocks hailed against the tractor, breaking the guide lights, and forcing the guards to hide behind the barricade. Shane pushed his way to the front for a better view. A crowd of mostly adult men formed outside the eastern Old 24 barricade. Armed with rocks mostly, they pushed against the tractor, climbing over the dead bodies of their own former front line.

"What do we do?" Anders shouted when he saw Shane. Down the line, the electrified barbed wire sizzled as someone grabbed it to try to climb over. The guy screamed and let go. Shane could hear women somewhere shouting "We need food. Our children are starving."

"Jason and the militia are headed to the other checkpoints." Shane watched as Murphy and two of his National Guardsmen opened fire on the front line again. In the sharp morning air, he smelled the iron tang of blood. He opened the action packer behind the tractor and pulled out tear gas containers and a couple of flashbangs. "We need to shut those women up. Whose got an arm to send one each of these into their midst?"

Rafe Conopher appeared from the crowd and grabbed the canisters before heading down the wire to locate where the women stood. Shane, staffed as he was by volunteers, didn't try to instruct the former high school quarterback on what to do.

"Murderers. You have no right to keep food to yourselves. You didn't earn this. Blood-sucking leeches." The preplanned chants might have demoralized Midwestern farmers a month ago. Now they checked their ammo.

Gunfire from the other side of the barricade made everyone scramble and duck and then the flash-bang boomed. Women screamed. Thirty seconds later, Shane smelled teargas. Murphy's men returned fire, now joined by a handful of Emmaus residents. Some of the mob disappeared into the drifting fog of teargas. The tractor shifted as the frontline pushed on it.

"Wire's down," Murphy bellowed. "Wire's down."

Shane glanced to the right and saw where the barbed wire sagged allowing three men opportunity to climb over it without risk of shock. He pushed through the stunned guards and leveled his AR15 at them. One-two-three-four and they and a fourth man who had joined them fell back from the wire, which now lay on the ground. Jos Osimowitz and Cai huddled behind the hay bales at the next fence pole, trying to reenergize the wire, but Cai signed the wire needed to be repaired. Shane snatched up a riot shield they had liberated from the National Guard and plucked at Jazz's bullet-proof vest.

"We need to mend that top wire. I'll keep them off you if you'll do the splice."

She nodded, eyes wide, but not panicked. Raised with brothers by a practical father, she knew a lot of technical skills, and Shane preferred she didn't have to kill anyone today. Huddled behind the shield, Shane discouraged the mob from approaching by randomly firing his AR while Jazz wrapped a splice around the separated wires. Cai anxiously watched them the whole time. The mob thinned as Murphy and his men, now joined by mine guards and farmers, shot the more aggressive, including someone who returned fire.

Shane covered Jazz so they could retreat to the relative safety behind the tractor. Cai shouted they were energizing the wire just as a man threw a blanket over it to allow access by four men. The cloth began to smoke as Rob shot all four of them.

Shane's radio crackled and Click reported the northern border guards had turned the incursion there. The mob here seemed to rethink the wisdom of attacking the wire. Women wept, begging to be let in. Jason Breen reported a smaller, more hesitant crowd pushing against the gates at the overpass dispersed after Jason's men killed a few. Cai bumped Shane's shoulder as he stared out at the killing field Old 24 had become.

"Post those bodies at the intersections with a warning sign?" Shane sighed, saddened by his brother's change of attitude.

"Yeah." He radioed Click to order the same thing at all intersections. "Did Mara get hit?"

"Not that they've reported. Stan shifted resources from his western approaches to the north and south. It must not be on a migration route."

"Migration route?" Cai hissed when Shane signed off. "These people are running away from starvation and freezing to death."

"And we join them if we let them inside the wire." Shane wondered what it felt like to still feel emotion.

"I *know* that, Shane! Did you not see me working to get the wire reenergized? You're not alone out here. We're protecting what belongs to us – our families, wives, children. But some of us still remember that those were once our neighbors and we should care that they're hungry, cold and running."

"I can't. If I let them inside my head, it becomes harder to convince you to not let them in the wire."

"You don't need to convince me, Shane. Marnie already did that."

"How?"

Cai sighed.

"I've been making her wait because – I don't know why. She's pregnant."

Shane's mind momentarily shut down and Cai must have thought it mattered to him.

"This is probably the wrong place to bring it up."

Shane rubbed a hand over his hair. Thick, dark and curly now that it outgrew his usual close-trim, it felt unkempt. He'd been so busy, he'd not noticed until now.

"Is there a good time to let me know we've got an extra mouth to feed? Dad know?"

"Mom does. Not sure if she told him."

"Then you probably should. I've got bodies to pile up

Tired beyond measure, having not slept and starting the morning with emotional turmoil followed by physical violence, Shane turned toward the security crews and began detailing men to help with body cleanup. He sensed Cai's hesitation and turned toward him.

"She and I were over a long time ago, Cai. I'm just ...." Shane couldn't think of the word to describe how thoroughly exhausted he felt.

"Overwhelmed?" Cai provided.

Shane stared at him. Talking with Jacob had rattled him. He didn't talk about the field. The impossibility of escape when you lived on a battlefield threatened to drown him. There had to be 20 bodies lying on the ground and his brother insisted upon producing babies when they'd all be starving by spring. He felt caught in a riptide trying to breathe underwater.

"I can't afford to be overwhelmed." His volunteers gathered to go out and take care of the bodies. "I gotta go."

Butcher's Bill

Rob Delaney scratched fingers through his beard while listening to Joe Kelly's assessment of that morning's damages. What he could gather of the town council and security forces huddled in his office overlooking Main Street. Their body heat made the room almost tolerable, though the smell of body odor nearly overpowered him.

"One of the dead wore Army fatigues. The rest were just people. Hungry, foot sore. One of the women who stayed with her husband said that they knew we had resources because we offered to let them stay if they had useful skills."

"They'd been here before?" Anders McAuliff's no-nonsense business style didn't waste time. Joe stumbled to a stop, nodding. "I knew vetting people to see who might be useful was a bad idea."

"It was the right thing to do." Jacob didn't really direct his comment to Anders. "And we got Walt Hamber from it and he's helping to fix the phone system so we can communicate instead of walk everywhere."

"It ain't fixed yet and that's another mouth to feed."

It was and he wasn't the only one. They'd let in a dozen people over the last few weeks – each one with a highly useful skill. Shane paid them from the corn he'd harvested from his fields – fields everybody wondered how he owned.

"Do we know where they came from?" Shane kept the objects in view and Rob appreciated that.

"Looks like there's a camp to the south of here." Joe sighed tiredly. "Maybe one to the north. The woman was from the southern camp. She said they're starving there and don't have the energy to keep going. They just got desperate. One of the guys was a soldier. He figured we were guarding the intersections and reasoned electrified fence wasn't going to keep them out. He didn't figure we were anything more than a bunch of farmers carrying guns. He's dead, by the way. One of the bodies had Army fatigue pants."

"We wouldn't be anything more than a bunch of farmers carrying guns if it weren't for Shane training us." Cai cast an appreciative look at Shane who looked exhausted.

"Why today?" Anders' gaze rested on Shane.

"Major force came from the east." Shane shrugged. "I'm going to guess they saw us come back with the trucks and figured it was a good time to hit us."

"Why?" Cai frowned.

"Because every incursion we've had so far was right after Jason and his crew came back with a truckload."

"Do you think it's been the same group all along?" Anders knew the right questions to ask if this were normal times.

"Maybe. Some of my guys have reported a guy in Army fatigues in a few of the mobs. My guess is that the camp reached critical mass. We saw that in some refugee camps in the Middle East."

Silence fell over the group gathered in Rob's office since the rest of the building had no heat.

"So what do we do about it?" Cai asked.

All eyes but Jacob's turned toward Shane.

"We killed a dozen people and posted their bodies, so I don't think we have to do much."

"They ignored the bodies at the northeast corner." Anders still looked annoyed with Shane. Some of his decisions, like posting the bodies, didn't sit well with some in the community. They didn't sit well with his father, but Rob couldn't think of any more effective alternatives.

"Not really. It was a much smaller mob. Starving people are going to get desperate. I can't do anything about that."

"We could take out the camp." Anders' suggested surprised Rob.

They all stared at one another before Jacob spoke up.

"We've no business outside the township line."

"And I didn't train my guys for offensive action." Shane's long fingers traced a figure eight pattern on the thigh of his jeans. "I'm not taking untrained people into a danger zone."

"And, Pa's right. We have every right to defend what's ours, but going after people in Beulah township is not right."

"They attacked us." Anders' jaw tightened.

"And we defended ourselves," Cai replied. "They know they can't get in without paying a butcher's bill, so --." At a loss for words, he looked at Shane as if his brother had the answers.

"We take militia off the borders to do this and we risk being attacked while they're gone. Winter's going to get them, or they'll mistakenly drink from Beulah's well, or any number of other things. Or they'll get smart and resume walking south. I can't authorize a raid on a camp that probably has women and children in it. I won't."

"And that's your decision, Rob?"

"You're outnumbered here, Anders. Most of us don't want war with our neighbors, not when we've got all we can do not to starve or freeze to death this winter. And Shane's the only one here who commands enough guns to do what you're suggesting and you've got his answer."

"The woman I talked to sounded defeated, but she'd just lost her husband." Joe looked like he'd aged 15 years just since this morning.

"Do you think they'll be back?" Cai directed his question to Shane.

"Not if they know what's good for them. My guys are no longer restrained. We'll give a warning and then fire into the crowd." He stood, stretching. "I'm going to go get some sleep now. I suggest you all do the same. What happened this morning was unfortunate, but we live in a war zone now and this is the price we pay for survival."

He left them there.

"He's wrong." Anders stared around the room. "Getting rid of those people would make us all safer."

"And more blood-covered," Jacob countered.

"Better than dead."

"We aren't and they will be." Cai stood too. "If you haven't killed anyone yet, Anders, good for you, but I don't need anymore nightmares with faces and I think Shane probably feels the same way."

"So we're just going to leave a known risk at our back door?"

"Yeah," Rob said, seeing the men he'd shot this morning falling back from the wire. "I got wood to chop. I say we adjourn."

Jacob stood and followed Cai out of the room. Anders growled under his breath and left as well.

"You okay, Joe?" Rob asked.

"Yeah," the young police chief said. "I gotta go too. Sharon Lafferty promised me some food if I add to her green wood pile and my folks are running real low."

"I'll talk to Shane about getting you some corn."

"Thank you. I've been thinking about starting some patrols. There's been some folks reporting breakins – food being stolen off porches, the like."

"Yeah, that would be a good idea. I'll authorize you to take on deputies if I can figure out how to pay them."

Joe nodded. He sighed and left the room. Rob closed the door behind him, walked slowly to the big front windows that overlooked Main Street. Tears trickled down his cheeks into his beard. He let them for about 10 minutes and then he decided to go find Lemuel to talk about what had happened that morning.

Making Yourself Useful

West Virginia – Next Day

The second morning at the quarry dawned icy cold and early when Katharine woke them because flakes of snow floated out of the sky.

They broke the tents down and packed up as quickly as they could in the grey predawn.

"How many days of food do we have?" Joseph asked as they loaded up the truck.

"We can go about four days." Andi had taken charge of the cooking because she needed to make herself useful to these people and Julian was apparently gay. Or, er, maybe just a bit more traditional than most guys his age. It turned out Katharine didn't cook, and she didn't seem to care if others went hungry. Exhausted from the night's guard duty, she just wanted to lay down and sleep, as evidenced by her crankiness.

She kept complaining that a fifth person on the trip made arranging the truck bed more difficult because you couldn't stretch out easily. Andi tried to accommodate her as much as possible, breathing a sigh of relief when Joseph offered to ride in the back with her.

But first, an episode of Ice Road Truckers West Virginia. They spent all morning laying down branches, driving forward 10 feet and then laying down more branches. They all breathed a sigh of relief when they reached the highway. Katharine then worried them all by running into the woods to puke.

"There's been flu in Iron City," Andi whispered to Julian while they waited.

"We've heard about it. Not much to be done, though. If she's got it, we've all got it."

Joseph helped Katharine climb into the back while the other three got in the front. A half-hour later they drove through a small town where a sign on a small grocery store announced they had "food for reasonable trade". By mutual consent, Perry pulled over and Andi and Julian went in to see the available goods. The pleasant grocery store mostly had canned and dried goods and the shopkeeper accepted jewelry as payment. Andi trusted the Sullivan group enough to part with some of the jewelry she'd scrounged up in Pittsburgh. The gang she'd been with the last two weeks had sent them out scrounging food, but a lot of people had abandoned good stuff in their haste to get out of town. She'd found a jewelry store that hadn't been looted yet and knew she'd found the means to leave town.

"You folks traveling south?" the clerk asked after she parted with a nice ring. Older than Perry, he knew the quality of what he bought, but seemed friendly enough for a capitalist.

"We're getting out of Pittsburgh."

"Good idea. We've heard some awful things about that. Where you headed?"

"Columbus," Julian said. The clerk nodded. "Do you know anything about the route there?"

"I know what I've heard. Most of the towns round here were guarding their borders when people left the cities headed south, but they're letting people pass. I heard Columbus is doing pretty well. It's a SullCorp hub and it got a shipment from Bunnell & Wilson early. You got folks there?"

"One of us does, yeah."

"Well, good luck to you. I probably won't remember you for a long time, but I'll pray for you while I do."

Andi felt her smile grow plastic. Pray for them? What the hell good would that do? She'd have argued six weeks ago. Now, they walked out with potatoes, three cans of Spam, and a mixed case of vegetables. Katharine looked better, sitting up, talking with Joseph. A thought occurred, but Andi didn't know her well enough to ask. Of the Sullivan group, she was the hardest to know.

The asphalt now stretched snow free to the west and the sun filtered through the leafless trees. The highway west beckoned, as good as any other route for now.

Seal Team D

Seattle, Washington – Week Later

Bunnell & Wilson didn't have Seattle under martial law. Or theirs was a kinder, gentler, corporate version of it. Geo hadn't seen any real sign of what a Navy Seal recognized as martial law. Security forces lightly patrolled the streets and most Knight Industries mercenaries seemed focused on keeping the city functional. With the electric bus system down and most of the grid smashed, they provided transit routes using trucks. You hailed one as it passed and rode in the back, often sitting on pallets of food. Of course, a lot of people no longer worked regular jobs. McDonald's or Pier One weren't open in a survival situation like this. However, B&W advertised new jobs – unloading food and fuel on the docks, for example. Electric pallet jacks had fried in the Pulse, so they needed human power to replace the broken equipment.

Geo milled around in a hiring group and learned that B&W weren't asking for identification and they paid you in food at the end of your shift, so he'd worked a couple of shifts last week, enough to replenish his supplies since Duke seemed to have a year's supply of dog food in the breezeway.

Geo cleared off Aunt Connie's scrapbooking board to use as an investigation board, then removed it from the wall upstairs and brought it down to the living room where he could work.

Note #1 - The Army had been doing something with citizens right after the bombs. Geo still didn't know what but suspected nobody survived being taken away out of the back of the command trailer. He'd sent a woman and her children to that trailer. He didn't know how to confirm his suspicion and that didn't make B&W the *good guys*.

Note #2 - Did a civilian outfit have authority to overrule military command? His training said no, while his father's voice in his head said yes. He'd been a SEAL long enough that the training had become second nature but sitting in this house brooding over the last couple of weeks had him remembering the lessons of his youth.

Note #3 - Constitutionally, the military operated under civilian rule, but with the President gone and the chain of succession destroyed, who knew who the civilian-in-charge was? Nobody had ever planned for an attack this devastating.

Note #4 - Last night he'd picked up a low-level transmission that sounded like coded radio chatter. Geo being Navy didn't know Army codes. He suspected troop movements. The Knights didn't talk in code. They were aware of small bands of military outside the city. They were keeping an eye on them to assure "no more abuse of citizens" consistent with their stated reason for taking over here in Seattle in the first place.

Geo stared at the four notes, not sure where to go from there. SEALS weren't really trained to work alone. They operated in teams. You could lose some members and still function. You could even be the last one left standing and still complete the mission. But when it came to implementation of plans, Geo struggled against the solitariness of his task. What if he missed something vital? What didn't he know that someone else might? He'd never been a lone soldier for a reason. The strength of teams thoroughly discredited the Army myth of the lone soldier.

Geo turned on the radio and started peddling the charging bike. He could always hop off to adjust the frequency, but he'd concluded keeping the batteries charged without using the generator called less attention to him and helped keep him in shape. The conversation came up between a tech at a power station and a guard on the outside of the station. The sentry recorded information for the tech, who worked to get the station going. It sounded like a lot of burnt relays.

"I need you to talk to me, Paskin."

"What do you want to talk about?"

"...just need you to keep me awake while I wait for this check to process." The tech sounded older than the sentry. "I've been at this for 22 hours and I'm starting to fade."

"What's the emergency?"

"We're trying to get power to the hospitals, so they don't have to run on generators. You send that message about relays yet?"

"Just texting it now."

"Round up. I'm nowhere near done and it looks like at least 50% failure."

"The linemen say all the transformers are blown."

"I heard. Thank God Bunnell & Wilson hardened its infrastructure, or we'd be back in the Dark Ages now. I need to quit talking or I'm going to zap myself and you'll have to clean up roasted electrician from the equipment. But you need to keep me awake."

"How?"

"Tell me a story. Something."

The sentry hemmed and hawed, and Geo felt for the tech. SEALs mostly practiced radio silence, but sometimes it helped to have a voice in your coms when you'd been awake for a day and had to diffuse a bomb. Some guys excelled at idle chatter and some made you wish you'd become a pastry chef.

"I'm missing seeing the ghouls."

"The ghouls?"

"It's Halloween."

"Is it? Dang Seattle weather, there's no real fall, hard to tell. No trick-r-treaters this year?"

"I haven't seen any. And it makes sense. Folks are worried about eating and getting the lights on. They don't have time to make costumes and the stores don't have them. When I was a kid, we'd start out at my aunt's house. She lived just down the street and she made the best costumes. She'd recycle 'em from kid to kid. The best – when you were in high school – was a wizard's cape. Black-grey with all these sparkling symbols in silver all over it. We drew lots for it and I got to wear it twice – freshman and senior year. We'd go from house to house and our neighborhood always had good treats – chocolate was my favorite. The air would be cool, but not cold and most years it didn't rain. Fallen leaves all over the streets. This tang – kind of spicy – flavor in the air. And Brianne Benson would dress as a fairy every year. She was a ballet dancer and so the costume changed every year and, man, could she carry that off – the body, you know, and she knew how to make costumes – they weren't childish, you know? One year David dressed as a soldier from the 300. Turned out to be commitment coz a cold front moved in. He turned blue in places, shivering. Folks felt sorry for him, though, so we got extra candy and one group had a bonfire on their driveway and they gave us hot chocolate. Good times. I wonder how everyone's doing back home."

"Sounds like a tight neighborhood. I bet they're fine. Thank you. The check is done, and I haven't blown myself to goo. Time to record the data."

The subject switched to numbers and Geo got off the bike to find another station. He encountered a low-powered ghost channel and recorded the coded speech, noting a longitude coordinate. He pulled out a map he'd found in the basement. Wes's uncle had planned for a dark future and then died before it got here. Geo had arms, ammunition, a radio, and maps – all of which helped him in his self-assigned mission of figuring out Seattle.

The longitude didn't tell him precisely what he needed to know, but it indicated a line to the east of the city, near the eastern shore of Lake Washington. There were no military bases there, but Geo's SEAL training said smart commandos wouldn't choose a base of operations that might become a target for a group of mercenaries who still had intact infrastructure behind them.

He found a station where a supply clerk took an order for goods to be transported to a market in Ballard. *The* market, where Geo processed citizens for ration cards when the Knights swept in, killing anyone in a US military uniform. Yeah, they seemed to be treating citizens with more dignity than the military had, but they'd killed a lot of his colleagues.

"There's supposedly a holding facility for your type at Seattle Center." Wes brought that news home from the market where he ran into a friend. Before Wes' death, Geo had planned to check it out. Should he still do that?

Duke dropped his big head in Geo's lap.

The risk of checking it out would occur if he got caught. His buddy would die here without food or water. Geo's honed sense of teamwork made him think about his comrades. Duke might only be a dog, but as the only other team member, Geo needed to consider his needs. On the other hand – maybe Duke could help him get close enough to check things out.

Stoking the Hearth

Emmaus – Two Weeks Later

The homebrew tasted too hoppy for Shane's palate, but he wasn't objecting to the buzz as he raked coal around the base of the furnace. He glanced sideways as a step creaked. He expected Mike to be checking on him, but Rob descended the stairs. Shane put the beer to the side of the heater. Rob grinned at him.

"Catcha!"

"Last I looked I am over 21."

"Then why are you hiding in the basement while you drink?"

"Respecting your sobriety?"

"You asking or answering? And since when do you 'respect' my sobriety? Or did you think I couldn't smell the pot you were smoking in the attic?"

The news surprised Shane, so he snorted.

"Yeah, I sucked as a teenager. Can I just apologize for that and promise to act like an adult going forward?"

"You can. And I accept. You did – suck – as a teenager, but so did Keri."

"Not Cai?"

"Cai was easier – until he wasn't. But you know that." They both smiled.

"Speaking of people who shouldn't drink." Shane licked his lips and then Rob surprised him by nodding. "You know that?"

"I do. And he mostly does too."

Shane considered telling him about Bart's bottle, but Cai was nine years past 21 and he didn't get the sense the bottle had its hooks in Cai. A shot ever so often wasn't an addiction. Right? *Can you toke ever now and again? Not advisable.*

"You ready to fire this thing up?"

"Yeah. I wish I knew the exact way to ignite it, but Grandpa says it just needs air and a spark. If a black cloud comes up the vents – I'm sorry in advance."

Rob grinned. The long silence that followed alerted Shane to a change of topic.

"I heard through the grapevine that you're working on Deke's Skywagon."

"Alex has a big mouth."

"Alex didn't really know it was a secret. Deke's been gone a few years, but that doesn't mean you can just take his plane."

"It's not his plane. Grandpa is owed storage fees – like a half-decade. So, I asked him and he said yes."

"And you're going where?"

"To get Mike's wife."

"I like Mike. He's a nice guy for a mercenary."

"Nicer than me."

"Yeah – you're not as nice as you once were."

"I was never really nice, Dad. I had an edge – it scared some people." He read Rob's expression, a subtle change in his eyes. "I guess you've noticed the edge has been finely honed since."

"The one who gets cut the deepest with that will be you. If you're not careful you could end up bleeding out."

Shane set aside the coal rake and dropped to his haunches.

"I've been listening to Grandpa."

"Is it helping?"

"It's stirring up shit, but – maybe that's right. I don't know."

"If you ever want to talk...."

"Yeah. It's not – I don't really talk. He does it mostly."

"I know that. He always warned me that someday I'd have to talk to someone else."

"Will I be your first?"

"Lemuel, but it's different because we both had largely healed it before we started talking. You're still bleeding."

And not likely to stop. Shane couldn't say that aloud so he focused on opening the airband.

"I wasn't joking about the black cloud. Is the door at the top of the stairs closed?"

"It is. It won't do much good if the vents are open."

"I know that. Covered the vents before I even started stocking. So here goes."

Turned out igniting coal took expertise beyond lighting a barbecue grill. The matches failed. The newspaper soaked in fuel failed. By the time the coal ignited from the hot end of a propane torch, a sweating Shane had almost convinced himself it wouldn't when it finally started smoldering. When a few of the chunks of coal started to glow, Shane whooped as Rob clapped.

"You did it!" They high-fived. "You going to celebrate by finishing that beer?"

"If you don't mind."

"You can drink around me, Shane. Like you said, you're over 21. I only objected to you drinking when you were underage. You got a right to celebrate."

Rob walked over to a shelf and pulled out a beer bottle, wiped off the dust and cobwebs, and came back to sit on the stairs.

"Is that the batch we made when I was in high school?

"Naw. Your mom and I made this – winter before last. But when you only drink it occasionally, it takes a long time to go through 72 bottles." He cracked the lid and gave an exploratory taste of the root beer. "It would be better cold, but yeah – Pa's recipe still rocks."

Shane sipped his beer. He didn't like pilsners warm. He'd started drinking darks in Central America where refrigeration wasn't always a guarantee.

"Just ask, Dad. You don't have to pretend to hang out with me."

"I'm not pretending." Rob took a sip of root beer. Shane waited, watching as his fire slowly spread. "You ever think about the future?"

"Not lately. The odds say not all of us are going to live to spring, so – the future – is that, like, next week? I've thought that far ahead."

"Santa Fe."

"Yeah. I owe it to him, and Alicia is my friend."

"And you don't have to convince me. I assume you're following your own rule."

"They have a stash of food and we're bringing it back. Might have to do two trips. Mom said we could make up the old bed down here and screen off a room. Not sure where her mother will go -- maybe the storm shelter."

"I'll work on that. You know, your great-grandfather was one of 10 kids. Can you imagine this house that packed?"

"I – no, I can't. I guess people shared beds back then." Shane tried to imagine sharing a bed with Cai and it just felt wrong. The fire burned pretty good now, so he added more coal, spreading it around. Jacob had said to damper it down after adding the new coal. He watched as the smoke stopped fluttering and then adjusted the air band and closed the service port.

"I don't suppose tossing this in the trash can would make Mom happy."

"I say toss both bottles in the trash and she'd figure out who was drinking which, but under the circumstances, we should wash the bottles out and reuse them." Rob shrugged. "I think it's been a long time since she worried overmuch about my falling off the wagon. Long as I don't get complacent, there's nothing to worry about. I mean, did you worry about my sobriety when you were a kid?"

"No. I mean, you guys never made any secret of it and I don't remember ever worrying about it." Rob titled his head and Shane knew he heard the lie. "Not until high school. Someone was talking about their dad – how they'd moved out here from Denver so he could get sober, but they always worried about if he was 10 minutes late or what. And, I gave a serious thought to if I was worried like that."

"And?"

"Only time you were ever scary late was when you were bass fishing with Lemuel, so --." Shane laughed and Rob joined him because fear of someone falling off the wagon while with their AA sponsor seemed ridiculous. "So, here's to – how many years of sobriety?"

"Eleven thousand one hundred and ninety-six days."

"Seriously? That's like more than thirty years."

"Almost three years longer than your brother's been alive."

"Wow. You're still counting days."

"They're an investment." Shane nodded.

"I don't think sobriety will ever be an issue for me, but it does give me hope. You learned to sleep through the night." Rob shifted uncomfortably and grew preternaturally still. "Or not."

"No, I did. For a long time. And mostly I'm dreaming about recent stuff. The hanging ... Ren's house ... the barricades. I know they were necessary, but it's not that easy to kill people."

"It's not. I don't dream so much about recent stuff. I guess I'm less conflicted about my recent kills."

"Makes sense." Rob drained the root beer bottle and set it on the stairs to take upstairs. "I gotta get to bed. So do you. And we should probably open those vents so some of this heat makes it upstairs."

"Sounds good. Dad." Rob stopped on the stairs. "I know we don't always see eye-to-eye and I sucked as a teenager, but you know I admire you, right?"

"Well, I hope so – coz I'm awesome ... this side of sobriety."

It felt good to laugh. It didn't make it to the deep recesses of his soul, but it acted like lotion on dry skin and gave Shane hope for the future he had not considered.

Safe Haven

Next Day

Circleville Ohio presented a pleasant collection of white houses with convivial front porches and it looked as good as anywhere to bed down for a while, but Perry had said to wake him as they approached the city, so Julian pulled over to let him drive the last few miles.

US-23 north ran flat and hardly curved along the way, mostly driving through fields and a small town or two. The outskirts of Columbus sort of surprised Julian. Perry slowed at a barricade under an overpass.

A Knight Industries operative politely asked them what their business was in Columbus, but he didn't ask for identification. He hardly raised an eyebrow when Perry said he worked for SullCorp. He asked if he knew the way. Perry did and they continued on their way.

"Interesting." The town beyond the light barricade seemed peaceful – some older cars creating easily-navigated traffic. "You could probably call your folks from SullCorp."

"That would be good. And B&W. I'm not actually due back to work until the Monday after Thanksgiving. I think that's next week. I'm hoping for a never-ending hot shower before then."

A gas station announced "We have gas!"

"Things look pretty normal here," Perry remarked.

The low-rise kind of town surprised Julian as they neared a section of taller buildings. Perry turned left without consulting a map.

"You've been here before."

"Yeah, a few times."

SullCorp's Columbus hub was primarily a shipping center with a small office block beside it. Julian kind of expected dozens or hundreds of semis just sitting idle, fried by the Pulse, but he was off by half and awnings covered several of the idle ones so mechanics could work on them.

Joseph gave up trying to comb his hair and when Perry parked the truck he got out to go into the building by himself. Perry slid out from behind the wheel to follow him. Katharine frowned after them while Andi got out of the bed to climb into the front.

"Now what?"

"We wait. Hopefully, they will reward us for getting the Sullivans where they should be by getting us where we should be."

Andi sighed.

"What if I don't have a destination?"

"Anywhere has got to be better than Pittsburgh, right?"

"Maybe I could come to Seattle with you."

Flattering, but --.

"It's only been about six-seven weeks since the woman I wanted to spend the rest of my life with left me at the altar, so – I'm flattered, but I'm making no promises for the future. We don't even know if Seattle is possible right now."

She stared at the building for a while before speaking.

"You must think I'm so childish."

"I don't. In a scary world, there is safety in numbers."

"I just feel really alone." Julian nodded. "Don't you?"

"I've felt really alone for a decade, but really – my parents are probably still alive – my siblings. Even my ex. I can't say I know what you're feeling. And, I can't just hop in the sack with you and make it all go away. That is not my superpower."

"What is?"

"Um, hacking."

"That's what you do for a living?"

"More or less." He straightened in his seat. "Perry's coming."

Perry walked to the door with a square-shaped man in neat tie and slacks with a SullCorp jacket over it.

"They have a guest apartment here. We can get cleaned up – sleep in warm beds."

"What about contacting Emmaus?" Katharine asked.

"Joseph's working on that now. This is Ramey. He's going to show us the apartment, get us clean clothes and food. It's taken us a long time to get this far. It's a safe place, so let's just take a pause for a night to get recharged."

"I want to talk to my daughter," Katharine sulked.

"I believe that'll happen, but it isn't so simple, right? The Pulse makes communication difficult. So, give them a night to work out the logistics, okay?"

Ramey indicated they should follow him, and Perry drove the truck to the far side of the complex, up some stairs above the warehouse to a two-bedroom flat with a small sitting room and tiny kitchen.

"Do we draw straws for the shower?" Andi quipped.

"Ladies first." Perry gave Julian a sharp look. It seemed chivalrous.

"What's another hour when I haven't bathed in hot water for a month?"

"You can go first," Andi said to Katharine. The door opened and Ramey came back with a stack of towels and wash clothes. Katharine grabbed a set and headed into the bathroom.

"Maybe she'll be in a better mood after she's showered." Julian kind of doubted it, but his own crankiness made him pessimistic.

They had just sorted themselves out in the small space when Joseph came in the door. The shower still ran.

"What's the news?" Julian asked.

"There's no way to contact Emmaus, but – well, my father is in Wichita, where he has apparently fought and won a revolution and been declared king."

Perry chuckled and Joseph joined him. That sounded like what Julian knew of the ultra-conservative businessman. Then Perry sobered.

"Where's Allison?"

"Safe in Emmaus, they think. There's good people in that town. I'm sure she's fine. Kind of glad Katharine isn't here, though, because she's not going to agree. So, just back what I say. Please?"

They all three shrugged.

"I think it's a really good idea," Perry said. "Whatever keeps her calm. And, I can't think of a safer place than Emmaus for a young girl."

Ramey appeared at the door again with a box of food that he offered to put away for them.

"It's fine. I've got it." Andi took the box and began to put the items in the little fridge and cabinets. Katharine came out of the bathroom wrapped in a towel. An attractive woman for her age, she showed enough skin that Julian grabbed a sofa cushion to hide his reaction. Ramey hadn't left this time. He unloaded another box filled with blue overalls.

"I guessed on the sizes, and there's two for each, all still in the packaging. I'll have undergarments for you tomorrow."

"Thank you," Joseph replied.

"Is there any sort of weather forecast?" Perry asked.

"There's no weather bureau or guys on television anymore, but the radio says it snowed north of here this morning and you can see how grey the sky is. So, I'd say you guys got here just the right time coz a big storm is blowing in."

Ramey closed the door behind him. Katharine took one of the overalls and went into the bigger of the two bedrooms.

"Who's next?" Joseph asked.

"Don't you own the place?" Andi pointed to the bathroom, bowing slightly.

"Ladies first," Joseph said.

"Seriously? Is this some kind of Midwestern thing?"

"Definitely." Perry jerked his thumb toward the bathroom. "I'll make dinner. You get cleaned up."

Andi shrugged, grabbed an overall and a towel, and disappeared into the bathroom. Julian turned to say something to Perry, who searched the cabinets for pots and pans. Outside the window, big white flakes drifted from the sky. Ramey hadn't been joking.

"Looks like we got here just in time for winter."

Perry sighed. Joseph flopped down on the sofa, stretching his legs out in front of him.

"At least we're not in the back of the truck tonight. Yay! Anyone want to lay a bet on how long winter is in Columbus, Ohio, and how long five people can live in a space this small and stay friends?"

The three men stared around the apartment for a moment and then laughed hysterically.

Sky Wagon

Emmaus – Next Day

Shane walked around the plane doing precheck. He'd had his head under the cowling for days and his current care before he took off didn't inspire Mike's confidence. He hated to fly anyway and Shane's caution just made him worry the plane might fall out of the sky. Yes, he trusted Shane's piloting and mechanical skills, but he didn't trust planes in general and he especially hated small planes. Who enjoyed riding in a compact car with wings?

And, no, it didn't help that Shane's grandfather wandered around in the other direction doing a second check. He'd been a barnstorming pilot. Just how committed to safety were people who flew through barns and did aerial acrobatics above crowds of people?

"Okay, checks out," Shane reported, looking at Jacob. The old man grunted. What did that mean? Shane seemed to know because he looked at Mike. "You ready?"

Mike nodded, swallowing tightly. He pulled the map out of his pocket and tucked it into the visor above the passenger seat. Shane slid a soft-side cooler into the space between the front seats and the back seats. It held their lunch. He noted its weight on his clipboard then signaled Mike to come over to the scale beside the wall.

"I've never weighed so little since high school," Mike grumbled.

He'd lost 20 pounds to the fever and hadn't gained it back. If he'd been a fat American, he might celebrate, but he'd lost solid muscle and the strength that went with it. Worse, it didn't look likely that he would regain it this winter. The whole country would be gnawing shoe leather by the time spring came. *Dios mio*, he quoted the old man now. He needed to get out of this town before he forgot his name.

"That's good," Jacob said. "Every pound you don't have is a pound of freight you can carry."

"It's going to be tight with four of us," Shane reasoned. "We can maybe bring back 100 pounds of freight."

"She has more than that."

Shane and Jacob exchanged glances.

"Now that Alex is back on his feet, I'll get him and Nehemiah started on another load of av gas." Jacob said. "Maybe you can go back for whatever you can't carry the first time."

"Maybe. We'll figure it out once we know what we have. I've got Jason looking for some lead as an additive so we're not wearing the pistons on these antiques." Shane stepped on the scale and added his weight to his calculations. He sighed and showed his math to Jacob. "If I had my druthers, I'd sub Jazz in for you. She weighs nothing. But I need you to find this house and Alicia is your wife."

"Once you burn some fuel, you'll be fine," Jacob commented. "They teach you moderns to be more careful than you need to be."

Mike swallowed bile and Shane grinned at him like a madman before he hugged Jacob and said he'd see him tomorrow morning. The old man fired up his truck to head into town.

"Mount up," Shane told Mike. "Sun's coming up and it's a four-hour trip. You got a bag just in case?"

"Shut up!" Shane cackled instead. The brightness of his laugh worried Mike. His humor didn't make it to his eyes. He pulled the blocks from the wheels. Mike climbed in and buckled up, eating a saltine cracker washed with ginger tea, waiting for Shane to join him in the cockpit. Mike watched as he worked his way through the startup process. What sort of insanity allowed the passengers access to a second steering wheel full of all sorts of buttons that could be pushed?

Mike didn't like flying, but he particularly hated takeoffs and landings. He squeezed his eyes tight as they raced toward the fence at the end of the still shadowy runway. Just as they left the ground, it occurred to him that Shane had only flown this airplane once – yesterday. What if he'd calculated the runway length wrong? What if they'd missed something when doing their precheck?

"You can open your eyes," Shane told him as the engine settled down. Cautiously, Mike peeked. In the surprisingly quiet cabin he'd not realized they'd taken off. "In fact, I'm going to need you to navigate for me since we're visual flight rules entirely. I got nothing on the radio. When I tried to file a flight plan last night, I got some guy in Nebraska and another in Colorado, but it's pretty much radio silence out there."

"You're the only pilot flying?" Mike asked. That didn't make him feel better. Maybe they shouldn't be doing this. And, wow, how close were those mountains to the west? How come he'd never noticed them from the town?

"All modern planes were probably grounded when the Pulse smoked their electronics, but there are thousands of GA planes that are old like this one that might still fly *if* the owners can find av-gas, *if* they have anywhere distant to go. I'm thinking there's not a lot of recreational flying going on right now. So here's the thing – I know you don't like to fly, but you have got to stay frosty for me. If you see anything in the sky, speak up. It might be a bird, but if it's a plane, I want to know about it as soon as you see it. Okay?"

"Why?"

"My cargo planes were never shot out of the sky in part because I don't get complacent. Maybe there's nothing to worry about, but I'm still not complacent. Could be a squadron of fighter jets scrambling to knock us out of the sky. I want to know as soon as you see it. Don't go 'oh, maybe that's a bird.' Say "Ric, what is that?' instead."

"If it is a squadron, what can you do about it?"

"Over open country like this – not much. I'm way slow compared to them. If this were Jacob's duster though – I could make it exciting for them. That's why you better have remembered to bring a bag because I don't want to meet your mother-in-law covered in your vomit."

"Shut up! It was one time, and do you remember the turbulence?"

Shane laughed. *He* liked turbulence.

"When you say 'exciting', what does that mean?"

"Empty, the duster really gets up and goes and it's great at flying low."

"Low?"

"Level of the highway low. I can't quite do that with the 180, but if I've got some warning and we're near some terrain, I can drop to smuggler level and maybe shake them. But I need some warning, so I don't have to terrify you. So, perk up so I have some warning. Now, pull out the map and orient yourself while I still know the landmarks."

Mike did as instructed. Although he hated to fly, heights didn't really bother him, so he looked out at the brightening prairie and identified I70.

"Why are we following the highways?" he asked.

"Because I don't have any towers to ping off and I've never flown this route before. I drove quite a bit of it every two months the four years of college, so hopefully I'll not end up landing us in Seattle."

"That's a joke, right?" Mike felt a band of tension tighten around his head.

"Mike, I cut my teeth on VFR and 90 percent of my flying in the Mirage meant visual only because they have no towers. Remember all those night flights? I'm really good at this. So please trust me."

"The way you trusted me when I wanted to scuba into that grotto in Greece?"

Shane snorted.

"I did trust you. I did it. Just couldn't stay as long as you wanted to."

"'Ric, you still have three-quarters of a tank of air. Calm down.'" Mike chortled at the memory of Shane insisting they needed to *go*. "I didn't expect the ceiling to be that low." Mike giggled. "We are a pair, that's for sure. Each fascinated by what the other finds terrifying. How did we become friends?"

"Bonded over that bottle of bourbon I couldn't finish after I decided my first kill didn't warrant becoming an alcoholic."

"It doesn't happen that quickly," Mike assured him.

"Long history in my grandmother's family and I grew up with my dad going to meetings."

"He doesn't seem stuck there."

"No. It's just a part of his life. And, I've never had trouble saying 'no', but some situations – that's when he lost control, so when I hear that voice in my head that says not feeling would be a good idea, I step back from the bar. Check the map. Is that Highway 25?"

Mike looked at the map, tracing the lines with his finger, then staring at the unrolling prairie below them. A marvelous patchwork of cleared and winter-seeded fields in shades of amber and purple unfolded as the sun climbed higher. The mountains to the west soared higher than the plane, topped with white.

"Yeah, pretty sure. It really looks different from up here." Mike glanced sideways as Shane maneuvered into a gentle bank. He smiled slightly at the ground visible from under the wing. Mike tried not to grab the door handle in terror. He *knew* they weren't going to crash. He grasped for something to distract him. "So why do farmers plant stuff in the winter?"

"Winter wheat is harvested in the spring. It grows under the snow." The plane leveled off and his heart settled.

"That can't be natural."

Shane's forehead furrowed.

"Yeah, probably isn't, though I've never known a time when it wasn't. Remember the Dustbowl?"

"Not personally."

"In school?" Shane laughed.

A decent student until he got into trouble for something stupid, Mike did vaguely remember the history of huge dust clouds in the 1930s.

"Yeah – 1930s, dust storms from the Rockies to the Appalachians. Picture of some lady with kids looking sad. What does that have to do with planting in the winter?"

"It was caused by opening up the prairie for planting during World War 1. As food needs decreased, farmers let their fields go fallow, but the soil had nothing to hold it down and when drought hit, the grass didn't grow back, so the winds took the soil. That was right out there." Shane pointed out under their right wing. "To keep it from happening again, crops were developed that would grow in the off season to prevent the soil from being wind-eroded."

"Wow. Farmers are actually pretty smart, aren't they?"

"Not all of them. It was farmers who screwed up in the first place. Some of them knew you needed winter cover crops. My great-grandfather Joseph Greyeyes, for example. The Lufgrens. But a lot of farmers, even if they knew, were greedy for the military food contracts, so they risked it and got caught. There's a reason why the Delaneys haven't owned a farm since 1935."

"Except you own a couple of fields now, you said."

"Yeah, but notice I'm letting Alex manage them. Next year, I probably will learn what I need to know, but right now – I'm a pilot who spends most of my life on the barricades and I just don't have time to learn farming too."

Mike called the next navigation change. Now they followed Highway 40 mostly west.

"Can you tell if fields are planted?" he asked.

"Yeah, that is one skill I have from spraying fields. There's some down there that haven't been. We just gotta hope we have a snowy winter and a wet spring or we're back to the Dustbowl and that's not good for any of us."

"Not Emmaus, right?"

"We're affected by our neighbors. Jacob lost a sister to dust pneumonia. Jericho County seems to be doing okay, but these other fields could be a problem. They're also not any of my concern at the moment. Stay frosty." Shane pointed out the right side of the aircraft at the majestic mountains there. "We're getting close to Cheyenne Mountain at this point."

"Your handler got any news on that?"

"They've had the flu and I've been keeping my distance so I didn't accidentally tell them about this trip."

"You don't belong to them, *hermano*."

Right then Shane's phone buzzed.

"You were saying?" he asked. He punched some buttons on the yoke. "We're on auto pilot. Keep an eye on the map. If we're coming up to another correction and the conversation is still going, interrupt." He slipped a blue-tooth on and touched his phone screen.

Help Along the Way

In the Air

Shane's contract with the Central Security Agency expired two months ago, so Mike had correctly assessed his obligations to them, but Shane knew he needed Grant Rigby's intelligence gathering in order to survive the winter. Advance reconnaissance put Emmaus a step ahead of surrounding communities. Being able to access the satellites meant he'd had a fairly good idea when the migrant crowds would pressure their borders, so they could mostly avoid bloody incursions. He *needed* the Rigby group as they needed him, so answering the phone was a useful obligation.

"Hey," he grunted.

"What the hell?" Grant Rigby growled. "Where are you going?"

"Taking Mike to get his wife and mother-in-law, who has food."

"In Santa Fe? And you didn't bother to ask for intelligence because you like surprises?"

"I didn't want to argue with you. How's Dylan?"

"Better, sort of. Not a good time to talk about it." Shane could hear him talking to someone, muffled by putting the phone to his shoulder. "If you're going to do these things, you need intelligence, so you come back alive. How are things going in town?"

"Non-farmers are starting to run out of food. Mae keeps bringing it in and selling it as fast as she can, but Jason's supply lines can't keep up and they say resources are getting scarcer out there. We're out of toothpaste and shaving crème at our house. Toilet paper's next. Chavez promised me he'd let me know if he figured out a way through my security system."

"He's learned a dozen ways to shock himself. How are you doing?"

"I don't have the flu yet."

"I would hope you wouldn't be flying to Santa Fe with the flu. I mean your head."

"Still attached. Haven't stuck a gun in my mouth lately. My grandfather is driving me crazy talking to me about World War 2. Maybe it's helping a little, but not as much as having something to do helps."

"Activity just masks it, kid, but you already know that." Shane rolled his eyes. Mike, who could only hear Shane's half of the conversation, made a mocking face. He'd been there the night Shane had nearly ended his own life in August. "Santa Fe has the flu and it's a nasty variety. Don't touch anyone while you're there. There's been some sort of military junta there. Chatter is mostly Spanish. Chavez has been monitoring it."

"Hey," Chavez said, coming into the line. "So, I don't think there's any command structure above the local. We weren't monitoring it at first and with Dylan down we have no fast way to go through the archives. It seems like *los chicanos* rule there. That shouldn't be a problem for either one of you. The head guy is a Sergeant Rojas."

"Sergeant?! Things are that bad?"

"What, you wanted to pick a fight with a colonel?"

"Technically, he picked a fight with me and since he was in civvies, I didn't know he was a colonel. Do we think all the officers are dead?"

"I don't know. Could be he's the highest-ranking Spanish speaker The way Americans been grouping up the last few years, a breakdown along social and language lines is kind of expected. Nobody trusts anybody who is different. You wouldn't think military discipline would break down at that point, but yeah, I think maybe the chunky melting pot is no more."

"And you think my Mexican accent's going to hold up to that?"

"Just because I teased you for not using the *che* doesn't mean that crowd will care. They're speaking *chicanos* for the most part but listen and adapt as needed ... or let your partner do the talking. Might want to keep your sunglasses on too."

Owing to the Greyeyes blood, Shane tanned dark enough to be a light-skinned *chicano*, but his eyes were green and that sometimes made people who cared wonder about his background. In the Middle East, he'd sometimes worn brown contacts to affect the illusion that he wasn't an American. It worked so long as he didn't open his mouth. Middle Eastern languages challenged him, but he'd fooled even *chicanos* with his Spanish.

"Ami wants to speak with you," Grant said. "Santa Fe Regional is your best bet for landing. There's a fellow there – maybe there. Carver – Ulysses Carver. He maybe can provide you with a vehicle."

"Good to know. Any news out of Wichita these days?"

"Sullivan seems to be keeping the peace. The Army's been disbursed to far corners. I don't know what he's done with the officers he detained. There's no chatter about executions."

"Yeah, my dad and grandfather say Ren would be reluctant to do that, so …. Good to know. I'll let them know when I get back. I'm ready for Ami now."

"Shane," she said. The other two lines dropped away. "I know we barely know each other, but I need your help."

"If I can. What's up?"

"I've got medical intelligence that says this flu might be bioengineered." Shane noted Mike's signal to redirect the plane and did it without talking. "Are you there?"

"Just executing a course correction while thinking of the implications of that news. Grant still listening?"

"He is."

"Sounds like all of this was planned. Multiple waves to hit us like a tsunami train."

"Yes." Ami's tone suggested she relayed Grant's answer, not her own opinion, and then she became more natural. "And, I fear it's not over. I can't get into an encrypted part of the drive I have because Dylan isn't able to help me, and Grant and Javier don't quite have the skills. Is there anyone in town who might be able to provide that help?"

"Maybe some of the teenagers. I can ask around when I get back. McAuliff's militia has a guy who is slightly legendary – Patterson. Ask Andrew Bennett if he'd be willing to do it. Might ask my brother Cai to ask Andrew, actually. Chavez and him know each other now. What else?"

"I need blood samples. I might be able to synthesize a vaccine if I can identify people with antibodies. You haven't been sick. You could be immune or immuno-aggressive."

"Right or just accidentally vaccinated against it. Knight Industries was pretty zealous in making sure we wouldn't catch anything. I'll see if I can round up guinea pigs when I get back. There's more, isn't there?"

"If you can get the authorities in Santa Fe to share information that might really be invaluable."

"I can ask. Email down?"

"I tried CDC there, but so far no response."

"EMP pulses will do that. We'll try analog." Mike tapped his arm and pointed to a dark spot in the north-western sky. "I gotta go. I might have a bogie on my right wing."

Grant replaced Ami almost immediately.

"It's a helicopter. Bell-58, according to sat intel, but it's not running a transponder. Not sure where it came from."

"Yeah. I can't scan radio frequencies and talk to you at the same time. And, I need to put on a headset to talk to them. Keep the line open and I'll let you know if I need anything."

The helicopter definitely paced them, but it didn't grow any closer. The 180 had a squawk box on the dash as well as a headset, so Mike could hear what Shane heard. Shane scanned through the radio frequencies until a single bandwidth steadied.

"N47G64 to the helicopter off my starboard at 177 degrees. What's your designation, sir? Over"

A long silence ensued.

"Maybe their radio is down," Mike suggested. "Could they hit us with one of those sidewinders if they wanted to?"

"That's not a gunship. It looks like an old Kiowa. They're scout copters that can be armed, but that one isn't carrying guns."

"You sound certain."

"It's the only helicopter I'm rated on." Shane tried his greeting again. Without an immediate reply, he opted for something sterner. "Look, you're making me nervous. Do you have a purpose in bird dogging me? Over."

The radio crackled, then fell silent. Shane considered giving up when a Southern-flavored woman's voice came on the air.

"G64, you're coming close to Cheyenne Mountain's restricted air space. Just assessing for threat. Where are you headed? Over."

"Tell me your designation and maybe I'll answer you. Over."

"This is Kiowa 170FR out of Cheyenne Mountain. Where are you headed? Over."

"I prefer not to answer questions. Over."

"What is your purpose? Over." Mike raised an eyebrow.

"Collecting a family member. Over."

"And where are you coming from? Over."

"My town has not authorized me to provide that information. Over."

A long radio silence ensued before the frequency crackled to life again.

"Noted. You have a nice flight, Cessna. Stay east of 96 and 287 on return. Over."

"I will try to do that. 64 out."

Shane pulled off the headset and donned the blue-tooth again.

"What do you think?"

"That's the first peep we've heard out of Cheyenne Mountain since the Pulse and no discernable ground contact," Grant explained. "I don't know. I need someone better than I am until Dylan recovers. You think Patterson would do it?"

"We both helped put him in prison for twenty-five years, where he'd still be for the next 20 if not for the end of the world as we knew it, so I'm not holding my breath, but beggars can't be choosers and maybe he'll let bygones be bygones in celebration of the end of the world as we knew it. That's why you want Andrew to do the asking. Don't wait on me to come back because they don't trust me."

"Got it. Good luck on your trip. Shane, I know I don't have to say this – be careful."

"You, my dad, Jacob, Cai, Marnie, my mom, and Jazz ... seriously, you folks need better hobbies than worrying about me. I'll make contact if I need it and probably on the way back. Over and out."

Shane hung up. The sun dazzled the Rockies and turned the eastern sky to a hard winter blue.

"How you doing over there?" he asked Mike.

"This isn't so bad. I've never flown in a plane so small and I thought it would be terrifying. It's still a little scary, but better than the big planes I've flown on."

"That's coz it's Kansas in November. Not a lot of storms. I'll try to keep the turbulence to a minimum."

"My feet are a little cold."

"Yeah. Cabin venting. It's probably right around freezing outside the canopy. I did warn you to wear wool socks."

"I did. They're not freezing. Just cold. And how do you stretch in this thing?"

"You don't when there are two tall guys in the front. If you're desperate to go pee, we can land, but that uses fuel and we have just enough to get there and back. The ladies offset the extra fuel on the way back and then we will be carrying cargo too."

"Couldn't you have gotten a bigger plane?"

"That still flies? That Jacob wouldn't give me guff about I don't own it? No. If Deke hadn't abandoned this plane with spare parts and done a good job mothballing it, we'd not be flying to Santa Fe at all. Is that a navigation waypoint down below?"

Mike looked at the map.

"No. Fly straight." He showed Shane the map just to put his mind at ease. "You hungry?" he asked after a while.

"No, I ate breakfast."

"I didn't, but I don't feel like puking now, so I think maybe I should eat."

Shane reset the autopilot.

"This thing doesn't have articulating seats, so I'm going to have to turn around to access the cooler. Don't panic. The autopilot will hold us. Okay?"

"I could get it."

"No. You are prone to vertigo and turning around backwards might make you hurl. We've discussed how I feel about vomit in the plane, so no. Just trust me."

Lunch consisted of two hunks of meat with hunks of cheese and bread and a baked potato each. Shane wasn't hungry, so he handed half the items to Mike before turning around.

"Nothing says how much stuff has changed like this does," Mike said gnawing the meat. "What is this, anyway?"

"Whatever my parents had in the freezer, salted so it won't spoil, rinsed so it is edible again and then roasted, although you could probably eat it uncooked since it's been smoked."

"So jerky?"

"Basically, yeah."

"We got fed better back in the Mirage."

"Of course, we did. We were contractors. Meanwhile the guys in the military units were living on MREs. And my dad and grandpa both love to talk about k-rations. I had some once when they were cleaning out the bomb shelter in Emmaus. Trust me, you've got nothing to complain about."

"But I still will." Mike grinned at him. "How long before we get there?"

"You only get to ask that question once per flight before I start turning the plane upside down. About three more hours. If you want to take a nap after you eat, be my guest. My turn in two hours."

"*Your* turn?!"

"Yeah." Shane grinned at Mike's terror. "I could nap and let autopilot handle it, but VFR – I probably shouldn't. I might do it on the way back though, so don't get all freaked out. Pilots sleep in flight all the time."

"Yeah, but I don't know that when I'm in the back of the plane. You got any water? My throat's dry."

Shane handed him a canteen. He knew Mike wouldn't sleep on this flight, but the invitation to be quiet meant Shane could enjoy touching the sky. He looked east and frowned at the horizon. Dark blue-grey clouds boiled against the clear blue sky, a streak of silver trailing along the ground.

"What's that?" Mike asked.

"Storm front. We should be out of its path by the time it gets here."

"Is it a problem?"

"Maybe for coming back. Rain I can handle, but without proper deicing, I might have to set down and wait it out."

"You mean snow?"

"Ice is worse. They fly these babies like cars in Alaska, so we're probably fine and I brought some jugs of antifreeze just in case. And, like I said, we'll be far to the south before it gets to us today."

He smiled, and Mike didn't panic. Air travel held risks and Shane had flown through some truly nasty weather in the past. He *liked* turbulence. If alone and carrying enough fuel, he might have flown closer to the storm just for the excitement. He could see flickers of lightning, which meant thunder, which felt like the power of the universe when you flew through it in a small plane. Mike would freak and they needed to stay on mission. He bumped the airspeed just slightly to assure they were well south when the storm slammed into the Rockies.

Earning Our Keep

Emmaus, Kansas

Brian Halloran stared out the window at the straw-strewn fields beyond the sod walls. Behind him, he heard the bed creak and he turned to see April sitting down, back from the bathroom.

"How are you feeling, honey?"

"Maybe better. It's just been hard to get over it. The drugs ... the sex ... it just hurt so much. All those men!"

Brian cautiously sat down beside her on the bed, surprised when she settled her head against his chest, her arm around his back.

"Thank you for being patient with me "

"I love you. You take what time you need."

She scratched a hand through her shaggy hair, looking up at the timber roof. The soddy housed someone since the advent of electricity and plumbing, but the toilet had an overhead tank and you turned the light switches rather than flipped them. Not that the electricity or plumbing worked since the Pulse. Heated by a cozy corn cob fire in the little wood stove in the kitchen area, the cottage wrapped them in snug warmth and would make a good refuge through the winter – if they could earn the food they needed. Cai explained the house on this lot had been mothballed some years ago and it would take too much to get it running and to keep it warm. *Beggars can't be choosers.*

"Can you stay here on your own today?" he asked.

"Yeah. Where you off to?"

"A boy with a head injury needs physical therapy. He probably needs speech therapy too. I'm going to go assess. If he does, are you ready to go back to work?"

April looked away a moment and Brian held his breath. They'd been here two weeks, but Dr. Delaney had said not to push her. They did need to start earning their keep though.

"Yeah. I'll – yeah."

"You rest for now. I'm going over there now, and I'll be back by sundown."

The dirt road that led from the soddy to the asphalt road felt hard under his feet. Cai had scrounged up some winter clothes for them. The boots were a little large, but nothing an extra pair of socks didn't remedy. Brian had reset a farmer's dislocated shoulder in return for a truck, but filling the gas tank required earning the fuel, so Brian walked. Cai said the girl he'd see today had horses and might be willing to loan one. The stable next to the soddy wasn't big enough for more than one.

A woman passed in a white van and stopped. She introduced herself as Nevada and when she heard he was going to the Vances, she went out of her way to drop him.

"Get David back on his feet. Nobody deserves what he's going through."

Was it standard for the barn to be larger than the farmhouse? Brian thought it weird, but they all seemed to be larger. He could hear male voices in the barn and a solitary figure walked far out into the fields. Brian knocked on the back door. The slender blond girl who opened it surprised him. He'd heard the Vance daughter had died during the USDA raid, so he didn't know who this girl was. He introduced himself.

"Dr. Delaney said you'd be stopping by. I'm Allison Sullivan. I'm just helping out here." She closed the door and limped toward a side room. The living room looked warm and cheery. A good-sized wood stove sat between it and the kitchen. Brian scrambled to keep up with Allison, who despite her dragging leg, moved quickly.

"Hang on a second. What happened to *your* leg?"

She paused outside of David's room to explain that she'd been tossed from a horse and suffered nerve damage. She'd just recently gotten the leg brace.

"And you have no idea how to use that brace. You're going to cause more damage. Will you let me work with you on this?"

"Of course. Sorry. I'm just here to help David and he seems to need you more than I do."

"I can work with both of you. So, show me the patient."

David attempted to spoon mush into his mouth using a spoon clenched in his left hand. His right one fisted on a pillow in his lap. His face was a mess from uncoordinated feeding. When Allison spoke, he focused on her, intent, clearly struggling to understand. He nodded awkwardly at Brian and didn't object to being examined. He answered yes-no questions by shaking his head, but most other attempts at communication clearly weren't processing. He grunted a few times, but he didn't attempt to say words.

"I think his legs are strong enough to attempt to walk. Not that you should try it unassisted. I'm going to gather some equipment and come back tomorrow – maybe the next day – to work with him. I do need to figure out transportation, though."

"You're on foot?"

"I have a truck, but fuel is an issue."

"Well, I have a stable full of horses I need to find temporary homes for." She explained her situation. She had feed and straw and folks who would deliver it where it needed to go. He described where he lived. She knew the "Greyeyes Allotment" and promised the horse would be there later today.

She'd provide the horse for the entire winter on promise that he would work with David and herself. When he mentioned April, she offered food for her payment.

Brian could feel the day turning toward evening and thought of the long walk back to his new home, but David's older brother James came into the house and offered to give him a ride.

"I was over at Nevada's visiting Kim and she told me you were here."

"Nice to meet you." They shook hands. No more than 17, with dark hair and liquid brown eyes, James had the oval face, high cheek bones and strong jawline that spoke vaguely of Indian blood, like a lot of other Emmaus citizens.

"The town needs your skills. We can't just drive to Beulah anymore."

"There's a hospital in Beulah?"

"It's a small one, but yeah. Everybody on staff there died when the Army poisoned the town well."

"So, there's equipment?"

"Was. Don't know if it's still there."

"Look, your brother and a whole lot of other people might benefit from the equipment there. Would you drive me over and see if we can get any?"

The boy considered the suggestion and then donned a pistol and put a rifle in the truck. They drove to one of the community gateways and explained their mission to a guard.

"That hospital was cleaned out of meds," the National Guardsman said. "But, yeah, there might be equipment that didn't mean anything to us that might still be there. I'll send a guard with you, just in case."

The guard climbed into the back of the truck and James drove the few miles to Beulah, the now-deserted county seat. Along the way, he explained his methanol production for his vehicles and told Brian a little about David's progress since his injury. It sounded like the kid had improved a lot from a few weeks ago.

The doors to the hospital hung open, making Brian pessimistic, but he found walkers, crutches and other orthotics in a storage room on the second floor. Orthotics were often custom, but beggars couldn't be choosy. He'd figure out ways to adapt them. He filled the bed of the truck with all the therapy equipment he could find. After they dropped off the guard at the gateway, James helped him unload everything into a shed at the allotment.

"Allison's horse will be a saddle horse, but if you kept the load light, you could use it to haul the cart in the barn." The boy showed him the small wagon in the huge barn. "I got a harness you can use."

"That's neighborly of you."

"Naw, I just want my brother back, best as he can be."

"I hope I can do that for you. It's gonna be iffy because we don't really know the extent of his injury and I lack some of the technologies we rely on. But I'm going to do my best."

"I hear your wife's a speech therapist."

"She is and I'm sure she'll be willing to work with him too. There are no guarantees though. What motivates your brother?"

"Music. Don't know what you can do with that."

"I saw the piano at your house. He play it?"

"Yeah, but he could make his guitar sing."

"Since it's his right hand that's affected, he can still finger cords. Might give him a reason to try to move that paralyzed arm and then it's just a matter of modifying something for a pick. People are incredibly adaptable. That's what makes my job rewarding."

Watching James drive away, Brian startled as his wife's arms came around him.

"You should come inside. Can't you feel that wind picking up?"

A chill wind from the east whistled across the fields, swirling around the old house and barn. It smelled like rain. Brian allowed April to draw him inside and for the first time since they were arrested by the Army, she kissed him.

A Mother's Duty

Life involved death and that knowledge terrified Emily Rigby as she bathed Dylan's arm with a rag dipped in warm water. His fever had reduced, but it remained elevated and general irritability, pain and vertigo left him unable to function. His hands trembled, he couldn't even feed himself. Not that he wanted to eat. His slender runner's body grew narrower every day.

"If you roll onto your side, I'll get your back."

"No," Dylan whispered. "I can't." He squeezed his eyes closed. "Stop moving."

She settled the blankets on him and started to clean up the bowl and bath equipment. Ami knocked on the open door.

"I'm here to check on him," Ami reported.

Dylan's left eye opened a slit and then he squeezed it shut, his hands fisting clumsily on his stomach. Ami gently examined him, giving him plenty of warning before she did anything. His vertigo worsened with every movement and speech became more difficult. Ami signaled for Emily to follow her into the hall.

"Is he getting worse?"

"He's about the same. Better than he was the first night. I've never seen these symptoms from the flu before. I think we need to suspect a secondary infection."

"Like a sinus infection?"

"Possibly, but that wouldn't affect his speech. This might have a neurological component. I don't suppose Dr. Callahan has more experience in that department than I do. He's young. He's got a good chance to heal. It'll just take time."

Emily nodded. Ami's swarthy face froze in a brittle fake smile.

"You're concerned about the information you can't access on the disk, aren't you?"

"That sounds insensitive, I know."

"No. You might find a means to treat my son, right?"

"I might. I hope so."

"Grant needs to find someone who can crack that disk and there has got to be something that can be done for Dylan."

"There's a lab at the college that I've arranged to use. Can I draw some of his blood? I want to see what his virus load is."

"Of course. Is anyone using the college?"

"No. It's like a ghost town. But the equipment is there and nobody is objecting." Ami looked in where

Dylan lay as if dead. "I will do my best to come up with some treatment for him. There are some anti-vertigo medications and Javi did ask Shane to look for some."

Emily nodded, glancing toward Dylan, her eyes misting with tears.

"He is actually your son?"

Emily giggled through her tears.

"I am older than I look, but I also had him very young. Grant and I were foolish. My friends said he would ruin my life, but I've never regretted for a moment that I had him."

Ami patted her on the shoulder and went back to Dylan to draw that blood.

Uncertainty

Santa Fe, New Mexico

The radio crackled to life. Mike jerked awake. Shane stirred. He'd been watching the sky behind them, now a stormy slate grey where that front from the east had met a weather system coming out of the Rockies, but it was time to concentrate on landing the aircraft.

"Santa Fe Regional tower, this is Cessna N47G64, requesting permission to land. Over."

They waited for an answer for quite a while as Shane made the turn into Santa Fe's airspace, keeping a wide berth from the Sangre de Cristo Mountains.

"Santa Fe Regional tower, this is Cessna N47G64, requesting permission to land. Over."

"What's going on?" Mike asked. Shane shrugged and repeated his greeting a third time.

"Okay, Santa Fe Regional – I came a long way to get here today and I need to land. Unless you have some objection, I'm doing that now. Over."

"N47G64, you really don't want to land here," a man drawled on the open line. "Santa Fe has the flu. Over."

"We're coming to collect a family member. And, I'm low on fuel. I'm landing. Over."

"We don't have fuel to sell you. Over."

"I brought my own. I'm landing regardless of the flu. Which runway do you recommend? Over."

A wind out of the south buffeted the plane and Mike stopped breathing.

"G64, Runway 15-33 is safest in these winds, but know there's no ground support and you need to land on the south-eastern end because there's dead planes near the terminal. You can taxi on the runway, turn right on 28-10 and stop near the ARFF building. Over."

"G64, keeping coms open. Over." Shane bumped the earphone off his right ear so he could talk to Mike. "You're going to like this. They're letting us land on the big runway, so I have all the room in the world."

The wind jerked the Cessna back and forth.

"You sure?" Mike asked nervously.

"It's just wind. You know, I've never even crashed one of these in the simulator and the guys at Emery had me flying a Cat 4 hurricane, so we're good."

Mike frowned at the yoke in front of him.

"Why would they do that?"

"They try to provide truly hard scenarios to make you a better pilot. I started flying when I was 10, so there wasn't much small-craft they could throw at me. I landed a damaged plane in that Cat 4, but I landed it. So, don't worry. This is a piece of cake for me."

Shane flew over the airport to spy out the town.

"What's the smoke?" Mike asked, pointing at a couple of big smoke sources.

Shane considered the plumes and shook his head. He suspected the purpose, but he didn't need Mike more upset until they got onto the ground. Fortunately, the wind settled down when they turned into it and Shane easily landed on the available half of the runway. The other half had a crashed commuter jet blocking it. Shane turned on the runway and, defying his training, taxied back to the cross runway as instructed.

A man about Rob's age came out to the field as they climbed out of the plane. Short, spry man with shrewd eyes, but laugh lines around his mouth, he embodied a Levi-Straus commercial.

"Uly Carver." He nodded but ignored the hand Shane held out. Shane withdrew it.

"We were told to look for you. Shane Delaney. Mike Sanchez."

"Know your grandfather – Jacob, right? And your mom – uh, Jill."

"Right, they used to stop here on their way to visit me in college. I forgot that."

"Haven't seen him since you graduated, but we still get a Christmas card from him. How's he doing?"

"Great considering the circumstances. And you folks?"

He sighed deeply, shook his head and looked away.

"This flu –." They waited while he got control over his emotions. "I don't have the means to stop you landing, but – we've had thousands die here. They're burning bodies."

"I'm so sorry," Shane murmured. Mike looked away, uncomfortable with the emotion or worried for Alicia and Magdala. "Have you lost people?"

"My wife." He swallowed convulsively. "My daughter survived it. My son didn't catch it, but now his kids have it. You don't have the flu up there?"

"We do, but we've only had one elderly person die from it and the town doc thinks the flu was a complication of old age, not the actual cause of death."

Uly nodded, swallowing again.

"Have either of you had it?"

"No. I've been exposed, but so far I'm asymptomatic. There's a theory about immunity, but I also traveled overseas in the last year, so I might have been accidentally inoculated against it."

Uly nodded.

"So, if you're going into town, you should dress so your skin isn't exposed and cover your mouths. Take proper PPE procedures."

"Yes, we'll do that. So, Grant Rigby thought you might be able to get us a vehicle."

"I can loan you a truck. I'm the only one here now and there are a dozen to choose from."

"I want to fill the plane's tanks and have her all ready to take off before we head into town. Mike will go with you while I take care of that."

"Do you know ... does Rigby know what happened? The bombs, the Pulse, this flu?"

"He knows something, but I don't know what he knows. It's beginning to look more and more like a complex coordinated attack. Bombs, EMP, bio. One alone was survivable, but three --. And the multiple-site nature of the bombs --." Shane sighed.

"We'd run our course," Uly said after a moment's pause. "It was a great experiment that had loaded itself with too much baggage, so was bound to collapse if someone hit us too hard in the right places. I thought it would be economic. I remember your granddad thought it would be political – the two-party system just squabbling until it collapsed into a food fight and new parties would have to form."

"Jacob thought that?"

"He didn't like it. That's just what he thought would happen. He and I would argue. I'm a minarchist. He really thinks we'd do better with just local community governments who were friendly with one another. I still think we need a national government to deal with everyone else."

"How's that working out for us now?" Shane returned Mike's question with an incredulous look. Mike growing a sense of politics seemed unnatural. "Show me this truck. Shane, you get started on refueling. I don't want to wait longer to go see Alicia."

"Yup," Too much time spent behind the cordon. They needed to concentrate on the job at hand. Philosophical thinking needed to wait until the snow fell and trapped everyone where they were for a while. "A couple things, though. Who is in charge in Santa Fe?"

"A National Guard outfit. They clashed with the Army and won."

Mike and Shane exchanged glances because that appeared to be a continuing theme.

"What's with only Spanish over coms?" Mike asked.

"They are majority Spanish and they sort of decreed that all official business would be in Spanish. It's kind of hard on those of us who speak better English, but it's keeping the peace. Most of them will talk to you face to face in English if you need it."

"We don't, but do things go better if you speak Spanish." Uly nodded to Shane's question. "Good to know. When this is done, you're going to want to be paid. What's your coin of choice?"

"Food or water."

Agreeing to the terms, Shane told them to go get the truck and he turned his attention to refueling the plane.

Mutual Admiration Society

Emmaus, Kansas

Rob used to like rain. Before the bombs had turned rain into a threat you needed to hide from, he'd go for a walk in this. The rad meter said they were fine in the house, but he refused to open a window to check the outside levels. He just hoped Shane and Mike were safely outside the weather shadow. After weeks of the house growing steadily colder, it now felt a bit too warm since Shane had stoked the coal furnace. Unfortunately, the ground floor heat hadn't reached the bedrooms yet. How long would that take? He startled from his reverie when Jacob rapped on the doorframe.

"Hey, Pa. What are you up to?"

"I finished my tasks for the day before this started. I'm headed to read a book. I wanted to talk with you before I did though."

"What's up?"

"Shane." The old man sighed before settling into the side chair. "As long as that boy has something to do, he's okay, but winter's coming."

279

"Right. Cai seems better."

"His damage is skin deep compared to Shane's. I've tried talking to the boy. Told him things I've never told anyone else. Almost feel like my conscience is clear finally. Anyway, he's stubborn and he resists me."

Rob nodded, then realized Jacob wanted him to reply.

"He won't talk to me about anything in the past, so it's good he talks to you."

"*I* talk to *him*. He *listens*. I don't think I can drag him out into the light like I did you. It's going to take more than just me."

Rob sighed. He'd known he hadn't atoned enough for his past, but that didn't make it any easier.

"I'll try, Pa."

"Good. Might have that bride of yours talk to him too."

Jacob stood up, put a still-strong hand on Rob's shoulder.

"I know you will try, son. It's just that you got to get over the idea that because he's quiet and self-disciplined, he's strong. He's like that chip in the windshield just waiting for a cold wind to crack across to the other side. Put some pressure on it then and it'll shatter into a million pieces."

"I hear him wake up from nightmares enough to know, Pa. I just don't know how to get past his reluctance to hear from me. Like I said, I'll try. It surprised me when Cai rebuffed my attempts when he first got back."

"Yeah. Young men always think old men don't know what we're talking about."

Rob felt his cheeks grow warm.

"I did think that. Of course, I wanted an excuse to stay in my misery. Shane?"

"He thinks he deserves it."

"What do you think?"

"I think there's redemption for everyone, but he may have done some things that are hard to forgive yourself for. You know how that goes. I'm going to go read that book now. And, Rob, in case I haven't said it enough – you're a good father. Shane's a tough customer and Cai makes phenomenal mistakes when he steps off the straight and narrow, but you did a good job. Keri, she's made of great stuff, but so are the boys. They just have to make some hard choices these days and that's bound to affect them."

"Thanks, Pa. It sounds a little self-serving, but you did a good job too. I know you've always felt guilty about EJ, but I really don't think that was your fault. Our war was very different from yours."

"No, war is war, son. The details change, but what it does to you doesn't." Jacob sighed. "And, I do still feel guilty for EJ, mainly because I didn't know how to reach out to him. I yelled instead of listened. He was my trainer, my setup for when it was your turn."

"And the demon?" Rob asked quietly just as Jacob turned away. Jacob breathed deeply before replying.

"I don't know. I caught hints about her from Lai, but I thought it was DTs. Vi mentioned her a few times, but she had no personal knowledge. Joseph talked about avenging spirits and I thought he was being poetic. Jill talked to Calla Thomas before she died and recorded everything she could remember. You never saw her?"

Rob sighed, pulling on his beard.

"Dark haired woman with knives stalking me. I thought they were Nam memories mixed into drunk dreams, so I don't know. And Carl isn't a very good source of information. Shane admitting to anything?"

"He's not denying. That's how you know with him. He won't outright lie."

Rob nodded.

"Should I worry about Cai?"

"Well, if you maybe saw her – supposedly it's a Greyeyes phenomenon, but – technically, you have more Greyeyes DNA than Shane, so maybe that's just a fancy and every male in the family is at risk."

"Family demons is definitely a fanciful idea. Or seemed like until Carl saw her too and I started seeing Shane shift his gaze to her. You said EJ did that too?" Jacob nodded. "What happened to Lai? Do you remember?"

"Dead before he turned 40. I'll have to ask Ed Greyeyes. I don't really remember. You know he's Lai's son, right?"

"I knew we were cousins, but I thought it was out further."

"I don't think Lai ever married his mother, but she gave the boy his name. So, him and Trish Vance, only she doesn't know it."

Rob stared at him for a long moment remembering a conversation from a few weeks before.

"Something?" Jacob asked.

"No, just a random thought. You go read that book, Pa. Times like this when we can rest are becoming rare."

"And people wonder what we did before television."

Smiling at his own joke, Jacob left the study. Rob stood up to stare out the window, asking God to watch over his sons – particularly Shane, but also Cai.

Mi Corizon

Santa Fe, New Mexico

The sky continued to darken toward the northeast and the Sangre de Cristo Mountains became wreathed in clouds as Mike tried to orient himself to find Magdala's house. Once he found the road they drove in on, it all went very quickly, except the main roads were blocked by broken down vehicles that they had to maneuver around. Finally they turned into a neighborhood of modest homes.

"This adobe is whack," Mike remarked. "Everything looks the same."

"Are you telling me we're going to be knocking on random doors?"

"I'll recognize my car, man. I left it for her."

"Your car is here? So, I could have come here without you and driven around until I found it?" Mike nodded, then frowned. "If you weren't my best friend, I might be annoyed by that."

"Sorry. I didn't think of it."

"You were running a fever. That it up there?"

"God, you have good eyes. Are those prescription?"

Shane adjusted his sunglasses and laughed. They weren't. His eyesight evoked legends – and he meant to keep it that way, thus the sunglasses. Jacob always wore them too and his eyesight hadn't deteriorated with age. Mike pulled over to the curb and they got out, both scanning the street.

"What do you think?" Mike asked.

"Feels deserted. Not entirely, but yeah. Mexico isn't that far away, and a lot of these people probably had relatives there. Let's get off the street."

Nobody answered the door immediately, though a small dog barked from the interior.

"Maybe we should go around back," Mike suggested, but Shane indicated the curtain on the front window, and then the bolt slid back on the inside. Alicia flung herself into Mike's arms, weeping, talking a blue streak in Spanish, so fast Shane didn't even try to keep up. Seeing vehicle movement at the end of the street, Shane swept them before him into the living room and bolted the door behind them.

"Ric, where have you been?" Alicia demanded.

"You got big, *chica*." Mike smiled, moving to touch her belly.

"I was beginning to think you were both dead." Alicia hadn't gotten that big, but she definitely looked pregnant. She marveled at her husband's new head fuzz.

"The Pulse kind of complicated life." Shane had drifted to the window to peer through a crack in the curtains as a military vehicle rolled by. It didn't pause for the truck they'd left at the curb, but Shane breathed a sigh of relief that he'd stripped the magnetic signs off it before they left the airport. "Just for grins, we should move away from the door. What's been going on here?"

"I'm not altogether sure." Alicia rolled her eyes upwards, as if trying to remember something from the past. "We've been told to stay in our 'areas'. The only time I've left the house has been to get water."

"Martial law?" Mike asked.

They sat down on the sofa while Shane took a side chair. A small schnauzer came out of a side room and growled at him. Shane bared his teeth. The dog ran away. Alicia stared at him like he'd lost his mind.

"Dogs don't get away with that crap with me." Shane loved dogs, but they needed to be trained and he wasn't going to apologize for responding to it like an alpha should.

"He's the size of a cat."

"And I wouldn't treat a cat with attitude any better than I treat a dog with one. Can we get back to the point?"

"Where's Magdala?" At Mike's question, Alicia's face twisted, and tears filled her eyes.

"She died about a month ago."

"The flu?" Alicia nodded to Shane's question, wiping her eyes. "Did you have it?"

"Yes, but not like she did. I just felt really punk for about a week and then I recovered."

"So, you had the milder version like we do up in Emmaus. And your mom?"

"High fever, cough, couldn't breathe. She seemed to just drown."

"Why is it different here?" Mike directed his question to Shane.

"My handler thinks it has been genetically manipulated and there may be different strains."

Alicia stared at Shane as if he puzzled her.

"Who are you really?"

"Shane Delaney from Emmaus Kansas, son of a feed store owner who is now mayor and a nurse. Most of the rest has always been the truth. Faraday's my mother's maiden name. Eric is my middle."

"And you don't work for Knight Industries, do you?"

"I worked for Knight Industries, but I also worked for the US government – the Central Security Administration – kind of an FBI/CIA/NSA hybrid that hasn't made it into the news. They sent me to spy on Knight."

"To spy on guys like Mike?"

"Broadly, yes, but I never reported on Mike. They weren't interested in individual grunts. They wanted someone who could check on the higher-ups and as a pilot, I occasionally got to talk to them. And within 24 hours of meeting each other, I wouldn't have reported on Mike even if he had done something my handlers were interested in."

Alicia looked at Mike, who shrugged.

"We've talked about it and I don't care."

Alicia took a deep breath and a moment of silence.

"Thank you for bringing my husband back to me."

"Yeah," Shane replied. "We're here to take you to where it is safe – well, safer. We hear food is scarce here and water is even tighter."

"Fortunately, my neighbors don't know about Mama's stash, but water is hard to come by. I've been raiding swimming pools, but even those are getting low."

"Emmaus has plenty of water. Not everyone has food, but my family is fixed okay and you're bringing food, so that'll be okay."

"You want me to leave here?" Alicia frowned at Mike.

"Yes. This flu is dangerous and it's not so bad up there."

"My mother is buried in the backyard."

Shane opened his mouth to say something flip, but Mike beat him to it with a surprisingly thoughtful answer. For a big grunt mercenary, Mike knew his way around Alicia well.

"And when things are better, you can come back to visit, but I want you safe."

Alicia paused, perhaps considering her arguments, but then she nodded.

"How do we get there?"

"We flew here. Let's show Shane the stash."

Alicia moved the bed to reveal the trap door that led to the cellar. The low ceiling didn't inspire Shane's confidence, but he looked at the neatly stocked shelves and the solar-powered freezer and made an estimation.

"I can carry about a third of this in the Skywagon. If weather permits, I can come back with Jazz and we can haul the rest of it home."

"Or we could pack what the plane can't carry into my car and drive it to Emmaus," Mike suggested.

Shane chortled and Alicia looked amazed.

"Your car is a lawn ornament, honey. I've been using my Popi's old truck."

"Would it make it to Emmaus?" Shane asked while Mike mourned. His Camaro had been a great car.

"I don't know. You're the car nuts. You want me to make dinner?"

"Oh, yes, please!" Mike begged. "That's the one thing with these Kansans. Their food sucks."

"I'm standing right here." Shane smiled through his protest.

"Your mom never heard of spices."

"She did, but she says she's holding the spices for when the food we've got starts to go stale. You guys get caught up. I'm going to do a perimeter check. Are all your neighbors gone, Alicia?"

"The Acevedos next door died three weeks ago and half the neighborhood bugged out after that." She took a deep breath instead of crying. "They helped me bury Mama and they were sick within 48 hours."

"I'm so sorry you had to go through that alone." Mike hugged his wife.

"That wasn't the worst of it. I started spotting and thought I might miscarry. Then I got sick and the baby wasn't moving. I thought she'd died inside of me until about a week ago when she started kicking again. In fact - ." She grabbed first Mike's hand and then Shane's and laid them on her belly. "I think yours is an elbow, Mike. Shane, I'm pretty sure that's a knee."

Shane had never touched a woman's pregnant belly before. He imagined a tiny human in a confined space stretching or --.

"Whoa. I think he just rolled over."

Alicia grinned like she'd discovered cold fusion.

"Something swapped here too," Mike declared. "Wow! What a difference two months make!"

"I feel every stretch mark, to be sure," Alicia said, laughing. "Time to make dinner. Mike, you should go with Shane. There's a pool about a block and a half down the alley that's still got water in it, so take buckets."

Shane followed Mike out the back door.

"I'm surprised she hasn't been raided yet. This house is totally unprotected. Lots of windows, low fence."

"Friendly neighbors and Magdala was clear that we were never supposed to tell anyone about it. She built her stash up slowly over the years."

"Sooner or later, people would have pushed in demanding the food. They would kill her to get at it, even if they couldn't find it. Before we go, we should board up the windows and doors just to discourage looting."

They moved down the alleyway. The darkening sky cast the neighborhood in shadow.

"It's going to rain," Mike indicated. Shane nodded in agreement, privately wondering if it had snowed at home.

Several houses had burned, smoke staining the adobe around their empty windows, roofs collapsed. Neighbors trying to control the spread of the flu? Some back doors of intact houses were just left open. There were no signs of looting, but clearly, nobody lived there anymore.

They found the yard with the pool that still had water, but they had to use one bucket to fill the other bucket. Shane wondered how much rain would refill the pool. They probably needed another source for Uly's payment. Returning by way of the street, they scanned for threats. A man came out from behind a house. Shane didn't care if it looked suspicious that he reached his right hand behind his back.

"*Who are you?*" the man demanded in Spanish.

"*Alicia Esquibel is my wife and this is my brother,*" Mike replied also in Spanish.

The neighbor looked from one to the other and directed his question to Shane.

"*What are your names?*"

"*Eric and Miguel.*" Harvesting corn had deepened Shane's tan and he still wore his sunglasses. He hoped his Chicano accent served him well.

"Nice to meet you. Bueno tardes."

"*Same likewise. What's your name?*" Mike asked, pausing at the end of their driveway. It looked more and more like rain as a chill wind blew from the north.

"Carlos Pedimente." Carlos now lapsed into perfectly schooled English. "I'm glad you're here. A woman alone is not safe here any longer."

"True that." Mike could sound just as American, but he kept a flavor of Sonoran in his accent. Shane doubted he could do that. Thanking Carlos for watching the neighborhood, they turned toward the house. They didn't talk until they were back inside the kitchen.

"Good way to establish the relationship," Mike complimented, putting the bucket in the kitchen. "You're dark enough you could be my brother. I never heard you pronounce your name with the Spanish 'I' before."

"It never mattered before. Carlos seems like a nice guy, but this place feels unsafe to me."

"The sooner we're out of here the better, I think."

"We need to go to the CDC tomorrow. Hopefully the weather will break because I don't like the look of this sky. Storms and small planes don't mix."

"In the meantime, we need to inventory those supplies, decide what we need to take with us and what we can get on the return run."

Shane doubted a return run. Winter loomed and the deadly form the flu had taken here made him intensely nervous. Alicia used bleach water on all the surfaces, but that didn't make the rest of the town germ-free.

He offered to wash dishes after dinner, pouring bleach into the rinse sink. He heard Mike and Alicia kissing soon after that and then they withdrew to what he supposed to be her room. That left the master bedroom and he wasn't sleeping there out of respect for a dead woman and the virus that had killed her. Looking for blankets and sheets, he climbed the circular stairs to the second floor. Outside rain pounded the streets, washing them with successive sheets of water. The solar system powered lights here and he stared around at the bold floral paintings decorating the walls. Magdala's signature proclaimed her artistry. He hoped Alicia understood they couldn't take them with them.

Finding sheets and blanket in a cupboard near the top of the stairs, he made up the couch and built up a low fire in the kiva. The house settled into the night doldrums, the neighborhood beyond shrouded in storm. The little dog jumped up on his legs. He kicked it off. It sulked. He dozed off with a smile on his face.

Windmills

Emmaus, Kansas

Mark survived the flu and Lisa would too, Keri thought as she scrubbed the door frame between the living room and dining room. When she'd moved into Alex' house she'd scrubbed the kitchen until it gleamed, but she'd stopped at the door between the kitchen and dining room. She couldn't exactly say why. Maybe respect for Alex's mother, whom she didn't really remember. A freshman in high school when the Lufgrens died, she'd not really been friends with Alex. Older than her by almost four years, her brother's best friend might have remained a virtual stranger if he hadn't needed a babysitter as he struggled with single parenthood. She'd admired him and even had a crush on him, but he'd been so grownup and busy trying to keep the farm afloat and have a little bit of a social life. He'd scared her a little bit when he'd come home with beer on his breath and offer to drive her home *in the morning*. He'd never seemed interested in her until she'd gone off to college.

They'd not seen each other in a few years when she'd been at the county fair last summer and he'd asked her if she wanted to dance. Such a tall man surprised her with so light a step. They'd been engaged by Christmas, married in June. They slept together on their first night as man and wife and he'd surprised her by being shy and tentative, admitting he was a virgin, as was she.

"Your brother tried to get me laid a few times, but I just never liked any of them enough to let him win."

He seemed not to suffer from the lack of experience. He admitted to picking the brain of every older and happily married man he knew. If Alex's gentle exploration was what inexperience wrought, Keri didn't know any different, and she didn't feel deprived.

The fingerprints finally yielded to her elbow grease. Alice Ramirez came down the stairs, carrying a fussy Lisa. Mark opened his eyes from where he lay on the couch. His fever had broken last night. Everyone else in the family needed to rest a day or two after the fever broke before their complete recovery. Everyone except Keri had been sick.

Marnie had a theory that men were more susceptible to the flu than women and it seemed to be harder on breeding-age men. The old and the young hardly seemed to get sick at all. Pete had been sick the shortest period of time. Lisa was fussy and uncomfortable, but her fever wasn't life-threatening, and she wasn't puking like the adults had.

"The mechanism is here in the cellar," Keri heard Alex say in the kitchen as a whirl of cool air wafted up her back.

"That storm is slamming down on us," Michael Tully said. Keri saw Alex disappearing down the basement stairs, followed by a man she didn't know and then Michael. She moved to the staircase to the upstairs, washing the railing and the wall on the opposite side. Then she did the doors and knobs in the upper hallway. By then, her bucket needed to be swapped out. She'd gotten the bathroom this morning. She returned to the kitchen to upend her bucket into the farm sink as Alex and his guests returned from the bowels of the house.

"My wife Keri, Abe McArthur and you know Michael."

"Heard from Jazz lately?" Michael asked.

"I saw her yesterday when I took milk and eggs to my folks. She's doing okay." Kerri didn't know if he knew about his sister's trip to Hays and she wasn't about to share what might be upsetting news. Jazz could tell her own tales. "What brings you our way?"

"Our windmill," Alex explained. "Abe thinks they can replicate it."

"And I think some of the components could be adapted to get the big turbines going again," Michael explained. Jazz's younger brother held a notebook with some extensive drawings on the page. "If I can figure it out, we might be able to get electricity locally."

"That would be great," Keri said.

Her visit to her parents resembled time travel to the 1880s. Fortunately, Jill had a coal stove to cook on. Some people made do with barbecues or open fires in the backyard. Meanwhile, Keri lived in an old-fashioned house that still had hot running water and a freezer that stayed cold.

"I need to find a way to stay viable this winter and providing people with house turbines may be one way to do that since we have the machine shop," Abe said. He shook hands with Alex. "Thank you for letting us stop by."

"My pleasure. Come back if you need to. And, Michael, you should try to see your sister sometime soon. This storm's just the start of winter roads."

The youngest Tully sibling nodded.

Pete and Poppy came clamoring in the back door. Snowflakes covered the scarlet cap Poppy wore over her blonde hair.

"Storm!" Poppy signed. *"Cows all in barn-there. Missing goat road far side found. Stubborn!"*

Born deaf, Poppy had never known speech and didn't seem to care if Michael and Abe McArthur could understand, though Pete interpreted. He'd really learned sign quickly. It hadn't been two months yet, had it?

"You two need to come with me to the far barn to help Abe load up some corn cobs for Stan Osimowicz's house," Alex said, signing simultaneously. "Keri, we'll be back in about an hour. Dinner?"

"Will be ready by then."

She'd fried up a pullet and the potato salad probably had rested enough. The rhythms of cooking on a wood stove still baffled her. Alex stoked it first thing in the morning and Keri could cook on it until mid-afternoon when he stoked it again for the rest of the day, rendering it too hot for cooking until past dinner time. She embraced the art of warming.

"Do you need help?" Mark asked from the door as she worked.

"Go lie back down. You're still sick."

"I know, but this is your home. We're just --."

"Family. Our kids are engaged."

Mark's mouth twisted. The adults had accepted the inevitable, but that didn't mean they had to rejoice over it. Even while he stood there, Mark's face whitened.

"You need to go lie down. It does no one any good if you get up before you're ready and make yourself sick again."

"It just never seems to end," Mark admitted, heading back to the couch.

Two weeks of successive sickness left them all fed up. Hopefully, Lisa was the last one and then they could settle down to a winter routine. Alex said winter meant less work, but farming was labor intensive, so there would be no down days now.

Keri paused by Alice's chair and touched Lisa's sweaty black curls.

"Her fever is holding around 101," Alice assured. "This is the – the third day?"

"Yes. You look so exhausted. Do you want me to take her for a while?"

Alice had just gotten well herself.

"No. You should get dinner on the table. She's trying to fall asleep. I'll nap when she does."

"Let me know if there's anything I can do."

Alice smiled. They'd only known each other six or seven weeks, but it felt like they'd known each other for decades. Keri washed her hands and got busy with dinner. The other half of the family returned in less time that Alex had anticipated.

"We're going to need more oil if I keep making things requiring mayonnaise," Keri told him as he helped her clear the table.

"I'll see what I can do," he told her. "Someone must have some they're willing to trade for eggs, milk or butter. Although, hopefully not butter for a while because we need someone to churn it."

"I just didn't have time when you were all sick."

"It wasn't a complaint. Just an inventory of what we have for trade."

He stomped on the floor for Poppy's attention. She and Pete signed so the adults couldn't see.

"You clean up here. Me shower, sleep."

Although he'd beaten the flu, his energy levels flagged by the end of the day. Pete and Poppy nodded and took over for Alex and Keri.

"You know your crazy brother flew to Santa Fe today?" Alex announced.

"I didn't. What's in Santa Fe?"

"His friend's wife. Ran into Jason Breen on our return trip. I'll talk to him tomorrow about the oil. If I'd known about it today, I would have mentioned it to him."

"We're not out yet. It's just that you don't think how much you need oil until you start making things like mayonnaise from scratch. I've never in my life fried chicken and saved the oil. It's just fortunate Alice knows that trick."

"I didn't want to argue with you when you threw out my fry oil this summer. I guess I would have said something eventually."

"I didn't know. I wonder if my mom knows."

"She's the one who taught me." Alex closed the bedroom door and started to strip off his shirt. "I know it's early, but you want to – uh, you know – while I'm showering?"

"You know, huh? We could save water."

"We could?" Alex blushed. "I guess we could." He experimented by unbuttoning her top button. "It's weird with other people in the house."

"Poppy has always been in the house." Keri unbuttoned his Carhartt's.

"Yeah, but she can't hear us."

"No, but that's never stopped her from figuring out what's going on. And, besides, Mark and Alice managed to create a baby in a camper, so you know even Pete knows what's up."

She kissed him. His anatomy responded.

"I'll meet you there," he whispered, reaching for his robe, still blushing like a farm boy. Keri silently thanked her mother for suggesting the implant in her arm that meant she wouldn't get pregnant this year and grabbed her own robe to follow him.

In Loco Parentis

The bell over the door tinkled and Jos Osimowicz looked up from the hand-written inventory, wishing for a working computer. Since they'd boarded up the windows, he could no longer see headlights coming and going in the little parking lot out front, so the bell gave him first warning of a customer. Max Albright helped them with the heavy lifting now that the power had gone out. Granmae appreciated his efforts. Jos disliked how the guy's eyes dwelled on him and he always seemed to stand – well, it was odd and creepy, oddly creepy.

"Where's Huffy?" Max asked.

"Flu. She tried to tough it out, but I sent her to bed about two hours ago."

"So, you're running the place by yourself?"

"I know what I'm doing." Jos hoped he told the truth. Granmae knew what she was doing. He would try to do what she did and hopefully it would all work out okay. Don't give away the store. Rule #1.

"Do you need help?"

The creepy vibe came and went and right now, it wasn't in the store. Jos handed Max two sheets.

"If you go to the far boxes, we can meet in the middle. Distribute things to the shelves and mark how many we have."

"Don't you have school work to do?"

"School's out, maybe permanently. Keeping the store open keeps us fed. I'll worry about ACTs next year – if those even exist then."

"When I was your age, my goal was on college, playing soccer."

"Yeah," Jos agreed. He hadn't been to the Silo climbing gym since the bombs and he tried not to think overmuch about what had happened to his mother and stepfather. He hadn't liked Bill, but he hadn't wanted him incinerated in a fiery hell. "I need to get to work."

While they worked, Max asked if he played soccer and got him talking about climbing and then some of the books that were – had been – popular. Jos supposed Amazon didn't exist any longer. Max said the building probably still resided in Seattle, but without the Internet, it would have a hard time staying in business.

"I guess Jason and his guys are the new Amazon," Jos joked. They were on the last few boxes, basically working in the same row. As inventory went, the hour had been pleasant.

"What's the building materials for?" Max indicated the stack of lumber over by the now useless coolers.

"This place is way too much to heat, so I'm going to build a wall to create an unheated warehouse and a heated storefront. If we're just heating that and the residence, we should be able to get through to spring."

Max nodded, looking sad.

"I'm looking for a place to live and a way to earn that and food. Drew hadn't filled the tank yet and my fuel ran out yesterday. Sounds like you could use help here."

The hairs on the back of Jos' neck ruffled as something creeped up his back. Max put a hand on his forearm.

"I know it's a lot to ask, but I'll earn my keep."

"I-I don't think I can hire anyone without talking to Granmae."

Besides the three-bedroom apartment they occupied, a second two-bedroom rental occupied the third story. Logistically, Jos knew he'd have to heat that too. Max wouldn't have to live with them. Still he felt nervous at the thought. The desire to snatch his arm back from the man's touch grew with every second. What was he supposed to say? Wasn't it rude to tell a gay guy to get his hands off him? Was there a polite way to say "I'm not interested"? They never talked about this in school and Uncle Stan had never mentioned it either.

"What's going on here?" Jason Breen asked, startling them. Max snatched his own hand back from touching Jos, but Jason had seen it.

"We're doing inventory," Jos explained.

"Sorry to screw that up," Jason quipped. "I have another truckload of goods – probably the last for a while. It's starting to come down pretty heavy out there. The roads will be hard after this" While he spoke to Jos, Jason's gaze dwelled on Max. "Where do you want the delivery?"

"Right here."

"I'll have my guys get on it. Um, yeah, this is awkward. Jos, are you gay?"

Jos's stomach dropped into his legs while heat flashed across his face.

"No. I definitely like girls," he mumbled.

"You sure about that?" Max asked, flashing a defiant glance at Jason.

"I've --." Jason nailed it when he said this was awkward. "—done some kissing and – uh, fantasizing." His neck could fry eggs.

"Max, leave the kid alone. If you really need a boyfriend, I hear Kowalcsky out at the McAuliff compound swings both ways."

"You don't have the right to tell me how to live my life," Max snapped.

"I don't, but neither can you run to a judge now and complain that someone is infringing on your right to diddle teenagers who just haven't liked a girl enough to fumble their way into her panties yet. What you do in your house with consenting adults is your business. What you do in public is the business of anyone who can see. And, I saw a white-faced teenager creeped out by you touching him and not knowing what to say to make you stop. So --."

Max's face turned purple and then he pivoted and slammed out the front door. Jason and Jos stared awkwardly in different directions until the silence became more painful than the embarrassment.

"Thank you," Jos said finally.

"No problem. Had to do that for myself when I was about your age – maybe a little older. They'll give you that whole 'if you're still a virgin at this age, you obviously aren't all that into girls' speech and it goes from there. Being young is not a sign you're gay."

"My uncle Stan – we've had that talk."

"Good. Just so you know, it's okay to tell men like Max that they need to step back. Or women, for that matter. And, in these current circumstances, you won't have to worry about a civil rights complaint either. And – well, it's not for everybody, but if you want to get that squared away, we have a couple of ladies available out at the hub."

Jos felt hot again. Jason laughed.

"Like I said, it's not for everybody. I'll get my guys unloading the truck. You need help building that wall?"

"I planned to start on it tonight after inventory, but now – what will it cost me?"

"Frank and Josh don't have anything to do tomorrow. I'll send them your way, included in my agreement with Huffy. Keeping this business viable keeps my business viable. You have insulation?"

"Yeah, it's back in the walk-in freezer. I needed the room."

"Sheetrock?"

"With it."

"Good. Anything you need to finish the project?"

"Uncle Stan said he'd bring a door, but I haven't seen him yet."

"The weather turned pretty quick. I'll send Josh that way tonight, make sure Stan's okay, bring the door if he can."

"Thank you."

"Mutual back scratching society. How's Huffy?"

"She's pretty sick. Lost her voice. Anyone sick at your place?"

"Not so far. Marnie's got her hands full."

"Thanks again for the help and – you know. I didn't know what to say to him."

"Yeah. In my day you could be rude. Today ...." Jason shook his head. "Better get my guys to work and I'll radio Josh."

Jos got back to work, clearing the last box so that he could receive the next inventory.

Touching Death

Santa Fe, New Mexico – Next Morning

Lightning sizzled across the sky as Shane poured water into a tank in the back of the airport truck. He'd stolen the tank from an abandoned municipal building. He guessed the building was abandoned since the windows were broken. Last night's rain had cleared this morning, but massive thunderheads formed over the Sangre de Cristo, promising a hard rain coming soon. The arroyo now ran half-full instead of yesterday's trickle. Shane and Mike exchanged buckets.

"Can you imagine what she went through looking for water every day?" Mike asked.

"The whole southwest is hard to live in without wells. And wells need electric pumps. You know, your mother-in-law has a cistern. Alicia was just a day away from having plenty of water right on site."

"But pregnant – hauling water --."

"She's fine. I don't know a lot about it, but if the baby's kicking, she's fine. One more bucket and we can call this good." Mike bent to fill it. Shane watched the sky nervously. Lightning storms and bodies of water didn't mix, and arroyos could go from tame to raging flood in a few minutes. Mike handed him the bucket.

"I'm going to take a whizz before we go." Mike headed up the bank, leaving Shane to dump the bucket into the tank and close it up for the trip. He operated the vent, listening while the air escaped before clamping it back down. He heard Mike yell. Instantly, he leapt over the side of the truck bed and ran into the scrub brush where Mike had retreated for privacy.

Mike grappled with a man in filthy clothes. Shane grabbed him by the shoulder and pulled him away from Mike, pushing him backwards after he broke his grip.

"The world is ending," the man raved in a ragged voice. Shane's brain registered what his hands had discovered – fever. "Repent or you're going to hell." He turned and stumbled off through the mesquite brush, pausing to puke before leaving their sight.

"We need to wash – like now." Without hesitation, Shane ran to the truck to pull out his go-bag. They washed their forearms and faces with soap and then antiseptic.

"He got spit on me." Mike sounded disgusted as he rinsed his mouth in the arroyo.

"It'll probably be fine." Marnie hadn't yet figured out the transmission rate. Not everyone got sick, but it seemed it hit whole households. Mike didn't need to know that. "We need to get over to the CDC, try to find this Dr. Perrin Alicia talked with. Load up."

People walked and drove here in Santa Fe. Alicia reported a steady stream of folks leaving for Mexico, but not everyone had deserted the town. Shane spoke to several people on his way to the CDC trailer set up outside of a hospital where Spanish-speaking military personnel guarded the gate. Nobody questioned Shane's accent so long as he spoke Spanish.

"You don't want to go in there." One of the guards on the cordon gate pointed to the hospital's main building. "People die in there."

"I need to talk to Dr. Perrin."

"And I'm looking for this guy." Mike showed him a drawing.

"That's one of the FEMA guys. I haven't seen him in a while, but if you go to that trailer over there, they might know where you can find him." The guard talked on his radio and pointed Shane toward another trailer.

Shane glanced at Mike.

"I'll probably be done before you are." Mike headed off around the fenced area while Shane went to the CDC trailer. Dr. Perrin looked exhausted, his reddish hair unwashed, his jaw shadowed in rusty scruff. Shane guessed him in his early 40s, but his blue eyes looked old. He listened when Shane introduced himself in Spanish, then asked if Shane spoke English.

313

"With a last name like Delaney, yeah." Shane laughed, effortlessly switching into English.

"Where are you from?"

"Midwest. - Kansas." Shane consulted his phone where Rigby had texted him the last known codes. "Alpha 57 Romeo 43 Foxtrot 72 November niner Yankey 34. I was asked to get as much information as I can about this flu."

"You're working with someone at CDC?"

"I don't know. I'm merely a grunt. There's a virologist involved – Amisi Ceylon."

"Don't know her but hold on a moment." Dr. Perrin had both electricity and computer access. Apparently, the CDC had at least partially hardened its infrastructure. "She worked at Northwest Memorial in Chicago." He sighed and smiled briefly, then dropped a disc into the CD tray. "This is going to take a while. Do you have the flu in Kansas?"

"It seems to be milder. We've had a couple of elderly people die of it, but mostly it just makes folks feel like crap for about 10 days."

"Have you had it?"

"No. My family has so far not caught it."

"Interesting. You willing to give me a blood sample?"

"Sure, if you'll tell me what's going on here."

Perrin prepped a blood draw kit while Shane took off his jacket and rolled up his sleeve.

"It's a variant of the H1N1 virus. What do you know about that?"

"Spanish flu, swine flu – not much more than that."

"That's a bit more than the general public knows. In 1917 to 1920-ish, it infected 500 million people around the world and resulted in about 75 million deaths. Five percent of the world's population at the time." The numbers boggled the mind. Was it really 350 million in today's numbers? That had to be more than the current population of the United States. "It's a nasty virus because it doesn't just kill the very young and old. Young adults are especially susceptible."

Perrin tightened a tourniquet around Shane's bicep and told him to make some fists. A veteran universal blood donor, Shane didn't really need his instructions.

"The good news is that the 20th century pandemic was spread by troop movements – it was World War 1. Given our current state, we aren't going to be traveling a lot for a while, so this may be contained. Before the Pulse, we were still able to talk outside the country and there were no reported cases."

"That can't last with so many people headed to Mexico."

Dr. Perrin slid the syringe into Shane's forearm and loosened the tourniquet. Blood flowed into the tube.

"We're hearing rumors that Mexico has closed the border."

Shane raised his gaze to Perrin's and they silently appreciated the irony.

"So far we've seen a 30% mortality rate here and it's only going to get worse as food becomes scarcer. I'm recommending people who are exposed to isolate themselves for the sake of the larger community. Transmission rate is at least 50 percent and you are contagious within hours of exposure. Keep yourself clean and wear a mask when you go out, but this is spread mainly by spittle and contact with contaminated surfaces." He withdrew the syringe and taped a cotton ball over the puncture. He sealed up the vial and asked Shane some questions including his name and town. When Shane hesitated, he laughed. "This is just so we can follow up if I discover you're carrying the cure in your blood."

"Doubtful, although as an overseas operative, I might have been accidentally inoculated against the flu."

"In the 2009 outbreak, they developed a vaccine, but this is a variant, so it probably wouldn't work. Do you have any information you can give me?"

Shane considered the ramifications of telling the CDC that this was a bioengineered weapon. His training said keep your mouth shut, but his head said something else. Dr. Perrin didn't even blink at the news.

"I suspected. Interesting that there would be two forms of the virus, however." He typed something into the computer while he talked. "Any idea how I get hold of Dr. Ceylon?"

"No, but if you have a way for her to get hold of you, I can provide it to her."

"Already included on the disc. You're going back to Kansas?"

"Trying to leave tomorrow morning."

"You should quarantine yourself for at least two days after interacting with anyone here who hasn't already had the flu and been symptom-free for three days. Do you have the means to do that?" Shane nodded. He asked about Dylan Rigby's symptoms, but Perrin shook his head.

"I'd guess a secondary infection, but the speech involvement worries me. I can provide you with a few types of anti-vertigo drugs. Trust the CDC to stock a place hundreds of miles inland with Dramamine." He left Shane alone for a few minutes and came back with a small box of several varieties of drugs. "Good luck."

Shane ordinarily would have shaken Dr. Perrin's hand, but the doctor didn't seem to want to touch any more than he did. His parents would say they'd pray. Goodbye and good luck were all Shane had.

Mike had just come back to the truck when Shane got there.

"How'd whatever you were doing go?" With nobody around to hear, Shane spoke in English.

"Ron Bannon, the would-be rapist, is dead." Alicia had told Mike who had told Shane, but they'd agreed that Shane didn't need to be involved in scaring the guy. He hadn't realized murder was on the menu.

"You okay?"

"I didn't kill him. He died of the flu about a week ago."

"Sounds like a good riddance to me." Mike nodded.

"How'd your thing go?"

Shane patted his pocket where possibly the most important disc on the planet resided, then indicated the box on the seat.

"It went fine."

Mike sniffed.

"What is that smell?"

"I'd guess they're burning bodies somewhere. We better get going."

The Future Doesn't Look Bright

Emmaus, Kansas

Snow blanketed Emmaus, but not so thick that the roads were impassable. Javi parked his Land Rover across from the clinic. He wore his sunglasses despite the overcast sky. His light sensitivity increased and decreased from day to day.

"I don't know if I'm going to be needed or not."

"You'll be needed. I'm going to reconnoiter the town, see if I can meet up with this guy Murphy. I'll swing back when I'm done, see if you need a ride home or if they're going to keep you for the rest of your natural life."

Ami laughed. He caught her behind the neck with a large hand and they kissed. Although they'd spent a good deal of the time since they arrived at the Jericho B&B either sick or nursing the sick, they had also gotten their mutual attraction squared away.

The medical center looked more like an office park than a center for healing, but Ami doubted they'd had more than broken arms and an occasional cold before the bombs. Now the lobby overflowed with people who probably had the flu. A harried looking woman looked up from the front desk. The nameplate on her sweatshirt read "Abigail."

"Can I help you?"

"I'm Dr. Amisi Ceylon, reporting in as I promised."

"Never heard of you. Dr. Callahan is down the hall in one of the exam rooms. The one on the left, I think. Knock yourself out."

Ami loved American idioms. She didn't always understand them, but she assumed Abigail meant for her to just go introduce herself. Dr. Callahan proved to be a tall woman with auburn hair pulled up into a bun. She palpitated a man's abdomen as Ami approached and introduced herself.

"Shane said you might come around. Palpitate this and tell me what you think."

Amisi found a pair of Nitrile gloves and did as instructed.

"That's probably an infected appendix."

"My diagnosis too. Hiram, that has to come out. We're going to start you on some antibiotics immediately and then we'll do the surgery this afternoon." Dr. Callahan stepped to the door and hollered down the hallway. "Chris, I need one unit of whatever IV antibiotic we have, Exam Room 2."

"Now, Marnie, isn't there something you can do besides surgery?" The patient was a late-middle-aged man with a weather-beaten face.

"Before the Pulse, maybe, Hiram, but right now it's all I've got to offer and you will die if your appendix bursts, so let's just get this out of the way. If you really did just start feeling the symptoms last night, you might not have perforated, so this should all go quickly."

"But, Marnie, I have a farm to run. I can't be down for weeks."

"Hiram, would you rather be dead." Of course, he wouldn't. "There's lots of folks in this town who need food and are increasingly willing to work for it. I'll put the word out that you're going to need some help."

Now Dr. Callahan – who apparently went by Marnie even with her patients – turned to Am.

"I assume you interned in an emergency room setting?"

"I did."

"This is like full service medical now – everything from birthing to surgery to – if we can find the meds, cancer treatment. I've been the only doctor since the bombs with four nurses, a vet who is great at setting bones and suturing, and a couple of EMTs who sporadically help out. Have you ever removed an appendix?"

"As an intern, I assisted a few times. I was never lead."

"Then I'll be lead since I've done one."

The door to the room opened and an athletic girl with black curls swept up into a messy bun strode into the room dragging an IV pole. She pushed past Marnie and Ami to get to the patient. Ami stared at her, dumbfounded.

"Christine?" she whispered, then repeated it louder. Her sister looked up and forgot all about the patient.

"Ami!" They embraced, babbling at each other in Arabic. *Where have you been? How did you get here?* By the time they were done, Dr. Callahan had hooked up the IV. Ami wiped tears. Circumstances had convinced her Christine perished in the bombs, but the commuter plane set down at Emmaus' airfield and she'd been here ever since. Ami gave a very brief overview of how she'd gotten to Emmaus.

"Where are you living?" she asked.

"I was at the church, but we haven't not had patients here for weeks now, so I moved in here a few days ago."

"How do you eat?"

"People pay us in food and fuel. We're probably doing better here than any other business. What about you?"

"I've – um – the man I came here with has friends and we're staying with them. I'm fine and – well, I need to stay there." Christine nodded. Abigail came to the door.

"We have six people in the waiting room. I sent Janna Thomas home with the flu. We can't do anything about it. But she's there alone with her children since her husband never came back."

"We are not Meals on Wheels," Marnie said in a comfortable voice. "Report it to Rob Delaney and if he can find someone to help, he will. Also report that Hiram needs someone to help him on the farm for a while."

Abigail wrote it down.

"How do you want to be paid, Ami?" Marnie asked.

"Food's fine. Perhaps I could look around before we perform this surgery?"

"Yes. Chris, can you walk her around?"

The building wasn't huge, though it clearly been built for more than one doctor and had rooms set up for dentistry, surgery and eye exams.

Ami started in surgery before Javi got there and expected to have to walk home or sleep the night at the clinic until she came out of surgery to find him sprawled in a chair in the lobby, a deadly tiger imitating a parlor cat.

"How long have you been here?"

"Long enough to meet your sister and have her interrogate me. Woman could teach the Taliban a thing or two."

"I heard that," Christiana said from where she did record-keeping behind the counter.

"What have you been doing?"

"Mostly staring at my feet. Reading gives me a headache now."

An older woman wandered up to the desk.

"Did you say there was someone who wanted to see me here, Chris?"

Chris introduced Ami to Dr. Verheil, Emmaus' only eye doctor. They took Javi back to the eye exam room.

"The equipment was fortunately shut down at the time of the Pulse, so it mostly works. Let's see what's going on with you."

Ami went to check on patients and acquaint herself with charts and wandered back a bit later to find Javi and Dr. Verheil in serious conversation.

"May I ask what your findings were?"

"Go on." Javi looked unhappy.

"There's permanent retinal damage, which wouldn't be so bad except he's developed cataracts, both eyes, rapidly progressing. There's surgeries, of course, before the September Attacks, but for now – I'm sorry to deliver bad news. I do have some NAC eye drops on hand and they might slow the progression. Otherwise, my estimate is he'll be blind in his right eye in weeks and in his left eye by spring." She patted Javi on the shoulder. Ami recognized that rock-hard posture. The man looked ready to tear someone's head off but knew that Dr. Verheil was not responsible for his situation. "I'll go get those drops. Maybe we can save your vision until treatment is available."

"Thank you," Ami said since Javi seemed at a loss for words.

When the door closed behind Dr. Verheil, Javi said a single swear word and then looked at her, anger swimming in the tears in his eyes. She'd suspected for a while because of an odd silvery shine in his right eye.

"Now what?"

"We try to slow them down and we try to find a way to get the surgery. It'll be fine."

"No, it won't and if you were the one going blind, you wouldn't make such platitudes."

Ami nodded.

"I'm supposed to see a patient. I'll be done after that and we can head home.

"Where a blind man is not very useful."

"You're allowed a bit of self-pity right now. Don't make a habit of it."

Ami crossed the hall to where Nevada Randolph, a lean woman with shoulder-length honey blonde hair starting to grow out darker at the roots, waited.

"Intermittent nausea," Ami said, looking at the chart. "May I call you Nevada?"

"Yes, of course. I thought it might be the flu at first, but it comes and goes."

"When did the first symptoms start?"

"Two – three weeks ago."

"Are your breasts swollen or tender?"

"Yes."

"Any chance that you're pregnant?"

"I've got an implant in my arm."

"They're usually effective. Occasionally they aren't. When is it due for renewal?"

"Um – oh, my – I guess it might not still be working. It should have been re-implanted in October. I had an appointment October 3rd, but things got complicated." They both grinned at the euphemism. "But I haven't had sex since before the bombs."

"There's supposed to be a margin of error for contraceptive implants, but sometimes things go awry. Pregnancy would be consistent for the symptoms you have now. Let me see if we can get a pregnancy test."

Nevada looked alarmed. Fifteen minutes later, Ami ended all guesswork.

"You are definitely pregnant."

"Well, that would be how I roll – always pregnant at the most inconvenient times. Thank you for letting me know."

Ami had gotten some prenatal vitamins when she'd asked Abigail for the pregnancy test. Nevada appeared stunned, but she hadn't asked about the possibility of an abortion. She walked out with the vitamins, so perhaps she wanted the child. The risk of neural tube defects so soon after the bombs – well, Ami didn't plan to get pregnant any time soon. If she were a praying woman, she might have offered one up for Nevada and her fetus, but she wasn't sure which way she would pray. Bringing a child into this mess seemed like a bad idea.

Dusk fell outside as they neared the car. Javi held the keys out to her.

"I think if I can't see the car across the street, I can't see to drive in the dark."

"It'll be okay," she assured him after they'd buckled in. "I have to believe this won't last forever."

"What won't?"

"The return to Little House on the Prairie.'

Javi dropped his face into his hands. He looked more tired than she felt. She reached across to touch him on the shoulder and he shrugged her off. He stared out the passenger window a moment before reaching to catch her hand in his, barely speaking above a whisper.

"I'm not used to having someone in my corner. And, I'm scared you're going to take off when I need you most."

Ami didn't know what to say. A product of foster care, Javi had more or less raised himself, possessed deadly skills and kept darker secrets, and was terrified of being dependent. She hadn't left him while truly helpless. His connections had secured her a safe place to live in decidedly unsafe times. They enjoyed spending time in bed together and he listened to her ramble on about biochemistry. Was that a basis for a long-term committed relationship? She didn't know. She'd never been in one before and she suspected he hadn't either.

"We can't tell them." Javi sighed. Ami realized he meant the Rigbys. "Not yet anyway. I guess it'll get obvious with time. Rigby is a practical man and if he suspects I'm going to be a liability, he'll put us out on the roads before he can't."

Ami nodded. It occurred to her that Javi might not be able to see that in the dark.

"I think you're right. I learned the community college has several labs that might work for me to study this virus. I'll make us useful, I promise."

He nodded, swallowing audibly.

"And maybe the drops will work until surgery is available."

"There's the spirit."

"So, I've had a headache for like two hours. Can we go home now?"

Fortunately, living in Chicago the last two winters had given her ample experience driving on snow and the Land Rover's 4wheel drive helped. Christine seemed to be in a safe place and the B&B had the computer capacity she needed. Now, if she could just find the equipment to go with it – yes, she would stick around.

I Need What You Have

G rant Rigby stood in the central recreation area of the silo complex, wondering how long he could be expected to wait. Nick Kletti had heard him out and told him to wait. Neil Patterson had yet to appear. Had it been half-an-hour? At least.

A converted missile silo, the compound consisted of several underground levels divided into apartments of various sizes with a mechanical level at the very bottom and this two-story modern testament to Scandinavian design, sweeping floors, curving walls, light colors. The smell of the communal dinner permeating the air made him wish for the seconds Emily and Mads called tomorrow's lunch. He vaguely remembered what this space looked like when the windows weren't boarded up. There'd been a little bit of light coming in from an upper window when he'd arrived. That was gone now, meaning the sun had set. Families and individuals gathered in small groups around the large room. The floors were linoleum broken with rugs and the walls were plywood stained a warm amber. The furniture was comfortable and modern. A man, wife and their two teenage children cleaned the kitchen. Two people worked on the mezzanine arranging books on shelves. Rigby could hear them discussing where genres ought to go and why and whether to alphabetize by author name or title.

"Mr. Rigby," Daniel McAuliff greeted, approaching with the tall, gangly Neil Patterson and the short, curly-headed Nick Kletti. "Please, do come sit down and let's discuss what we can do for you."

He ushered Rigby to one of the dining tables, far enough from a father working with his kids on a project that the conversation would be at least somewhat private but making it clear that they meant to keep the meeting public.

"Let me begin by saying that I have no desire to disrupt your community here. Our previous interactions were part of my job. That job no longer exists. I hope we can move forward on that basis."

McAuliff smirked.

"Take a man's life away and put him in a box for having ideas you disagree with – or even that your employer disagreed with -- and then expect him to forgive and forget. We aren't going to do that, Mr. Rigby." All three men nodded firmly. "However, for acceptable remuneration, we are willing to not act on our anger. Agreed, Neil?" Patterson nodded, face impassive. "Tell us what it is you need from us."

Now for the part Rigby really didn't like.

"My computer tech suffered some sort of side effect from the flu and is unable to fulfill his duties at this time. I've got several databases I need to get into and lack the skills necessary to do that. I want to hire you, Mr. Patterson, to substitute for Dylan."

"And what do you have to trade?" McAuliff asked.

"Scotch whiskey?"

All three mouths twitched as if suppressing smiles.

"Two cases," Patterson said.

"One."

"Two."

Rigby leaned back in his seat. Shane estimated Patterson's legend accurately, and the man knew his worth. Rigby could walk away now, hoping Dylan would recover soon, but if he had to come back, he'd lose his bargaining advantage.

"One to start. If I need your skills past one month, you'll get a second one, but you'll have to work at least a total of three months."

"I can agree to that. Terms?"

"There are no secrets. What you find, you share with me, or my team, but you agree to an NDA. You don't share info outside of my organization and you don't write any trapdoors or other boobytraps into my system."

"No more than eight hours a day at that price," Kletti said. He directed his comment at Patterson and McAuliff rather than Rigby. "Five days a week."

It paled compared to Dylan's contribution, but slavery had been outlawed a long time ago.

"Agreed."

"You provide two meals a day on the days I work," Patterson said.

"Agreed. If weather prevents you from coming, that day is counted against the total time worked."

Patterson nodded. McAuliff typed into a notebook computer. He paused, hands over the keyboard.

"Anything else?" he asked.

"I don't want to know anything about your community here, so that if my employer somehow still exists, I can't be used against you."

McAuliff smirked again.

"Yes, very wise. One last provision – if anything comes up affecting this community, you will share it."

Rigby hadn't expected that clause, but truthfully, it made sense. They had a right to know if trouble headed their way.

"Yes. *I* will share it. Mr. Patterson, you understand that means you aren't permitted to share it? It's my decision."

"Agreed."

They each read the document and then McAuliff printed it and all four of them signed it.

McAuliff asked the kid who'd been doing his science project to make copies.

"I'll come tomorrow, assuming the roads remain open, and we'll get started on it." Patterson stood. "Dan." He nodded and walked away.

"Dr. Kletti, what was your area of treatment expertise?"

Nick Kletti stared at him for a moment. He and McAuliff shared a gaze and Dan nodded slightly.

"I started as a neurologist, ended up in psychiatry. Why?"

"What do you know about this flu that's going around?"

"We haven't had it so far and we're trying to keep it that way. Why?"

"Just adding to my knowledge store if I can."

"Do you have information about it?" McAuliff asked.

"Beyond what swept through my house and my programmer is still affected by it – no."

"If you did, would you tell us?"

"My job is to keep secrets, so you know my default position, but I have just agreed to share information that affects the community. What I know currently is that a form of this flu has apparently cropped up in Santa Fe and it is quite deadly. The strain we have here appears to be milder."

"Until it mutates," Kletti muttered. "You were saying everyone in your house had it?"

"Yes. We've all had it."

"What are you thinking, Nick?" McAuliff asked.

"It's more virulent than many flus. I would suspect that if you're exposed and contract it, you are contagious before you have symptoms. That's standard for flu. It's why pandemics occur."

"Would this flu have neurologic effects?" Rigby asked. "My programmer is suffering severe vertigo, seizures, he had difficulty forming words initially."

"What does Dr. Callahan say?"

The hairs on the back of Rigby's neck stood up. He knew a test when he heard one. He wasn't quite ready to reveal Ami, not to the militia anyway.

"She hasn't had time to get out to see him and he can't sit up without vertigo, so we're kind of stuck."

"That doesn't sound like the flu. He might have developed an ear infection secondary to the flu – but you said he's had seizures and dysphasia?" Rigby nodded. "Are the symptoms getting better or worse?"

"I'm no doctor. They're better than when he collapsed initially. He can talk now, and he hasn't had a full-blown seizure in a few days."

"Tremors?" Rigby nodded. "More on one side or the other?"

"Yes." Rigby hadn't really seen it, but he trusted Ami to know what she saw.

"He might have encephalitis." Kletti exchanged a significant, but inscrutable glance with McAuliff.

"If it's viral in origin there's not much to be done beyond keeping him comfortable and waiting it out. Lots of rest, healthy food, time. Antivirals if you can get them, but that's a stretch now."

Rigby hadn't been able to get any antiviral on the short notice for going to ground. Dylan would have to heal the old fashion way, if it was encephalitis. Shane would bring back information from Santa Fe. Perhaps involving Kletti would not be necessary.

"I think our business is concluded," Rigby said, standing. "I'll give Patterson the first case when he comes tomorrow."

"As agreed. I'll walk you out." McAuliff nodded to Kletti and followed Rigby out to the compound yard. Moonlight cast the dark sky and snowy ground in silver and charcoal. McAuliff paused at the gate. "This deal doesn't mean we trust you and you might want to ask yourself what changed while we were in prison. Don't think you can screw us, and we'll be all zen about it."

Ice water slid down Rigby's back. McAuliff meant what he said. Rigby nodded. McAuliff opened the gate and closed it between them, turning toward the building. A figure on the balcony above the main entrance shifted and moonlight glinted off a rifle. Rigby shivered and headed for home.

Uneasy Negotiations

Emmaus, Kansas – Next Day

Javi wondered how long he'd be able to see to drive. Already the vision in his right eye clouded in places. He didn't really notice it in his left eye, but he believed Dr. Verheil's diagnosis. You didn't need perfect eyesight to navigate Emmaus's traffic and you didn't need to be able to read street signs to get around. He drove along the rural highway that formed the northern border of the township. The barbed wire fence to his left was energized to discourage the migrants, who had all but trickled to a stop. In the predawn grey, the men and women on the barricades at the intersections paid little mind to him. Perhaps, they'd been through enough now to not care what their neighbors were up to compared to what strangers might do to them.

Murphy manned the northeast intersection, which made sense as they saw more migrants there than at any of the other barricades. He dropped down from the bus they were using as a gate and approached Javi. Shane introduced them briefly a few days ago and Javi spoke with him yesterday.

"Glad to see you, man. I need someone with experience to go out beyond the wire with me."

"Why?"

"We've seen some kind of movement out there from the tower, but we don't know what's going on and I think we need to check it out."

Attracting attention to the town sounded like a terrible idea to Javi, but he wasn't in charge and Cai Delaney wasn't arguing. He joined them in the LTATV and they drove out about a half-mile until they could see the silhouettes of tents and vehicles against the lightening sky. Javi really couldn't see even with field glasses, but Cai and Murphy both saw it as a large group, including RVs and at least one MRAP.

"We should probably go talk to them," Murphy said.

"Or not," Javi suggested. "Why draw attention to the township? With enough vehicles they could just drive through the barbed wire, right?"

Cai looked at Murphy.

"They could. Not sure we could stop them if they did."

"So why even let them know we're here?" Javi asked.

"What makes you think they don't already know? That's a pretty big town bristling with rifles at the entrances?"

Murphy had a good point. He looked at Cai.

"Chavez, you want to go with me to talk with them?" Javi nodded. "Murphy, stay back in case there's trouble. They're Army, you're National Guard, and right now that's not a fun party." The National Guardsman inclined his head. The shift of leadership surprised Javi, but it made sense. A lawyer, Cai must have trained in negotiation skills.

The mess tent next to the MRAP gave the camp a larger footprint than truly needed. A couple of women tended a fire in the middle of the camp, but not much else moved around the dozen tents. Cai slid his rifle around to his back and held up his hands.

"We just want to talk."

A guard stepped out of the shadow of the tent. He wore an Army uniform and an M4 carbine held at the ready.

"Drop your weapons."

"No, we won't." Cai's voice didn't waver. "We're from a nearby town and we want to know what your business is since you're parked on private property."

"Eminent domain." It sounded a practiced response. Javi continued to scan the camp, but so far nobody else had come out of the tents.

"Eminent domain requires judicial action. I'm sure you're familiar with the third amendment. May we speak with your superior, please?"

Another Army noncom stepped out of the tent and they conferred for a moment before the second soldier returned to the tent. After several tense moments, the soldier returned and gestured for them to come in.

"What do you think?" Javi admired that Cai deferred to him on this issue.

"It's a tent. I can cut us out of it if I have to. Best to keep it friendly."

Lieutenant Daglin, 30-something, blond and short, greeted them and offered coffee. Cai turned down the beverage and explained the town's concerns.

"You're aware we're the US military, right?"

"I'm unimpressed after spending a week as a slave under a rogue unit in Hutchinson."

Daglin controlled his wince, but he knew about Hutchinson.

"We're not doing that here." His tone was firm. He'd clearly been living rough, bags under his eyes, cheeks hollow. "We suffered devastating losses in a clash with a rogue National Guard unit a few weeks back. We've been all around this area and the communities are refusing any aid."

"Can't really blame us since you confiscated our food." Cai held up a conciliatory hand. "I get that you had orders, but we have our own perspective, which is no less valid. That said, our town has opted to accept immigrants who have useful skills. Border security would be one of those. How many are left of your unit?"

"Four of us are still standing. One is still healing from wounds suffered in the battle at

Beulah. Two more have the flu. One seems to be on the mend, the other is still pretty sick. Plus we've picked up a group of civilians."

"Do you have any food to support yourselves?"

"No. We've got about two more days of rations left."

"What happened to the food you confiscated from Beulah?"

"Taken by the USDA, probably to a facility at Wyandot Lake."

"Have you tried there?"

"No. There's been no reply to radio communication."

Cai stared at his hands in thought.

"Then here's the deal. On the Wendat Reservation, there's a man named Ed Greyeyes. He's asked our help with a raid on the Wyandot Lake facility because the USDA confiscated reservation food. If you successfully negotiate a fee with him and liberate his stolen food, Emmaus will honor a commitment for you to enter our wire. You have to bring your own food or figure out a way to get more because the City of Emmaus has opted to not play nanny state even with our own people, but we will banish you if you're caught stealing food."

Daglin stared at Cai, a weighing look in his hazel eyes.

"That it?"

"The offer is made to the military personnel. We'll fold you into our security forces. The civilians can come in with you, but we will expel them if their food runs out. I hate doing that, but our head of security and the mayor are clear on this."

"Ed Greyeyes? Wendat Reservation? You sure they're not going to just turn me away at the gate?"

"Not if you say I sent you. Just be aware that if we hear you're exploiting the Rez folks, my brother will organize a party to come kill you and, trust me, you don't want to piss him off."

"You his *brother*?" Daglin asked Javi, who snorted because they clearly weren't siblings.

"I take orders from his brother."

Daglin's eyes flared slightly. Yeah, he knew Javi's type and that could only add to Shane's credibility. Shane being a sane badass could only make the town safer.

"I'll check in with this Greyeyes fellow. You're spread pretty thin on your borders. You do know I could roll right through your electrified fence?"

"I do, but you know the percentage of Midwesterners who have served in the military, so you got to know you'll meet resistance and you're outnumbered. We may only be shooting ARs, but we know how to use them."

Daglin's eyes flared again.

"I'm not trying to be belligerent. I'm pointing out that we didn't do that. We're looking to cooperate. I'm also pointing out that you need us."

"I wouldn't argue with that, although winter's here, so I think the migration will stop."

"Yeah. There's a group that gave up a few miles north. About 20 people. We were there yesterday. There was one woman living. We brought her in, but she needs to be warm."

Cai hesitated for just a moment, then surprised Javi.

"And, you have my offer. I wish we could do better, but we can't. We've got a little less than 5,000 people in town and estimates are 3,000 will die by spring. I just can't offer shelter to people who can't feed themselves."

Daglin sighed and nodded. Cai stood up.

"Ask for Cai or Shane Delaney or Murphy when you come back. I'll make sure the town leadership is apprised of your reward. Um, you should make sure Ed Greyeyes gives you a code so we know it's been accomplished."

"I will."

Outside, it had begun to snow again. Javi had lived in New York long enough to walk on this slippery stuff, but he still didn't like it.

"Murphy's not going to be happy about this," Cai whispered as they trudged southward.

"He's not in charge. How will Shane feel about it?"

"Fine so long as Daglin recognizes his authority. Shane said you trained him."

Javi nodded. Was he proud of that? It was just a fact. He thought Shane had turned out okay – deadly, but not cold-blooded.

"Some people are born to do what we do. He's one."

Cai cast him an incredulous look. Murphy emerged from a ditch and Cai told him what they had negotiated.

"These are the pukes who poisoned Beulah's town well."

Cai blinked.

"What?"

"Yeah. I mean, maybe not this guy, but someone ordered that. You didn't know?"

"I wasn't here. Dad and Shane told me about the battle. They poisoned the well?"

"Yeah. It killed most of the town. We were on another well, so we weren't poisoned, but when we fought back to save the people's food, the losses were heavy."

"A Pyrrhic victory?" Murphy nodded.

"Your father taught me that word, actually."

"What do you want to do?" Javi kept an eye on the camp as he spoke.

"Dad and Shane will have to make the decision if Daglin follows through. Carl said he's talking with someone on the Rez, so we'll talk to Ed if conditions allow tonight. Let's get back inside the wire."

Jacob handed out hot coffee as they slipped back through the barricade. After Cai's report he announced he would fly the perimeter.

"We need to know what's going on out there. Groups getting this close without our knowledge could be a problem."

"Do you need someone to go with you?" Javi asked. The old man fascinated him because Shane spoke so highly of him.

"I don't take passengers unless they can fly an airplane."

"I can keep a GA in the air and land if there's lots of room. I don't have a license, though."

"That never bothered me. I let my grandson solo at 12."

Cai snorted.

"He could barely see over the cowling."

"And he brought the plane back in one piece. If you want to go up with me, that's fine. We'll take the duster. I pulled the hopper so you'll just have to help install the seat."

"When?"

"Half hour at the field."

"Which is …?"

"Right at the end of your road, just go straight."

"And what about barricade duty?" Cai asked.

"Doesn't look like you need him right now." Jacob stretched a languid arm toward the snowy horizon. "Winter is the best security system we've got."

"We don't need him," Murphy echoed. "Not right now. I suspect you made all the difference back there in the tent."

Javi nodded. He'd not gotten a sense of hostility from Daglin. That didn't mean the man hadn't ordered the poisoning of a well. You did things in war that weren't good because it was war and only the winners got to tell their stories. He told Jacob he'd meet him at the airfield and headed toward the Land Rover.

Bad News

Santa Fe, New Mexico

Mike slid the first cases of canned goods to the very back of the truck, cautious not to hit his head on the underside of the canopy. He swallowed, throat feeling vaguely tight. Shane took his time returning, so Mike dropped out of the truck to gulp from his water bottle.

Shane finally returned.

"Where's Alicia?"

"She's taking a nap." Shane hefted a case of groceries and slid it into the truck. "Marnie's been struggling with being tired too."

"Some kind of pregnancy thing?"

"Yeah and she might still be run down from the flu." Mike nodded, then reached over and pulled the breezeway door closed. "Something you want to keep secret?"

"Yeah. My glands are swollen."

Shane halted in pushing the case into the truck bed.

"You're sure?"

Mike presented his throat and Shane palpitated with deft fingers.

"Those feel a little swollen. You're not running a fever."

"Yet." They stared at one another. Denial played a major role before you went out on assignment. You had to believe you'd come back. But there were tough decisions to be made in the field.

"What do you want to do about it?"

"Well, first, you can't tell Alicia. She'll want to stay and if this is what killed her mother -- we just can't put her through that."

Shane pulled a bottle of hand sanitizer out of his jacket pocket and applied it to his hands.

"You're right, but if this is the flu, it gets worse. So, what do you want to do?"

"We're going to board up this place and then discover we can't cover something – a window or whatever. It means I have to stay."

"You're going to try to tough out that nasty flu by yourself? No way!"

"The alternative is that I take this nasty version of the bug back to Emmaus and kill a third of the town."

"Rigby's group has already had the flu. We can quarantine there."

"Yeah but think about this. We need someone to stay here and guard the stash. And you're tempted to run that plane overweight. So, you can come back. Get that crazy man in Emmaus to radio here. I don't know if you've noticed, but Carlos has a tower. I talked to him. He's one of the resistance, doesn't think what's going on with the National Guard is a good thing. So far they haven't shut down communications and he said nobody is monitoring the Morse."

"That lasts as long as he lasts. Meanwhile, you're ground-zero in martial law and sick to boot. I don't think that's a good idea."

"What's the alternative?" Shane frowned. "You know there isn't one. You have to help me sell staying behind with Alicia. I'll let you know that I'm able to return and you'll come get me."

"If the weather allows it. Winter is a fact, man. I don't know if I'll get back here this side of Christmas."

"It's fine. Do what you have to do. Alicia is important. I'm not."

"Don't ask me to do this, Mike."

"I'm asking you to protect Alicia, even if it guts you."

"And, it will." Shane sighed, scratched fingers through his hair. "I can't think of another way to do this. Let's get this finished. You have about 24 hours before the symptoms worsen. We have to fake Alicia out and get her in the air before the fever hits. She'll know then."

Mike nodded. His chest felt odd and his nose began to run. Shane swallowed audibly, turned back to the truck and continued to transfer the cases from the hand cart to the pickup bed.

"Go get the plywood ready. I can handle this on my own. I'll meet you out back in an hour."

Mike wanted to say something. Shane's posture said not to bother. Angering Shane came with consequences. At the very least, the silent treatment followed.

"I'm sorry to put you in this position." Mike left then because he knew Shane needed some time to calm down.

An hour later, he'd lugged a couple of sheets of plywood to the neighbor's house so Alicia wouldn't know what he and Shane planned. He'd arranged the plywood so they could just lift it into place and secure it with screws. When Shane came out of the garage, Mike began the ruse for Alicia's benefit.

"I must have miscounted. We don't have enough sheets to cover all the windows and doors."

"I should have double-checked your count." Shane prepared a screw on the power drill while Mike lifted the first sheet up to cover half of the front window. He felt weak, whether from lingering effects of the knifing or from the flu. Alicia came out the front door.

"Can we get more?" she asked.

"Don't know," Mike grunted. "We'll get this done and then we'll go see if we can get some more."

"Math is not dumb-ass's strong suit."

Alicia laughed at Shane's comment.

"I'm going to make some sandwiches. You can grab them when you want. I'll be packing those boxes."

"We'll be lifting and screwing." Mike really felt the weight of the plywood in the raw scar on his side.

"Men are so cute when they're working."

"Would you like us to do a striptease?" Mike freed one hand to pretend to flip long hair over his shoulder.

"I'm a Midwesterner. We don't strip." Shane leaned into a screw.

"Mama would be so angry that we're ruining her *casa bonita*."

"At least it'll still be here when we get back. Next window, Mike. We gotta get this done."

Alicia went back into the house. Mike and Shane exchanged glances. Operation Protect Alicia had a good start.

Youthful Indiscretion

Emmaus, Kansas

Keri slid off her horse and untied the ropes that tethered three goats who'd wandered across the road. Goats went rogue all the time, driven by their intelligence to seek adventure. Seemed they escaped more often as the weather turned bad.

She turned the goofies out into the fenced field and made sure the gate securely latched then led her horse into the barn.

The warmth of the animals enveloped her as she unsaddled her horse and began to curry the mare down, losing herself in the rhythm of the work. As she stroked, her mind wandered into a prayer of repentance for the life she'd taken just a month ago. Intent upon robbing her, he'd taken aggressive action and she'd defended herself. A reason did not constitute an excuse. Grandpa told her to pray without ceasing, taking responsibility for her actions and asking God for forgiveness. Would that work? Maybe someday, maybe not. Shane's shuttered eyes could be her fate.

The hair on the back of her neck stood on end and she slew around to see who was there. This part of the barn had a mezzanine linking the lofts at either end. Nothing moved but dust mots. She could hear cows chewing their cuds in the milking theater below. She almost turned back to her horse Penny, but something caused her to look up to the loft. She didn't see anything, but the feeling of being watched still prickled. She climbed the stairs and walked around a stack of hay bales. Pete and Poppy lay curled together on a blanket between two stacks, their clothes disheveled and hay in their hair.

Keri cleared her throat and Pete stirred, then snuggled deeper into Poppy's embrace. Keri kicked Poppy's foot and her eyes came open. Her convulsive reaction woke Pete. Keri signed and spoke at the same time so there would be no question that they understood her.

"I said this – oh, yeah. Foolish. You and you – far too young. How many times have you screwed?"

The concrete nature of American Sign Language meant she couldn't use a euphemism. Two bodies lying one atop the other formed the sign for sex. Graphic. Uncompromising.

"This is the 1st time." Pete touched his thumb with his forefinger.

"Uh-huh. Well, go tell your parents. Go now." Poppy started to scramble up, her clothes still half-undone. "Not you! Pete, go."

Keri sat down on one of the hay bales and sighed. Parent of a teenager when you were 23 – exhausting.

"Tell me true. You want marry him?"

Poppy frowned, then nodded emphatically.

"Love him."

"Marriage lasts forever."

"Know that."

"You sure? Maybe you just attached – infatuated."

"Love – have an age?"

"No. But mature, wise, still young."

"Sorry we marry already. Sex, marry."

Keri sighed, knowing it and her arguments to wait fell on young and foolish soil. She couldn't argue with the Biblical definition of marriage and both kids had shown some maturity in suggesting this as the best course of action if they couldn't control their urges.

Down on the main floor of the barn, the door opened and closed.

"You here?" Alex asked.

Keri sighed again before alerting him to their location. Poppy couldn't really read lips, but she felt Alex's tread on the loft floor and looked at him.

"Decided?" he asked.

"We may be zero-in-mind. Love each other. Married already."

"Promises before church?"

355

"Yes."

"Are we sure Pete wants this?" Keri asked.

"House go to. Talk family," Alex said.

Mark and Alice waited with Pete at the kitchen table. Mark looked annoyed. Alice sighed.

"We love each other," Pete said aloud, signing for Poppy. "The Bible says we're married already."

"Yeah," Alex agreed, also signing. "If you sow the wind, you'll reap the whirlwind. I'll let Noah and Brad Snow know you'll want to tie the knot. When do you want to do this?"

Pete and Poppy looked at each other.

"Saturday," Poppy said. Pete nodded. Alex looked at Mark and Alice. Poppy stomped her foot. *"Not your-all decision. Ours."*

Keri cast a warning expression at her irritated husband.

"Fine. You're right. Since you're already married, are you just moving into her room tonight?"

Pete stared at him. Mark and Alice looked like they might just die of embarrassment. Pete signed what Alex had said. Her delicate forehead creased.

"Yes. We do this. Done. Done."

Pete's eyes widened and he shot a glance at his parents.

"It's your decision," Mark said. Fumbling, he signed *"Think yourself."*

"Yes," Pete decided. "It's already been done."

Alex sighed, broad shoulders rising and falling. Signing and talking at the same time were second nature to him.

"Good. Just remember, there's no mulligans. This is a life-changing decision."

Pete held his hand out to Poppy, and it was done.

Skimming the Treetops

Jacob Delaney had clearly flown out of Emmaus Field a million times and probably installed the copilot's seat at least several hundred. That explained why he'd moved Javi out of the way and finished the last two bolts himself.

The old man skimmed over the trucking company and then executed a long slow turn over the interstate and passed over a large house on a tree-covered rise.

"That the Shack I've heard of?"

"It is. You know about Ren Sullivan?"

"Everybody knows about Sullivan. He's like Koch or Soros. Rich men."

"I don't know him that way. Always just been a person to me." The duster skimmed over the converted silo. "You know about that?"

Javi grunted in a sort of non-answer.

"What do you think of anarchism, Mr. Chavez?"

"Javi. I don't know much about it. I'm a soldier, not a philosopher."

"You know enough to know there's a difference."

"I spent a bit of time squatting in a shack with your grandson, Mr. Delaney."

"I'm Jacob. Those three farms ahead are the Bennetts. You met any?"

"Andrew and another one, but I don't remember his name."

"They're the other anarchists round here – well, and the Conophors. I guess you could say this community doesn't really have much use for rulers or their hired guns."

The old man looked and sounded humored. They passed over the northern wire.

"I don't think I've ever flown so low before."

"Kind of exhilarating, ain't it?"

Javi thought it a little scary. Although he could keep a plane in the air, his skills were loose and needed some flexibility of altitude. He'd crash if the old man died now. The old man's hands on the yoke suggested he didn't need to worry about his imminent demise.

"I'm thinking we're not on this trip to be friendly."

"True enough. Kind of wondering about that house – all of a sudden a lot of activity, just when the world as we know it goes poof."

"We knew about it."

"Did Shane?"

"I don't know. I wasn't with him."

"Why are you here now?"

"I needed to go somewhere, and Shane and I share the same handler. I knew he came here. Just looking for safe haven."

"Shane let you in the wire and that says something is going on."

The prairie gave a slight swell and then they flew over a camp of tarps and unzipped tents. All that Javi could see of the people who had once lived in the camp was a swelling of churned-up ground – a mass grave. He wondered if the civilians in Daglin's camp were there by choice.

The old man swept to the east, executing a slight rise. They flew over a small collection of buildings. Javi didn't see any people.

"Are people abandoning their towns?" he asked.

"Not the little ones like that – not recently. That used to be a town, but it died about 50 years ago. Then a man started a tourist trap there and he was doing pretty well when the bombs went off. He's spent winters in Emmaus for a couple of decades. He's safe enough."

They passed over another town. Here Javi could see people in the streets.

"Is that like a suburb of Emmaus?"

"Used to be a water stop on the rail line. Now it's mostly farms. There's a good mechanic living in that town." They crossed the interstate again and passed over a small town with an impressive courthouse.

"Beulah."

"I heard about that."

"It's a tragedy. Emmaus grew by 80 people on account of what they did. Lovely what humans do to one another just being human."

"Lawless times lead to lawless behavior."

"You think? I think it's coz folks aren't used to thinking for themselves – not used to thinking morally. If you look around, you don't see many folks in Emmaus doing stuff like that. It's folks from outside. The Army without its chain of command. Men don't know what's right and wrong because they expect someone else to tell them."

They passed over a vast section of fields and Javi saw the tarps. Blinking, he tried to bring it into focus. Something flew by the window, nearly clipping the wing and Jacob heeled the plane over, climbing.

"What was that?" Before Jacob could answer, a hole opened in the fabric tail.

"Someone's shooting at us. We're out of range now."

"Are we okay?" Javi watched as the old man scanned through the few gauges he had on the instrument panel.

"Not losing any fuel, no liquids spraying. I think we're okay. Gonna have to get out my needle and thread to repair that rip." The old man's calm amazed the mercenary.

"Were you a fighter pilot?"

"Barnstorming. We used to do a stunt pretending one of us was the Red Baron. Naw, in World War 2, you had to be a college boy to fly. And, I'm glad I didn't. If you're going to kill men, you ought to see them face to face."

When he'd had the flu, Javi had dreamed of the 30 million people who had died in the terrorist attack he'd failed to stop. He didn't do guilt, but he knew he had some responsibility for those deaths. He wondered how the old man knew that.

"You broke my grandson."

Jacob didn't sound angry. It occurred to him that a man this old might not be afraid to die and they were so close to the ground that if he decided to crash them, there was nothing Javi could do to prevent it.

"I trained him in a nasty business that he mostly volunteered for."

"Mostly?"

"I don't know the whole story. Something to do with a representative's son and pot."

"That's why he infiltrated McAuliff's group, but why'd he go back?"

"He took a job when he got to California."

"Yeah, the son and grandson of an old buddy of mine."

"Apples sometimes roll far from the tree. They were running guns into Central America. When his name came up, they sent me to tap him as an asset. He was a natural."

"How'd he end up in Miristan?"

"After the hammer came down, the airline was bought by B&W and Shane was under contract, so they kept him on, but the CSA wanted to use their asset so they encouraged him to join the Knights."

"Mike's outfit?"

"Sanchez, yeah. I think he was in Central America with Shane before everything went down. Knights have a lot of long fingers. CSA doesn't like companies with long fingers."

"They could maybe compete with the US government."

"Exactly." Javi's eyes watered as he looked out across the frosted fields. Ahead, the Rockies stood bright and brilliant. He adjusted his sunglasses as a headache began to niggle behind his eyes. "What are we seeing?"

"There are a couple of those camps, but Shane was right that the numbers would drop as it got colder. And, they're beyond us. Can't imagine they'd be headed north. I got enough fuel to check out over Kanorado way. What's wrong with your eyes?"

Javi's startle verified the accuracy of his question.

"They were open during the Pulse – looking right at the sky. I can see, but they're not the same."

"So are you in this plane on false pretenses?"

"No. I can still see well enough to land."

"You got any skills besides killing?"

No, he did not, but he'd soon have to face the necessity of learning other skills.

"Times like these, those are useful skills."

"Unless you can't see out your right eye."

Javi chose to stay silent as the mountains grew closer. Jacob dropped low again, probably to avoid any potential radar. They passed over smaller towns. The Geiger counter on the dash began to tick up slightly.

"We're good." The old man grinned at him then executed a port turn. Now Javi became well aware of how badly his right eye had deteriorated as the Rockies blurred to an impressionist painting.

"Where are we going?"

"Testing a theory."

"That Colorado Springs ahead?"

Javi had thoroughly researched the town for his cover story of an ex-wife in the Springs. The skyline was familiar to him. The old man smiled and kept flying. The squawk box on the panel crackled. Javi contemplated a ground-to-air missile obliterating them when Jacob executed a sweeping turn to the east, gaze scanning the ground below them.

"What was that about?"

"There's people down there, but I didn't see any Army and their communications ability is severely limited. Streets full of broken down vehicles too. I won't risk getting that close to Cheyenne Mountain, but I'm thinking it is either shuttered or dead."

Should he tell him about the helicopter Shane had encountered yesterday? Turned out he didn't need to because Jacob's radio crackled to life.

"This is Kiowa 170FR out of Cheyenne Mountain to GA aircraft." It was the same Southern-honeyed voice from Shane's encounter. "What is your designation? Over."

"Hello, Kiowa. I had a stuck aileron. Didn't mean to get so close. Headed back my way now."

While he talked, Jacob dropped even closer to the deck, causing Javi to swear.

"I spent 80% of my career only about 20 feet off the deck, son, so you don't need to worry."

"Why are you riling up a gunship, old man?"

"You really are going blind. That helo's not armed." While flying 30 feet off the deck. Jacob scanned through the radio frequencies. "That's what I thought."

"What?"

"No ground chatter. I suspect the folks you work with already know that. Boy, what I wouldn't give to be able to spy on them!" Jacob skirted a lone barn and then a grove of trees.

"Let's not give our lives." Javi couldn't see the helicopter anymore, but he could feel it.

"She turned back when I dropped. It's not that she can't follow me, but I get her fuel is limited. She's got a single door-gunner."

"If Cheyenne Mountain is dead or shuttered, what's she doing out there?"

"Don't know. Maybe they were outside the facility when the Pulse fried everything. Shane's place times a thousand. Can't get back in so they are doing what their orders say to do."

That would be consistent with the old man's theory about the Army needing a hierarchy. Jacob did a sweep over Mara Wells and then turned home to land safely at Emmaus Field.

Empathy & Dog Biscuits

Santa Fe, New Mexico

Shane kind of felt sorry for the little dog as it cowered near his leg while Alicia screamed at Mike. Shane sipped bourbon and tried to just screen out the Spanish swear words. It wasn't that he'd never heard them before, but that a Chicana woman in full sail could bite like an adder and he never wanted any of those words to pop into his head when having a knock-down-drag-out with a girlfriend. Too easy for thought to become word when you were angry. He hated that his brain put Jazz in the place of the mythical girlfriend. He knew himself to be totally inappropriate for her and, if the world weren't spinning out of control and circumstances didn't keep throwing them together, he'd run off somewhere she couldn't follow until they both forgot what their bodies did whenever they got close to one another. That led to babies and rings on fingers and probably a whole lot of pain and agony considering that he knew he wasn't a fit partner for anyone these days.

Pepe shoved his way behind Shane's legs, whining. Shane still thought the little dog was ridiculous, but he also felt sorry for him, so he moved his feet forward so the dog could hide there. He glanced at his phone. Eight minutes into the tirade. He'd wait another seven and then just quietly go about his part of their business. Mike looked tired, maybe because he hadn't slept enough last night, or he might feel the illness.

"So that's your decision?" Alicia sniffled.

"It is. We need to pull our weight in Emmaus and that means bringing the food. Shane will come back to get me in a few days."

Alicia heaved a deep sigh, then turned to Shane who figured it was safe to look up now.

"How long did you know?"

"Today."

"And?"

"There is no and."

Alicia glared at him. Shane felt confident in his poker face, but he also knew that Alicia spoke fluent mercenary. That's why he'd insisted Mike do the lying. He wasn't married to her. He had no obligation to protect her from the cold hard truth. In fact, he'd tell her about Mike as soon as they were at altitude.

"C'mon, honey, *mi corizon.*" Mike plucked at her blouse. "We need to get some sleep."

"Such a charmer."

She followed him. Mike would get lucky tonight, but maybe not as lucky as he'd been last night. She was pissed. Shane finished the glass of bourbon with a single gulp, enjoying the mellow heat that spread across his chest. He made up the couch and stripped to his shorts to sleep. He'd reached the level of sleep where pleasantly anxious dreams about Jazz and things he'd never done with her would morph into dreams of whatever horror was on tap today when distant sounds woke him. He blinked into the darkness. The fire had burned down to a mere glow in the kiva. His heart turned over in his chest and he reached for his gun on the end table. The house lay quiet. Shane slid on his jeans and sweatshirt. The sound grew closer as he pulled on his boots.

They'd boarded up the front windows, so he couldn't peek out that way. He could see light flickering off the walls of the upstairs room. He eased up the spiral staircase to peek out at the street. A truck had stopped at a house down the street a bit, perhaps in front of Carlos' house. Shane had no reason to break china for a virtual stranger. He moved to a side window that would give him a better view and eased up the blinds Yeah, they were at the house with the radio tower. Damn!

He heard Mike before he topped the stairs.

"What's going on?"

"They're at Carlos'."

371

They watched as men dragged what they presumed was Carlos out onto the lawn. They kicked him, shouting questions in Spanish. Shane leaned his head against the window trim and watched.

"Shouldn't we do something about it?" Mike barely whispered.

"Nope. I can take three. In your condition, could you manage one? There's five. We're outnumbered and we don't want to alert anyone else. These guys aren't alone. They're just all we can see. We need to let them think we can't see them."

"This feels wrong with one of our own."

"American?"

"Chicano."

"How am I included in that?"

"You might as well be. You're going to take care of her, yeah?"

As if to emphasize the seriousness, Mike stifled a sneeze.

"Of course, I will and when I come back, I'll take you to her and you'll take over for me."

Mike leaned back against the wall and swallowed tightly.

"I hope so."

The sound of a gunshot rang out and Carlos slumped to the ground, no longer moving.

"Shit," Mike whispered. Shane didn't move as one of the men scanned the street. Had he heard Mike? They both sat perfectly still until the men from the truck loaded up and drove away, leaving Carlos lying on his lawn.

"I probably won't be able to radio you."

"Uly can probably help you. But I'll come back soon as I can even if I don't hear from you."

"You can't bring Jazz, though. She doesn't speak Spanish, right?"

True enough, but Chavez did. Shane did a quick factor of how much weight they lost with three tall guys and decided he would solo.

"We need to get some sleep. You especially need to if you don't want Alicia thinking you're sick."

"Right. Like I'm going to sleep after that."

"I'm going to."

"You didn't really talk to him, man."

"No. Maybe a good choice, you know?"

Outside, some neighbors collected Carlos' body. Shane wondered what they would do with it.

They eased back down the spiral staircase and Shane moved to throw some more wood on the fire. His hand hovered over the pile when he heard footsteps outside, hands-on the plywood. Pepe flitted toward the door. Mike scooped him up, holding his snout closed with his hand. The footsteps circled the house. Although they hadn't yet boarded up the backdoor, they'd firmly bolted the door from the inside. Still, whoever banged tried the knob, rattling the door.

"Neighbors saw us working today." Mike barely spoke above a whisper, trying to keep the dog quiet.

Now the would-be intruder banged on the backdoor, whisper-hollering in Spanish, which Shane answered in the same.

"Open the door!" a rough voice whisper-hollered.

"Go away," Shane replied in a loud voice. *"It's the middle of the night. Leave us alone."*

"Let me in, please."

"He sounds young." Alicia's voice from the bedroom door startled both men. "It could be Carlos's son."

"What's your name?" Shane asked in Spanish.

"Alejandro. My father said to come here. Please, let me in. I've got nowhere else to go."

Muttering Anglo-Saxon expletives under his breath about neighbors obligating strangers to take care of their kids, Shane unbolted the door while Mike leveled his gun at the face of whoever came through it. Alejandro, maybe age 16, flinched and put his hands up.

"Please don't kill me. My father said to come here. I swear."

Shane shot the bolt and the four of them stared at one another.

"Where are your mother and sisters?" Alicia pulled a shirt on over her nightshirt, which stretched tight across her belly.

"They didn't come home from the market today. I think they've been taken to the camp."

Alejandro, medium height and gangly with a wild shock of dark curls, his face stained with tears, looked pulled together ... calm under the circumstances.

"I thought they were only locking up *gringos*," Mike said, rubbing his shoulder in lieu of rubbing his swollen glands.

"I don't know. People keep disappearing. Maybe they're leaving for Mexico. Maybe they're going to the camp."

"And, we cannot help him." Shane just wanted to get that out of the way immediately.

Alicia's eyes flashed in the dark. Mike shifted his weight from one foot to another.

"No, but he can stay the night. *Acordato?*" Shane didn't like it, but when Alicia nodded her head, he really couldn't say no. He got blankets and a pillow for the kid. By the time they'd made a bed for him on the floor, Mike and Alicia had gone back to bed. Shane kicked the little dog off his legs then looked sideways at Alejandro. In the light of the fire, he could see tears glistening on the boy's cheeks.

"Are you okay?" Shane asked.

"He heard them coming and he sent me out the back. I hid up on the roof and watched as they ...." He shuddered.

"Yeah. I'm sorry. Your father seemed like a good man." The kid snorted despite his tears. "What?"

"I think good people will be the first to die now."

Shane sighed and refrained from agreeing with the kid. He didn't truly remember being that age, but he suspected he'd been a lot more naïve.

Alejandro didn't have that luxury and Shane dozed off mourning that on his behalf.

Team D Surveillance

Seattle Washington – Next Day

The rain stopped around midnight, replaced with fog that softened the edges of the buildings and hid the disc of the Needle in misty drapery. Headlights expanded into blurs as cars neared. The steady rhythm of his tennis shoes slapping damp pavement was broken by the counterpoint of four sets of nails running beside him.

Every time Geo had been here before, Seattle Center buzzed with activity. Now trailers graced the plaza below the Space Needle. Duke glanced up at him, asking him what they were doing next. More trailers lined Broad Street to the restaurant parking lot. Geo paused to retie a shoelace that didn't need to be re-tied. He used the break to scan the area. Lots of people came and went, some in Knights uniforms, others in civilian clothes. He saw no evidence of a detention for Special Forces soldiers.

Duke licked his ear as the first light of dawn blushed the eastern sky a misty pink.

"You're a great dog, fellow, but you need to keep your tongue to yourself. I don't French with other guys."

He rubbed the dog's floppy black ears, using it to continue to take note of the area. There were security cameras, which wasn't suspicious. Cameras recorded life before the Pulse. Geo and Duke continued around the block, only to find 2nd Avenue blocked by more trailers. He still hadn't seen any sign of mass incarceration. By the time he got back to Thomas Street, it seemed as if you could walk right into the area without fear of anything. Now the eastern sky blazed the neon mango shade of a tequila sunrise.

He'd decided to turn back to the improvised bus route he'd taken to get here when a Knight came striding in his direction.

"Can I help you?"

"Naw, I'm just jogging, man."

"We get guys like you coming around here."

"I'm going."

Geo and Duke ran directly away from the Knight. Fortunately, a bus-truck passed. He rode it for two blocks and then got off, ran two blocks over and caught another shuttle headed north. Well-trained and eager to please, Duke hung in there all the way back to the house – the perfect partner.

Allies

Santa Fe, New Mexico

Sleeping through the night wasn't happening for Shane. He cooked breakfast when Mike came into the kitchen.

"You okay?"

"I think I'm running a fever and I have a headache."

Shane put a hand on the side of Mike's neck.

"Yeah. You're warm. If you want to pull this off, you should probably take some aspirin and a cold shower. Are you absolutely sure you *want* to do this?"

"She'll forgive me."

"I'm more worried that she won't forgive *me*." Alejandro came to the open doorway from the living room. "We should probably stop talking if we don't want to be overheard."

"I'll go take care of that, go to that little arroyo down the road."

Mike headed out the door with his shaving kit.

"What are your plans?" Shane asked the boy.

"I don't know. I could go to the base and ask to join. They would take me, and I could get close enough to the man who got my father killed and take care of him."

Shane looked in his eyes and saw resolute rage. He believed Alejandro knew this man and would try to do just that.

"Yeah, live a lie until you get close enough and then murder a man. If you want to do it, go for it. Just know you won't feel better when you've done it and you might lose who you are while you live the lie. I've had experience with that myself."

Alejandro smoldered. Shane continued making breakfast.

"I'd have to kill other people before I got the chance, wouldn't I?"

"Probably. Maybe there are other ways you can honor your father's memory."

Alejandro watched Shane scramble eggs. Shane refrained from giving unsolicited advice.

"My dad had a good radio setup."

"We saw the tower. Too bad that's gone. If you're serious about a resistance, contact with the outside world is helpful."

"It's not gone. The radio is hidden under the house. Dad had it set up as if it was no longer there. They maybe cut the cable, but they didn't burn down the house, so I could repair it. But I don't have Dad's contacts, so I don't know what I would do with it."

Uly's face flashed through Shane's mind. He slid the pan off the heat and put a lid on it.

"Come outside with me for a second. I've got a suggestion for you, but I don't want Alicia to overhear it."

He took the kid into the alleyway.

"Mike's sick. You overheard that?" Alejandro nodded. "He's not going with us. Have you had the flu?"

"Yeah. We all did – I guess that doesn't matter now." Alejandro blinked back tears.

"It does matter, if you're willing to work with me."

The boy weighed him with light brown eyes before nodding.

"Yeah. I want to honor my father and maybe find my mother and sisters."

"Good man. Listen up."

Tripping the Light Fantastic

Emmaus, Kansas

The rug weighed at least 20 pounds, so Jazz labored up the stairs carrying it over her shoulder. Keeping up with housework without electricity required a lot of labor and Jill pulled longer hours at the medical center, so Jazz had offered to clean Shane's room while he and Mike were gone. Since Rob had declared vacuuming a power extravagance, she'd taken the rug to the back yard and beaten the dust out of it. Her hair curled damply with melting snow, trickling icy water down her neck as she topped the stairs.

Jacob startled as she strode into Shane's bedroom. He'd been in the act of sliding a white envelope into a burgundy leather Bible that inexplicably rested on top of Shane's highboy. Jazz had seen it before when she'd come to check on Mike, but it made no sense to her that Shane would possess a Bible since he seemed hostile to the entire subject.

"Didn't mean to startle you." She laid the rolled up rug next to the bed and flipped it open. Dark green and gold woven wool edged with a blue border, the rug looked striking against the mellow orange of the pine floor.

"It's fine. What are you up to, young lady?"

Jazz explained. The old man grinned.

"That's one way to show your affection. Vi knitted me a sweater."

"I can crochet, but my mother declared me hopeless with knitting."

"Just takes practice. It's like dancing. Two-step looks complicated, but once you've practiced a few times, it really isn't that hard. You danced with me at Keri's wedding, didn't you?"

"The reception, yeah. You danced with all the young ladies."

"Vi would have wanted me to."

"She liked to dance?"

"Oh, yeah! You?"

"Sure. I took a decade of ballet, jazz, tap, highland, modern."

"Any ballroom?"

"A little bit, but guys today don't want to dance."

"Pfah, that ain't true. Shane dances some."

"Like what."

"You know the foxtrot?"

"I know the steps, yeah."

He stepped out into the hall and gestured for her to follow him onto the wide landing

"There's no music." She giggled because she knew she was going to dance with a man old enough to be her great grandfather – who *had* been friends with her great grandfather. But dancing without music just seemed silly. She should have known better. Delaneys never wanted for music.

"Blue Moon, you saw me standing alone ...." Jacob's voice still rang clear and strong despite his age. Since he held out his arms, she met him, and they moved smoothly around the landing. She didn't worry about him leading her wrong. He had done this a million times. "...you knew just what I was there for ...." She closed her eyes for a moment, trying to imagine what it might feel like to be swung gently in the smooth steps of a foxtrot by Shane Delaney rather than his grandfather. " ...The only one my arms will ever hold." His voice wavered. She opened her eyes and saw tears in his blue depths. "The moon had turned to gold ...." She doubted he danced with her at this moment and a gasp of the import of this gesture escaped her lips. "...without a love of my own."

Jacob brought her to a safe landing and placed a grandfatherly kiss on her forehead.

"Thank you for indulging an old man, young lady."

"Well, thank you for the dance, kind sir. You are the best couples' partner I've ever had."

"We danced a lot in the days before TV. I should – got a few things to finish up in my room. You?"

"Barricade duty." She pulled up her sleeve to reveal the watch he'd given her a couple of weeks ago. He explained it was Vi's everyday watch and since cell phones no longer worked as timepieces, he thought she'd be timelier with a windup version. She'd wanted to say "no", but Jacob Delaney was a force of nature in his generosity. "I have about 10 minutes before I have to leave. I should take Glister out. I'm sorry dancing with me made you sad."

"It didn't. Remembering Vi fills me with almost as much joy as time with the Lord. I miss her – and I'll be with her soon enough. Thank you for helping me to remember her. You remind me of her."

"Really?"

"You don't look like her – well, you're about the same height, but that's really it. She had dark hair – Shane dark. Her eyes were a golden brown – like topaz."

"Reddish brown and green." Actually, her roots showed a lighter auburn since she hadn't rinsed it in weeks.

"I have eyes. Your resemblance is at the soul level. There's a toughness – a pluckiness – in you that was in her. If her house blew up, she'd grab a dustpan and broom to clean it up. She took care of her father's allotment without my help until just a few years before her death. She could ride better than I could – and rope. Used to win barrel races at the fair. Taught all of our kids to drive – and to dance. She could change a tire and sew a dress and castrate a bull and not make any of it look hard."

"I never asked. Were you high school sweethearts or ...?"

"No. She didn't like me in school. Most of us left school in the 8th grade back then. She stayed in. Her father had already lost one son to suicide, a daughter to pneumonia and his other son was an alcoholic. He doted on her and wanted her to be all she wanted to be. So while I was convincing my father to turn one of his fields into an airfield so I could be a pilot, she was learning all that school had to offer. We'd see each other at the town socials, and she liked the way I danced well enough, but I wasn't a believer and she wasn't going to waste her life on a temporary relationship with a dead man. You understand what I mean by that?"

"Unregenerate, sure."

"Like Shane." Jazz sighed. She knew her crush on Shane was horribly ill-advised and he had never encouraged it. "She'd have married Billy Logan if World War 2 hadn't intervened. We all went off to war, but I returned, and Billy didn't. She cried for a while, but one day she looked up in a Sunday School class and realized I'd been sitting across from her for six months and she complimented me for getting my head screwed on straight. I invited her to a dance and three months later we were married. Shane ain't got his head screwed on straight. You know that, right?"

"I do. I sometimes wish I could just ignore that, but I know I shouldn't, and I probably won't."

"Good. But if at some time, you look up and see he's changed his mind, I hope you'll forgive him for whatever blockheaded nonsense he's done in the interim. Remember that not everyone is born grownup. It takes some of us longer."

"I will remember that."

He nodded as if that settled the matter once and for all, which of course it didn't because she lived in the same house with her crush and it seemed like they just couldn't get away from one another. She had to practice discipline and discipline meant work even if it bore a lovely reward at the end.

"Well, you get on about your duties, young lady. I got important things to do."

"Thank you for a moment of relaxation and friendship. I'll see you at dinner tonight."

"Mmm. Get going before you're late."

She patted him on the shoulder and clapped for Glister, who came bounding, as excited to go outside as if he'd been cooped up for days instead of hours.

Outside the world swirled with white flakes like a child's snow globe set roughly upon a shelf. A crisp bite to the air teased her nose and kissed her lips. Winter had come.

Making the Hard Choices

Santa Fe, New Mexico

Mike appreciated Shane's willingness to go along with what made him uncomfortable. Alicia knew. He thought so anyway. Her attitude spoke volumes. She no longer seemed angry. She'd grown quiet. When she kissed him, her eyes conveyed concern. The wife of a soldier, she knew when to hold her tongue. Shane drove the airport truck and Mike and Alicia followed silently in her father's ancient pickup that gurgled and wheezed the whole way.

Uly had expected them and met them at the Skywagon, pleased to get the water in the tank and the fresh gasoline Shane had liberated from Mike's now-defunct Camaro. If he weren't sick, he'd spend his time waiting for Shane in trying to get the car going. Uly gave him a weighing look as Shane spoke with him privately on the other side of the plane.

"I don't like leaving you." Alicia had busied herself strapped down the cargo as Shane had instructed.

"I know, but it's the only way this works. I put us too far over the weight limit."

Her brown-eyed gaze bore into him.

"I love you."

"I know. I love you too. It's why I'm doing this."

She knew. He knew she knew, and she knew she had to pretend not to know. It remained the right thing to do.

Shane gestured for Mike to join them. His body ached and the headache pounded in the back of his head.

"I gotta go."

"Yes. Go say goodbye to Shane. Don't make this harder than it needs to be." She leaned in and kissed him on the cheek. "Go."

Shane's expression didn't give a lot away as Mike walked up to him and Uly.

"Uly is going to keep an eye on you and Alejandro will stick around and work on his father's radio. Stay low and get well and I'll be back as soon as the weather allows."

"I know you will. I'm starting to feel really shaky, so I should go. Don't tell her. I mean, unless she knows. I think she might. But don't tell her otherwise. Okay?"

"Jury's still out on that." Shane's usually lush voice grew hoarse. He'd never cry, but Mike knew he wanted to. "Go say goodbye to her."

"We already did. She told me to come say goodbye to you. That's why I think she knows."

"She's a soldier's wife. She knows. So, Alejandro will make sure you have water and food and finishing boarding up the back so you're secure. He'll check on you and so will Uly. And, I'll be back when I can." Shane's voice grew husky again. "If I can. I hate this."

"I know, so do I, but it's what has to happen. And, I gotta go before I pass out. Get her to safety and no Irish farewells."

Mike got into the old truck, wheeled around and left the airport as quickly as he could. In the rearview mirror, he saw Shane walking toward the plane. Would he tell Alicia not to watch him out of sight? Would he do the same? Mike blinked tears out of his eyes.

A few blocks from the house he started coughing violently. He pulled over to the side of the road and held onto the wheel while his body wracked with convulsive coughs until he had to open the door and spew his stomach contents onto the pavement. The headache roared now and every muscle in his body ached. He needed to get back to the house and lay down before he became too sick to walk.

"I love you, Alicia," he whispered. "Take care of Ric."

Perfect Memory

Emmaus, Kansas

Jacob set his Bible in his lap. He'd been up since before dawn, trying to get the coal furnace adjusted so that it would provide heat to the bedrooms, but had finally admitted they'd have to move mattresses to the living room because Rob had removed old ducting during his remodel of the heating system. He'd done it to install an air-conditioning system, clearly not foreseeing nuclear Armageddon and EMP pulses. Jacob couldn't really blame him. He'd thought gaining that extra space in the powder room was worthwhile too.

"Consider the lilies of the field ..." That passage in Mark 6 had a clear message. "Don't worry about your lives. God's got this." Did He? Jacob worried that current events might be beyond even God's great provision. Cold and snow descended, and he couldn't protect his family, let alone his friends and it all seemed so overwhelming. He believed Rob, Shane and Cai would improvise their way through this, but the future just seemed a mystery that defied solving like no other time in his life.

"Don't worry about your lives." Jacob leaned his head back on the lounger and just meditated on that. "Don't worry about your lives. You can't make them better. God can."

"God, I believe. Help my unbelief."

***

A swish of yellow fabric caught his eye and so easily he slid back 70 years into the City Hall ballroom. November 1946 and he'd been home from war just since spring. The band played "Until the End of Time" as Vi Greyeyes and her friend Bethany Shoenfeld talked behind their gloved hands by the punch bowl.

Jacob had been watching her in church ever since he got back. He didn't want to intrude upon her grief for Billy, but it seemed long enough for her to mourn. And she came to the social, so ....

She danced with three other fellas before he got up the courage to go over and get a cup of punch. Since she stood right by his left elbow, he screwed up his courage and asked her if she'd like a cup too.

"You'd think a man who'd been halfway across the world and fought in a war wouldn't be afraid of asking a woman as delicate as me to dance with him."

Her long dark lashes lowered to shade her eyes and then came back up so she could meet his gaze boldly.

"You have a point there," Jacob admitted. "Do you know how to foxtrot?"

"Of course, I know how to fox trot. Do you?"

"Give me this song to prove it to you."

The band shifted to "Sentimental Journey" and they moved out onto the floor. Vi moved like they'd been dancing together forever, and he soon stopped paying attention to what his feet were doing and just focused on her face. Her deep-brown hair, lashes and brows and slightly sun-kissed skin hinted at her Wyandot heritage. Her eyes were a light silvery grey. The yellow of her dress set them off perfectly, bringing out the slight blue hints. She'd taken the new-fangled fashion of piercing her ears and wore tiny seahorse dangles and a simple string of pearls. He liked her Frenchy perfume and her small earlobes and how she smiled while they danced. They danced four songs in a row before taking a break.

"It's been good to see you back," she told him as he lit her cigarette before lighting his own. He hated the taste of cigarettes and meant to quit, but it seemed like every social occasion demanded a cigarette. He wondered if she thought the same thing and that's why her delicate nose wrinkled as she took a drag.

"It's good to be back. I see things very differently since."

She nodded, her gaze boring right to his soul. Unlike a lot of girls her age, she still wore her dark hair long and she'd coiled it up in a braid on her head.

"I noticed. Must be six months since you weren't in church."

"Couldn't be more than that since I've only been back since May."

"I don't remember seeing you there before."

"I wasn't … much…just didn't hold my interest."

"But it does now. Why?"

"Places I've been, things I've seen. Could have died a few times. It makes a man think. I did some talking to God and He let me know that I needed to make things right with Him. I always figured I was good enough, but you know, I'm just a man and I sin. Only Jesus could fix that." She didn't interrupt him. "I got that part of the repentance out of the way in France, but now I'm just trying to understand how He wants me to live my life."

"How's that?"

"I don't know all of it yet. I'm flying a mail route and that gives me a lot of time to think. Chuck Lewdosky and I are working up a barnstorming act too. We're performing over in Hutchinson next month."

"I didn't know you were a pilot. Was that what you did in the war?"

"Naw, you had to be a college boy for that. But I flew a mail route before the war, so --. The future is in the sky."

"Do you think so? Seems kind of scary. A little unnatural."

"You've never been up?" She shook her head, smiling slightly. "Maybe you'd like to do that some time – you know, even tomorrow morning. We could catch the sunrise over the prairie."

"Oh – uh, yes. That sounds exciting. Scary. But, yes."

"I'll pick you up at your house at 5:00 am, then."

"It's a date." When she said it, two delicate spots of pink darkened her high cheekbones. The band shifted into "Strangers in the Night." She smiled larger. "I love this song! Do you want to --?"

They put out their barely smoked cigarettes and moved onto the dance floor and Jacob remembered swirling in a swish of yellow and drowning in her silver eyes.

***

Caught

Seattle, Washington

Geo pinned notes to the investigation board. If a secure holding facility for Special Forces existed in Seattle, it wasn't at Seattle Center. B&W seemed to be providing transportation and working on getting electricity to some sections of the city. There were food distribution centers and occasional work paying food. He doubted the evidence. He'd not been trained in investigation. Misinterpreting the evidence could easily lead him in the wrong direction.

He sighed, rubbing the back of his neck with both hands.

Duke whined at the front door. Geo slewed around just as someone knocked on the door. Duke wagged his tail, then he barked. Geo got up and headed toward the basement. There were two Knights standing at ease in the backyard. Even if he abandoned Duke to hide in the radio room, he suspected he wasn't getting away from this. That meant bluffing his way through this.

He untucked his t-shirt and slid his gun into the back of his jeans, grabbed the can of beans he'd been eating and opened the door, hoping he looked like a college student squatting at his aunt's house.

"Hi?" he said to the man in casual slacks and an oxford shirt standing on his porch.

"Petty Officer One George Tully?"

There were two more Knights standing behind the man, eliminating any hope of escape.

"Can I come in?"

Geo stepped back from the door, setting the beans down on the entry table. The Knights stayed outside.

"Liam Carson."

Carson, about 35, fit, medium height with blond hair shot with caramel streaks, bent to pet Duke.

"You got me on camera?"

"There's a few working around the Center – yeah. What got me here was this fella. He's chipped and we picked it up on a scan."

"There's still a database working?"

"B&W is EMP hardened, yes, although we were lucky to find this guy's chip ID and address."

"Can you find him a good home?"

"Good home? Looks like he has one."

"You're arresting me, right?"

"No. What gave you that impression?"

"Four Knights and the rumors I've heard of guys like me being detained."

"For a few days after we took control of the situation here in Seattle, we did detain a lot of soldiers and sailors. Most of them chose to be absorbed into the Knights. I'm here to make an offer to you to join us."

Geo stared at him, dumbfounded.

We Could Be Family

Emmaus, Kansas

Jos Osimowitz crossed the bridge at Wolf Creek Run, eyes burning with the need to sleep. He'd been up all night listening to Granmae coughing and he'd started out far too early this morning delivering food to people whose cars weren't working. He counted it luck that there was even food to sell to them. Alternatively, he worried about all those bags of corn and salt piling up in the warehouse. He had a definite trade deficit. He needed fuel, but farmers were the only ones producing it and they really didn't need his corn. What should he do about that? What could he do about it?

He pulled up before the neat frame house with the detached garage. A light shown in the kitchen window, so he grabbed the bags out of the back and knocked on the kitchen door, nearly falling off the step when it opened because he hadn't expected to see Max Albright there.

403

"Morning." Max looked comfortable – sweats, a mug of coffee in one hand. "Hey, groceries! Come on in."

Jos thumped snow off his shoes before he set the bags on the counter.

"Eggs and milk, crabapple jelly, a jar of citric acid, potatoes, salt, and some carrots."

"Great. Any butter?"

"No, but Alex Lufgren promised to have some after the weekend and Poppy's also working on cheese."

"Sounds great. What do I owe you and what is the medium of exchange?"

"Nevada welded a security bar for me, so this just about makes us even – after I bring the butter and cheese."

Max looked anywhere but at Jos and Jos still didn't know what to do about that. While he filled out a receipt, he opted for a change of topic.

"I didn't know you knew Kim and Nevada."

"My husband was Nevada's business partner. I needed to find somewhere to stay and she offered."

"I'm glad you found somewhere warm to live."

Nevada Randolph came into the kitchen, breaking the awkwardness.

"Oh, you are a life-saver!" She started looking in the bags. Everybody in the town called her the "bohemian" behind her back and she kind of deserved it. When she'd arrived in town her hair had been died pink. Now it was a more normal brown with blond tips and cut kind of spiky, though it was growing out. "Those freeze-dried meals Jacob Delaney gave us are okay, but they get old quick. Thank you."

"Thank you for the work you did. Folks are mostly telling me what they hope to get on the next truck. Any ideas? No guarantee at this point."

"Anything but corn and freeze-dried meals. Toothpaste, deodorant." Nevada's gaze wavered between Max and Jos, her hazel eyes trying to read their minds. "Something wrong?"

Max set down his coffee cup and leaned back against the counter, his fingers tight on the edging. Jos stared at the toe of his boot.

"You know he's the same age as Kim, right?" She handed one bag to her daughter as she entered the kitchen. Jos had always thought honey-blonde Kim was pretty, but like everyone these days she hadn't taken a shower in a while. She disappeared with the bag into the pantry.

"It's different," Max muttered.

"Is it?" She looked at Jos now. "If a cougar like me bedded him it would be wrong. Why is it different because you're gay?"

"I'm not," Jos retorted.

"No? Okay, but he is. He's also like 20 years older than you." She jerked her head toward Max, then looked right at him. "Why is it different because you're gay?"

"You don't understand." Max's jaws bunched. Jos's ears burned in the stocking cap. "Gay kids

405

don't have the opportunity to come out without anxiety and family drama, not in small-town Middle America and I don't want to see any kid suffer because he's outnumbered and expected to adhere to an outmoded social convention."

Jos knew he needed to go. The store wouldn't open itself and if he didn't do it, Granmae would get up and do it herself. But he also needed to deal with this now and get it over with.

"I don't know how you got the idea that I'm gay. I'm not. Never thought I'd have to argue that, but yeah."

Kim came out of the pantry and stood there with her mouth open, making Jos' ears burn hotter.

"I was getting mixed messages from you."

"Yeah, because you were creeping me out. My grandmother really appreciates your help and so do I, but when you say things like you did the other night – you made me uncomfortable."

"I did not intend to do that. It's just – most of us go way too long in the closet. Drew saved me from that and I just ...." He stared at the refrigeration door, struggling to formulate his thoughts.

"There's no hard feelings or anything. I just – quit bringing it up. If something changes, I'll let you know, but – kind of think I want to try girls first before – before. Okay?"

Max nodded. Kim closed her mouth. Nevada handed her another bag and pointed to the pantry.

"Thank you for bringing the groceries, Jos. I wish I had fuel we could give you."

"No, it's fine. I'm trading corn for fuel. Nehemiah says he'll trade anyway. So – gotta go. The store is supposed to be open in 15 minutes and it'll take 20 for me to drive there. Nice to see you, Kim. How's your wrist?"

"Still weak, but it's healed."

"Great. I'll see you – sometime." With no school, those times were much less frequent. There was no organized meeting time.

"Yeah." Kim knew that too. "Nice to see you too."

"If you know anyone else who wants welding work --."

"Of course." Jos liked Nevada. And truthfully, he liked Max. He just wished the man would keep his interest to himself.

Outside it snowed and he had to wipe the windshield off before setting off down the dark road toward town.

Loss of Waypoints

In the Air

The Sangre de Christo had a light dusting of snow as Shane maneuvered the plane around them. Alicia had field glasses to her eyes, scanning the desert below.

"I don't see a camp," she reported.

"Yeah. I didn't see one on our way in."

"What does that mean?"

"A wild guess that they're transporting prisoners somewhere else. Alamogordo maybe." A hollow formed in Shane's chest as another possibility came to mind, but he determined he wouldn't mention that to the woman whose husband he'd abandoned.

Wind buffeted the small plane as he turned her north. Alicia cast him a nervous glance.

"Just a little turbulence. You'll feel it more in a small plane than you do in a jet."

"I bet you like it."

"Small planes are definitely more fun than jets, not the least of which is that I own it and so I don't have someone else to answer to."

"Do you own this?"

"Guy abandoned it about a decade ago and my grandfather is owed storage fees. The owner lived in Florida, so if he survived the bombs, he's died in the heat by now, so – yeah, my grandfather owns it. I suspect it is part of my inheritance."

Alicia rubbed a hand over her belly and her eyes misted with sudden tears.

"Is he going to be okay?"

Shane stared at the clouds forming ahead.

"I don't know." He heaved a deep sigh. "I didn't want to leave him and --."

"Eric – Shane, stop! I know that you didn't want to, and I know he is the most stubborn *pendejo* in existence and there's nothing you could do to *make* him do anything. There's no need to convince me of that. I just wish you were there to guard his back."

"I had to fly the plane. Alejandro and Uly are going to watch out for him and I'll get back there as soon as I can."

Wind rattled the small plane again. Alicia gave a little shriek.

"Sorry. I'll try to warn you when those are coming. See the clouds ahead?" She nodded. It would be hard to miss that wall of black and purple cotton balls. "It's probably snowing ahead. There's nothing to worry about. I coated the wings with antifreeze before we took off and I have quite a lot of winter flying experience, but I don't want you to be scared. The fuel had me worried on the way down since it was made in my brother-in-law Alex's barn, but the water-finding paste says we're good. It's going to start getting cold in the cabin because we don't have a heater, so that's why I told you to dress in layers. Now, for the part you're not going to like."

Her eyes widened as Shane dropped the Skywagon to slip under the clouds.

"We're on visual flight rules, which means I have no way to see where we are if we're above the clouds. So, you're used to jet travel and it might freak you out as to how close we are to the ground, but you're going to have to trust me that we won't hit it."

Shane followed the dark line of a highway, fairly confident that he was following Highway 25 because of the mountains off his port wing. He plucked the map from his visor and handed it to her. He showed her the route.

"If I seem to be going off course, speak up because it's easy to lose your way when you can't see the roads. I70 ought to just leap out at you, however, so we can always follow that home."

"You're not inspiring my confidence." She giggled. She wasn't a nervous flyer like Mike, but it was her first GA experience.

"Been flying since I was 10."

Shane hoped he knew what he was doing as the ceiling behind them dipped, clouds curling ominously as if to close their line of retreat. Alicia stared out the window as if afraid she might miss the highway. Shane grinned. He liked engaged passengers. They didn't chatter as much.

"Sing out the towns as we pass them."

"Is that why we're using a road map?"

"Yep."

They'd been flying a few minutes and she'd already named off two towns when she pointed.

"What is that?"

A long train of people bent into the wind as they struggled along the highway, dragging wagons, pushing wheelbarrows, some even had horses, the family dog and men and women in harness, doing whatever it took to get themselves and their children away from winter. They hadn't outrun it, but they still moved forward.

"Refugees. Emmaus has been dealing with them for weeks."

"Santa Fe will turn them away."

Shane hoped she was right. A wide open town that hadn't put up fences, he wasn't sure how they would keep such a large crowd of people out, but if they didn't speak Spanish, it would be easy to identify them and either expel or kill them.

"Yeah. We had to. We can't afford to feed them."

"They'll die out there on the roads," Alicia whispered.

"And we all die if we try to feed them. It's horrible, but this is not an era for wimps."

"And you're a do-whatever-it-takes kind of guy."

She knew him. He glanced at his fuel gauge. He could go back to Santa Fe and figure out how to get fuel to get back home. He had enough fuel to do that. He continued on the northerly heading.

"Sucks."

"I know. Mike doesn't dwell on it, but you do."

"I'm not complaining. It's just a fact of life."

"I know what you mean."

She dashed a tear away.

"I'm sorry." Shane opened his mouth to tell her what he and Mike had decided.

"Eric, don't apologize for Mike's decisions. You had to fly the plane and limited choices make for complicated decisions. I'm scared for him. He was scared for me. And, you'll go back for him."

Watching the clouds ahead turned Shane's stomach. Even if he'd been flying alone, weather concerned him. He didn't really have an option for waiting it out and he kind of thought he needed one. He set the autopilot and pulled out his phone.

"What are you doing?" Alicia demanded.

"Don't worry. It's fine. I'm just going to make a phone call."

"How is that thing working without towers?"

"Not well today. Must be a heck of an electrical storm above us." Outside the plane, snow began drifting down. Shane had bars, but barely.

Lela Markham

"Where are you?" Rigby demanded.

"Northern New Mexico, almost to Colorado. Weather is looking crappy. Do I have any sort of option for set down where I can replenish fuel if it gets worse?"

"There's a safe house there with a runway in El Moro. Used to be a drug transfer site for the Medellin drug cartel. Can't guarantee anything, but there should be avgas."

Shane felt a tremor in the airframe.

"Turbulence," he warned Alicia, putting a hand on the yoke in case he needed to make a correction. The wind grabbed the plane and shook it like a plastic toy. Pepe growled from his carrier.

"I gotta go," Shane told Rigby.

"I need to tell you something when you get here. Come here before you go home."

"Yeah, maybe. Call – or whatever – Alex. Tell him there's a good chance I'm going to need to land on the road between his and Nehemiah's place. I need him to run his plow down between my two fields and I might need some light to land by."

"Call me before you need to land, and I'll make sure he has someone there who can light for you."

"It'll probably be text. I barely have reception now."

The turbulence tossed them, and they dropped about 200 feet in the space of a second. Shane dropped the phone to override the auto pilot as

Alicia screamed and Pepe howled. The plane settled, tremors quivering through the airframe.

"We are going to have a rough ride, Alicia. I'll try to keep it steady, but the fact is the plane needs to be able to wriggle a little. So, try to stay calm and please make use of your bag if you need to."

"I don't need the bag, not for that anyway."

"For what?"

"I might need to pee soon."

"That'll be awkward because unless I have to, I'm not going to set down."

"I know. Mike told me. I'm fine with it if I have to."

"That's good." Shane tried not to think of it as his anatomy remembered that one and only time they'd kissed.

"You really are a Midwesterner, aren't you?"

"I always was. I never lied about that."

"Did you really graduate from Embry with a degree in aeronautical engineering?"

"Yes. Living lies is easier if you don't tell that many, so I kept it simple. And, I'm sorry I had to lie at all. When I accepted the job, I didn't realize the collateral relationship damage."

"Mike's forgiven you, so I can. Just – I guess I can't ask you not to lie. I still don't know my husband's real name."

"You know mine." Shane's throat tightened. He'd said he'd tell her the truth when they got in the air, but now --. He stared out at the passing

415

scenery and decided the weather was a good excuse to not tell the truth yet.

Death Comes Stalking

Emmaus, Kansas

With the reduction in stock, Granmae had planned for shorter hours at the store, which meant Jos could lock the doors at 5 pm. The hours were posted on the door so nobody should be surprised that he'd closed up.

He toiled up the stairs to the apartment his grandmother kept above the store. He'd come up to check at Granmae in early afternoon. She'd fussed at him. What if someone wanted to buy something while he wasted his time on her? He'd refused to be intimidated and made her soup, even stayed to make her eat it. Her cough worried him, but it was the flu and Dr. Delaney couldn't do anything about that. It would run its course in about seven or eight days.

He paused at the top of the stairs to yawn. He'd locked the door earlier because Granmae always locked the door. They kept the key in the fire extinguisher box on the landing. It might not be the most secure burglar-prevention system possible,

417

but he was sure how many burglars would knock over an apartment above a grocery store.

The living room felt cold. He'd stocked the woodstove during his break, but he hadn't gotten the hang of optimal wood placement. The woodstove had been his grandfather's thing. He and Granmae hardly used it since his death. He wished he'd paid more attention. He'd master it in time.

He pulled out some bread and warmed the soup from earlier. Grandmae wouldn't want much to eat, so he figured a grilled cheese sandwich would tide him over to morning.

A sound from the main bedroom caused him to straighten from pulling a pan from the cabinet. That sounded like --. He pushed the door open. The remaining light from the sky bathed Granmae's room. She lay on the floor by the bathroom door, her pajamas soaked in sweat.

"Grandmae." He dropped beside her. She felt hot, her ashen face drawn, as if all the moisture had been sucked from it.

"Bobby, what are you doing here?"

"Granmae, it's Jos." Something was wrong with her. Her brother Bobby died before Jos was born. He reached for his cell phone to call 911, but of course, his fried cell phone resided in a drawer, a useless piece of plastic. The stupid 1970s phone on the kitchen wall didn't work either. He scooped her up and turned toward the door. She wasn't a fat woman, but she weighed as much as he did, so that it took every bit of his strength to carry her to the top of the stairs. He thought he'd drop her on the way down the stairs. His arms screamed as he lowered her into the passenger seat of Granmae's Taurus.

She started coughing until she nearly puked. One of the few things Granddad ever did that Granmae approved was when he'd expanded the garage to make room for the family car. He pulled the door open, hopped in the driver's seat and backed out. He cursed silently that he had to get out to close the door and then wheeled the car around to head for the health center. A block from the grocery, Mae grabbed her throat and gasped for air.

Hard Landing

In the Air

Outside the world looked like a snow globe. Shane looked at his outside gauges. It was colder than expected and despite the snow, humidity was low. A strong wind out of the Rockies pushed on their port wing. They'd left Santa Fe later than he'd wanted and they were going to be approaching Emmaus in the late afternoon. He'd have to land into the wind. He could only hope the sunset wouldn't be blinding him when they got there.

Ahead, something blue peeked out of the blowing snow. Shane dropped a little and asked Alicia to view it through the field glasses.

"It's tarps. Maybe a campsite. Nobody is moving though."

Shane took the glasses and dipped the wing to view the camp. Alicia braced herself on the roof. Nothing moved in the ramshackle wind-blown camp.

"Maybe that was the group we saw on the road?" Alicia offered.

"Maybe, days ago." Why wouldn't they take their shelters with them? The obvious answer bothered him.

Another crosswind jolted them sideways. Shane rode the wind, leaving the highway while maintaining it in view, slowly turning the plane into the wind so that they soon returned to their course.

"We're going to get pushed east soon and that's okay. The compass is working. We'll head due north to I70 and follow it to the town. We're going to land on a road between two farms."

"Wh-at? No!"

"There's no traffic. We'll be fine. And I've done it before. When I was in college, I brought a plane back for Ren Sullivan and got caught in a snowstorm like this. I did exactly the same thing."

"And your friend Alex plowed the road for you?"

"Yes. It's safer than trying for the airfield where there's a finite end of the runway and buildings on both sides. Even if I put her in the ditch, it is wheat fields, so we'll be fine."

"You're just saying that so I'm not scared, aren't you?"

Shane laughed. Alicia joined him, her laughter nervous.

"It was worth a try, but really, I do know what I'm doing."

The wind rattled the plane again and for a moment, as a downdraft drove them toward the prairie, Shane hoped he knew what he was doing.

"We're moving east to get away from this wind. Look at the map and familiarize yourself. That's Garden City down there, right? We're going to follow that road."

"What road?"

"Yeah, if I didn't know it was there, I don't know if I could see it. Nobody is plowing and probably not a lot of people are driving. It's amazing to see so much uniform white."

Referencing the GPS, they found I70 at Quinter and Shane turned into the wind. He judged his air speed and factored their fuel consumption. He could do this. He'd still have a margin for error. He hoped. He handed his phone to Alicia.

"Text Rigby and tell him I'll need Alex to light up the road about 4:45 pm."

He gave her the password for his phone. Below, ahead and above was an almost uniform grey-white. Shane could make out I70 only because it mostly stood above the surrounding landscape. Alicia pointed to a Walmart parking lot at Oakley. More blue tarps and campers. If there was anyone living down there, they soon wouldn't be because the temperature outside drop into sub-zero range.

"It just turns your heart to ice, doesn't it? Having to do what is needed to assure the survival of some? How come you keep getting those jobs?"

Shane resisted the temptation to look over his shoulder as his hair stood on end. He glanced at Alicia, but she silently watched the unfolding landscape. Sera couldn't possibly be in the back seat.

He hadn't had a flashback since leaving Emmaus and he'd thought maybe he'd finally turned the corner on that, but of course he'd indulged in wishful thinking. PTSD rarely just magically stopped, even if your grandfather talked to you a half-dozen times and you felt like maybe you were ready to talk to him. Alicia yawned, so normal a gesture that the odd electrical charge in Shane's skin dissipated.

"My feet are getting really cold," Alicia reported. "Wool socks notwithstanding."

"Yeah, mine too. We'll be on the ground soon."

It seemed to take forever to reach Emmaus, but the wide curve of I70 just east of town finally came into view. Shane's chest tightened as they passed over the town. So few lights seemed ominous.

"Tomorrow's Thanksgiving," he announced. "Doesn't look like we'll be playing flag football in the backyard."

"Is that a tradition?"

"Any year it doesn't snow."

At the western edge of town, Shane throttled back as he dropped to tree top level over Old 24.

"Those trees seem really close. What if we hit one?"

"We won't, but if we did, it would be a rough landing. We might not even walk away from it. But I know what I'm doing."

Far ahead a light flared. Shane saw Alex's house and the airfield pass below the plane and then Jericho Ridge pass to their starboard. He dropped even lower as he saw a series of fires lighting the ditches on either side of the farm road. He lifted the nose and set the Skywagon down on the gravel. The plane bounced, hopping forward. Feathering the flaps, he tried to slow the plane, which fishtailed and then slid along the road until they were way past the light of the guide fires. He spun the plane and headed back toward the airfield. Within 10 minutes, he helped Alicia out of the cockpit and was showing her where the hangar bathroom was, when Alex pulled up in his truck.

"Don't tell Alicia who was terrified most of the way, but that was a fun piece of flying. Who came up with the campfires?"

"Poppy and Pete worked on it."

"Those two are becoming quite a team."

"They'd better. They're getting married on Saturday." Shane blinked at him, confused. They were way too young to get married. Why was Alex so cavalier about it? "Shane, I need to talk to you."

"You should meet Alicia."

"No, Shane, really, I *need* to talk to you."

"Something wrong with Keri?"

"No. She's fine." Alex heaved a deep sigh. "Your dad let me know a few hours ago."

"What?" There'd been so many crises of late that Shane automatically felt his stomach twist now.

"It's Jacob. He – he died this afternoon." Alex continued talking, but his voice drifted off on the wind as the whole damn planet tilted off its axis and a dozen hijab-wearing women with AK47s appeared behind his brother-in-law and leveled their rifle barrels at him.

Brother's Keeper

Emmaus, Kansas – Next Morning

Cai pulled Marnie into his chest as she settled under the covers, letting in a waft of icy cold.

"Long night?" he asked as she snuggled into his chest. He'd been cold most of the night, waiting for her. It had to be about dawn.

"Mae Osimowitz spiked a 104 temperature and scared the beeswax out of her grandson."

"She going to be okay?"

"Probably. How's Shane?"

Cai snuggled his face into her neck, making her giggle. She'd been pretty physically affectionate with him since he'd stopped running away from her. His hand slid over her belly, which now rounded noticeably. In a couple of months, she would look like Mike's wife Alicia.

"You don't have to worry when I ask about him," Marnie assured him, turning so she could see his face. "He's your brother and we've moved beyond our past."

"I'm not worried. I see the way he looks at Jazz when he thinks nobody can see. When she says something funny, he gets this little twinkle in his eye." Cai sighed. "Or he did."

"How is he?"

Cai considered her question and tried to come up with exactly the right word.

"Dark. Broken." Marnie finished rolling over so that they were facing each other. "I finally left him up there because he was drinking and acting – I don't know – weird."

Marnie's smooth forehead creased.

"He had to know Jacob wouldn't live forever. It's an extremely unrealistic expectation from an extreme realist."

"Yeah. He's – there's something wrong with him." She waited for him to continue. "You know how he sometimes seems to look beyond you, like there's someone there?" She nodded, but not definitively. Maybe she didn't trigger him like some did. "He's acting like whatever he sees is all around him now." He couldn't read her expression in the low light. Was she thoughtful? "What are you thinking?"

"PTSD – post-traumatic stress syndrome. Soldiers come home with it."

"I know what it is. My father served in Vietnam. And one of the symptoms that the sufferer has been triggered is drinking. What do we do about it?"

"Nothing much without his cooperation. He feels continually vulnerable and unsafe, which leads to anger and irritability in someone who is already testy and closed off. He mistrusts us. And he would never show me this – have you seen evidence of depression?"

"I don't know. Mike hinted at something a few times. I thought he was saying I wasn't alone, but he drew some parallels between us, Shane and me."

"You seem to have gotten past that."

"Mostly. But I'm a lot different from Shane. What do we do to help him?"

"You asked that already and I told you – Shane isn't easy. He never was. You can't pressure him into talking. If anyone could have gotten him to talk, it was Jacob and that is probably why he's triggered now. For now, you need to be patient with him."

"That's it?"

"Normal activities, but that's not likely to happen these days. Just ... whatever he says, whatever he does ... you have to control your reactions. Don't treat him like he's sick." She rolled onto her back and rubbed her eyes. "God, it's freezing in here. I thought firing up that coal furnace was supposed to warm the house." He helped her cover up again. The basement was toasty and the living room tolerable, but the heat wasn't making it up the stairs now that the outside temperature had dropped. "In September, we would have been using those BS red flag laws to disarm him. But he's the town security chief now, so ....

Don't do things that startle him. You said he was still up at Beulah?"

"Ground's frozen, so he built a bonfire. We should be able to dig the grave today."

"Innovative."

"Dangerous when he's drinking."

"Yeah, but that's – you gotta let him grieve." She yawned, practically unhinging her jaw. "And you gotta let me sleep."

He kept the covers tucked about her as he rolled up to his elbow and kissed her on the mouth.

"I'm going to go up there. I gotta quit letting him push me away."

"Just remember what I said." She pulled the blankets around herself and curled into a ball. "I love you. I'll love you more if you can find us somewhere warm to sleep."

"I'll work on that." Cai pulled on his pants, hissing as the cold fabric enveloped his legs. He layered on a t-shirt and a flannel overshirt and slipped out of the room, sweeping aside the sheet he'd tacked up so they could have a modicum of privacy even with the door open. Shane's bedroom door was open, his bed empty. He could make out a vague shape in Keri's bed that would be Jazz. Jacob was laid out in his room and the dark shape sitting in the chair had to be Rob.

"Hey," Cai said as he came to the doorframe. He'd grown up not startling people like Rob. Jacob looked peaceful, like he was just taking a nap. Rob shifted and looked at him. He wore a jacket, gloves and a hat *inside* the house. "How you doing?"

"I'm okay. I think he knew. He had conversations with all of us in the last few days."

"Not Shane."

"They talked a lot the last few weeks. Shane probably feels like he should have been here, but.... Death always takes us by surprise."

"He left me a letter. I found it in my Bible last night."

"He left me one too, in this big binder that he's been working on for years. That's how I knew. I found it on my desk, and I went looking for him. He was just asleep in the recliner, only he wasn't."

"You read it yet?"

"No. I need time to grieve. You?"

"He told me I'll be a good dad and to take care of Shane."

"Is that where you're headed now?" Cai nodded. "Don't worry about me. Your mom's going to join me soon. We're going to get him ready for burial."

"I'm going to head out then."

"Good luck."

Getting up the hill to the cemetery proved difficult, requiring shifting into low-gear and gunning the engine. Shane obviously heard him coming. Bundled up in layers of dark clothes, Shane almost disappeared into the grey morning. Raking the glowing coals, he resembled some sort of

Greek myth – Hephaestus – dark and fiery – dangerous.

"Have a nice sleep?" Shane asked. He didn't sound like someone who'd been drinking all night.

"Have a nice drunk?" Cai shot back. The bottle of bourbon disrespectfully set atop Vi's headstone had nearly been full when Cai left last night. Shane had always had a capacity that amazed the guys at school. Cai got drunk and stupid too quickly and easily. Shane didn't. But he also knew when to stop in a way that Cai did not. That the bottle was nearly empty did not bode well.

"He wouldn't have objected."

"No. He knew you really well and he trusted you. He apparently trusted me too because he told me to watch after you."

"I don't need you to watch after me, Cai. You want a drink?"

"No." Cai involuntarily shuddered as Shane took a swallow and then a second one. "Maybe you shouldn't be doing that while playing with fire."

"Fuck off! I don't need you to look after me!"

"I'm here to dig a grave."

Cai glanced over his shoulder as snow crunched under a boot. Alex stood there in his tan Carhart's, a shovel and a pick across his shoulders.

"How you doing?" he asked neither of them in particular.

"Should be soft enough to dig." Shane probed the ground with a piece of rebar. "Yeah. It's ready."

He grabbed a coal shovel and began scooping up embers into a metal garbage barrel. Alex and Cai worked on organizing the embers for easier scooping. While they worked, Jason Breen walked up the road and stood watching them. Shane straightened from his work and blinked at him.

"You know who I am, right?" Jason asked.

"Yeah. I'm buzzed. Not out of my mind."

"You threatened me with a shovel last night. I assume you're also packing."

"Nope. Left it in the car. Never carry while drinking. Stu Mackler's first rule."

"So you aren't out of your mind, good. This is the only one you're getting so use it well." Jason set a bottle of liquor beside the one Shane was working on. "You sure you wouldn't rather have some cannabis?"

Shane shook his head. Jason shrugged and started to turn away. Cai strode after his father-in-law.

"Yes?" Jason asked.

"He's kind of listening to you. Why don't you help us talk him off the ledge?"

Jason's craggy face pulled with amusement.

"He's grieving. He's not coming off that ledge until he's good and ready. And all your efforts to make it happen sooner or to keep him from taking the edge off when he's in pain are just going to backfire on you."

"He's going to hurt himself."

"Yes, but do you know why?" Cai didn't know what he wanted to share with Jason. "I've seen this before with him, the day the USDA tried to kill him. This is about more than Jacob and, frankly, I don't think you have a clue how to help him, So if you don't want to have to dig a second grave in the week, I suggest you stay off his back, because you don't want him mistaking you for whatever demons he's seeing right now."

Jason headed back down the road. Alex cracked the earth with the pick and Shane followed with the shovel to toss the soil up on a tarp. As Alex moved along the perimeter, Cai started digging too. Their breath fogged the air as the sun rose above the trees, turning the silver and white world gold and purple. Alex spread a second tarp and began digging on the other side of the grave.

Something about digging a grave felt cathartic. Cai and Alex both stopped occasionally to wipe tears. Cai tried to imagine not seeing Jacob every day as he had for most of his life, not being able to call him on the phone and ask for advice or hear his rich baritone bouncing off the church walls. More tears flowed.

Shane didn't cry. He didn't look like he'd ever cried. His eyes looked sunken and his mouth set in a grim line. No tears allowed. He concentrated on digging, cocooned in his thoughts, mostly ignoring Cai and Alex until Alex huffed as the pick turned in his hands. He stood waist deep in the hole they'd just dug.

"Ground's getting cold again. Now what?" Cai looked at Shane to explain his plan. People must have done this in the old days. Cai gained new respect for grave diggers.

"That's why I saved the coals." Shane held out a hand to help Alex climb out of the grave. Both he and Alex wore leather gloves, so they grabbed the barrel to either side and dumped the coals back into the hole. Shane wiped snot off his upper lip with the back of his hand. "Go warm up, guys. I'll stay."

"It's cold out here, man." Alex set his tools behind a headstone. "You should come eat something at my house and take a nap."

Shane poured another drink while Alex spoke.

"Remember the last time we were all together like this?" His green eyes glittered with a taste of madness. "Do you remember, Cai?"

Cai nodded. They'd been at Maggie's bar because Shane rented a room from her. They'd started drinking and Cai's memory remained fuzzy after that, but he knew the basics. Somehow, Alex and Shane left him alone with Marnie's little sister and he'd ended up in Shane's bed with her.

"I'll always regret that night."

"It was the night you killed Marie, surely as I did by driving her to Denver. You ever look in your wife's face and feel like a fraud?"

"Shane, don't!" Alex paused in the act of tossing an armload of wood into the hole. "A lot went wrong that night and bringing stuff up a half-decade later isn't right."

"It's not later." Shane's voice rasped like sandpaper and his gaze shifted from headstone to headstone.

"Wh-at?"

He's stuck in Miristan and if you're reading this, I ran out of time to unstick him. I need you to look out for him now that I'm gone.

"It's okay, Alex. He's right. Marie's still dead. And the answer to your question is – I used to feel like a fraud, but Marnie cured me of that. And I get that you're grieving and that looks different for everyone. No surprise you're lashing out. I wondered what happened to that temper."

"What else is going on with you?" Like most Deaf, even those whose ears worked just fine, Alex read body language and expressions. Surely, he saw Shane reacting to stimuli that wasn't there. Shane chucked wood into the hole in lieu of answering. "I have to get back. I'll be back – what – around sundown?" Shane nodded. "Cai, can you give me a ride to the bottom of the hill?"

When Cai hesitated, Alex jerked his head subtly toward the truck. They started walking down the hill.

"You can't force yourself on him. He needs company, not control."

"He's scaring me."

"Yeah, but he's always scary and one thing about grief is it takes time. I wanted to be alone when I did it and Shane is even more so."

"I don't like leaving him alone."

"He won't be." Alex nodded down the hill where Jill parked a City truck and started the long climb up the slippery hill. "It's Thanksgiving and we're all meeting at your house in a few hours. I know it's not the usual way you roll, but he needs to grieve his own way. Let's go."

Cai sighed and moved to unlock the doors. He imagined Jacob saying, "I told you to look out for him, not annoy the piss out of him."

And maybe he did need to approach his brother with a softer hand. Shane wasn't just grieving Jacob after all. If Jacob was right, Shane couldn't move beyond all the murders he committed. Cai didn't know how you dealt with that, but he knew members of his family did. He stopped to speak with Jill on the way down.

"Who's watching the turkey?"

"Turkeys are easy," Alex and Jill said at the same time, then laughed together. "Your dad's there. How's he doing?" Jill inclined her head up the hill.

"Crabby."

"Some people experience grief as anger. I'll go see if I can quell some of his fire. What's going on with – the grave?"

They explained they were halfway through and waiting for the ground to thaw some more.

"Dinner at 3 then will work for you. I know it's hard, but Jacob would love the idea of being buried on Thanksgiving."

"He's getting an upgrade." Alex's voice rasped hoarsely with suppressed tears. "I gotta get back to the farm." Cai nodded and put the car in gear again. Life would move on no matter the circumstances and death didn't take holidays.

Regrets Old & New

Shane had doffed his coat as the day warmed and gone for a run looking for Marie's grave. He'd not been before, but death surrounded him today, so he might as well embrace it. Jill had brought him breakfast, but he had yet to eat the biscuit and bacon. He'd never felt less like eating in his life. So far the booze kept him from sliding over the abyss into the depression that had dragged him down into blackness after his return from Miristan. It lingered just beyond his fingertips, as palpable as the cold air. It wouldn't take much to tip him back into it.

The Callahans didn't have their own section of the graveyard dating back five generations like the Delaneys did. The long-time manager of the salt mine, Maggie's father came to town when Maggie was little. He'd died of a heart attack when Maggie was in junior high school. Jason had been in her English class and he'd been kind. That had produced three children. Josh had gone to jail because of Shane's entanglement with the feds and

Marie died because of his negligence. Shane sought the niche where Marie's ashes were interred along with dozens of others, including her grandfather. Maggie's mother still lived in town.

"You left her like you left me." Mike sat atop a gravestone, dressed like he was still in Santa Fe. Shane remembered a television show where ghosts were stuck in whatever they died in. That had to be uncomfortable for nude sleepers. Shane knew Mike wasn't there, so he turned his back on the specter of his imagination, though the hair on the back of his neck lifted.

"You just drove her to Denver and abandoned her on the sidewalk."

He contemplated several speeches he'd give Marie if she could hear him, but they all seemed like excuses, so he left them unspoken. Jazz found him standing there staring at the niche. She approached with a simple "hello" and just stood beside him. Time passed in silence. Shane liked that Jazz could be quiet for a long time. Liking her held dangers and danger attracted him like a moth to the flame.

"Why are you here?" Shane looked down at her, dressed in a blue ski coat and a scarlet woolen cap.

"I brought you hot coffee. Figured it might balance the booze."

"Who says I want to balance the booze? Booze might be keeping some shit at bay."

She nodded.

"Maybe the people who love you could keep that bad stuff at bay better."

"And maybe you-all aren't safe anywhere near me."

Her gaze dwelled on Marie's name. Niches weren't big enough for epitaphs. Hers displayed just her name, birthdate and death date.

"This isn't about Jacob, is it?"

The old man leaned against a headstone near Mike as if eager to hear what Shane would say.

"Go away, Jazz. I can't do this."

"Do what?"

"*This*. Normal life. Grieving with a buddy. I can't. And, you know that and yet you keep showing up. Go away, Jazz."

"Yeah." She grinned, not put off in the least by his prickles. "I'll do that, but I won't stay away. You know that, right?" Annoyance flared, but Shane controlled it. "None of us who care about you are going to stay away." She handed him the thermos. "And if you decide to Irish that, I won't tell."

"Yeah? How un-Baptist of you."

She laughed.

"Jesus turned water into wine, Shane, and it was *good* wine. But then, you know that. I'll leave you alone to try and blow out your liver and kill a few brain cells. Had to improvise on Thanksgiving this year. Hope you'll come down to give it a taste."

She strode off along a path. Shane looked at the sky. It had to be around noon. He headed back to

Jacob's grave. He had a fire to tend and a bottle of bourbon to drain. Jacob and Mike followed him. Vi stood beside the bonfire. The hijab-clad woman sat atop Vi's headstone. Marie stood just the other side of the grave, forever a teenager with long dark hair and big sad eyes. Shane drained the one bottle and cracked the seal on the second one.

Empty Seats

They all tried to ignore the empty chairs. Jill invited Jazz's brother, Michael, before Jacob died and with the inclusion of Alicia in the family Rob decided they should go ahead with Thanksgiving dinner. Alex's entire household were invited too, so Jill added both leaves to the huge Delaney dining table that once seated Jacob's father's nine siblings.

"It was Pa's favorite holiday," Rob said. "He'd want us to go forward with it."

When Vi died only a few days before Christmas two years ago, Jacob said the same thing then. He and Vi grew up in a different era – one where death lingered close to life. You mourned, but life went on. Jill struggled with the reality of that when Vi died, but now she kind of understood it as Rob echoed his father's words. If they didn't do Thanksgiving this year, it would forever change a holiday Jacob had loved. It would become a day of mourning instead of a celebration of life.

As Jacob did the Christmas Vi died, Jill had set Jacob's place this year. That left Shane's seat empty. He knew what time they were eating. The freezer with the turkeys in it had not been opened and with judicious use of the generator, they'd stayed frozen until Jazz pulled them out just a few hours before Jacob's death. Keri brought sweet potatoes and Alice pulled together a stuffing/dressing. Marnie managed angel salad with fruit cocktail and Alex's whipped cream. Jill pulled the rolls out of the oven of the cook stove. She'd made bread twice in the oven with differing results –the first time undercooked and then overcooked when she'd put it back in to finish, the second time just plain overcooked. The rolls looked okay this time. She checked internal temperature with a thermometer. She guessed they were okay.

Jazz's bicep rippled as she lifted the lid on the turkey. She contributed potatoes provided by Michael from their parents' pantry. Alex brought pies. As a young single "father" he'd been forced to learn to cook and he'd gotten good at it.

"Where's Shane?" he murmured.

"Being Shane," Marnie shot back.

"Grieving," Jazz said simultaneously.

"He's taking Jacob's death hard," Cai said a moment later.

"Don't make excuses for him," Marnie hissed, taking her bowl out of the fridge.

Cai looked confused but went back to pumping water for a pitcher.

"Pregnancy does that to women." Jill kept her voice low.

"I heard that," Marnie called from the dining room. She came back, sans bowl, to the opening. "I'm sick of Shane sucking up all the oxygen in the room. We all miss Jacob and we're all grieving. He's not the only one. He needs to stop acting like a jerk."

"We all grieve differently." Rob came up beside her in the doorway. "I'm worried about him, but Pa would say we shouldn't let Shane's inability to cope ruin Thanksgiving, so – we bury Pa tonight and then we can deal with Shane. Let's eat."

Alicia helped with setting the table and provided canned green beans and mushrooms for a casserole. She seemed to be self-contained and calm, but Jill had seen many a soldier's wife when her husband was reported MIA. The sadness just below the surface resonated from her. Mike hadn't come back with them and Alicia seemed unwilling to touch it.

When they'd all sat down, Rob took Jill and Keri's hands. Keri took Alex's hand, who took Poppy's hand and Jill took Cai's hand, who took Marnie's, and soon they were all linked.

"I once asked Pa why he loved Thanksgiving so much, and he said 'When you get a chance to praise God for all the blessings He gives you, you should do it no matter what day it is – but ain't it grand they made a holiday so people don't think you're crazy?' I know it probably seems a little strange to pause in the middle of mourning to thank God for stuff, but – we've all lived through some horrible times and we're still here, so even if Pa has passed – well, that man knew where he was going, and I believe he's already there. We've had a ritual in this family – goes back a long way – I'm not sure how long, really. We pause before we eat to each say one thing that we're grateful for." Rob looked sad. Jill squeezed his hand and he squeezed back. "I'm grateful Pa has passed. This may be the last real feast we have for months. Half this town is going to starve, and I can't do anything about it. I wouldn't want Pa to live through that. It was a kindness that he's gone to be with the Lord without having to suffer."

He squeezed Keri's hand. She'd released Alex's to wipe tears from her cheeks.

"I'm grateful I live on a farm where there's always a lot of hard work to do, but there's also a steady supply of food. In a survival situation, that means everything."

"Dang, you seriously stole my answer." Alex laughed. "I'm grateful Shane was here when this crisis got underway. Glad to have my best friend back, but also glad to have someone so – so, badassed."

Poppy was next and she released Alex's and Pete's hands to say, through Alex, she was grateful for the Ramirez family joining theirs. Alex and Keri both blushed. Jill wondered what that was about. Pete said he was grateful to be somewhere safe when the bombs went off, studiously not looking at

Poppy as he said it. They continued around. Mark was grateful Lisa was over the flu. Alice was glad her husband and son had recovered. Lisa giggled. Now it was Alicia's turn.

"I'm grateful." She wiped tears away. "I am. I'm grateful Shane brought me here. I feel safe here and I needed to be somewhere safe when the baby's born. I'm grateful for my husband --." She wiped her face again. "Sorry. I didn't plan this."

Michael expressed gratitude his parents had stocked the pantry before they left. He didn't cry, but he blinked hard a few times. Then it was Jazz's turn.

"I'm grateful Jacob invited me to stay here. I'm grateful that you've adopted me."

"That was Pa," Rob said with a smile. "We're glad to have you here."

"We are," Jill assured her. She looked at Marnie.

"I'm grateful my brother is no longer in jail."

Cai nodded.

"I'm grateful for the new life we're bringing into the world." Marnie blinked as if surprised. Cai smiled at her and she smiled back. "It just took me a little time to get over what happened in Hutchinson."

"Well, I'm grateful that our family is growing," Jill said. "This house was meant to be full and we're working on it. That feels right."

"Let's eat." Rob grabbed a platter of turkey and served a bit of food to himself before passing it to Keri. Alex already helped himself to sweet potatoes and passed it to Poppy. Alex remembered aloud the first time he met Jacob – a funny story about chasing a plane to the airfield and meeting Jacob and Shane. Jacob had taken Alex back to his parents and he and Shane had become fast friends.

Jazz told a funny story about the days in the old aircraft factory during the first rain after the bombs.

"We didn't know each other, really, but you spend days in the dark with strangers and you emerge friends. He felt like – like he could be my grandfather."

"He loved you like a granddaughter," Cai announced. "He – uh, twinkled when you were around." He blushed.

Jazz stopped passing food to blow her nose.

"You know, Grandpa didn't have any other granddaughters." Keri smiled at her friend. "I was it. Aunt Ada has boys. So does Inez. Being the only gave me some lovely privileges. There was no way I could live up to that. So I'm glad he got a second granddaughter. You're a sister from another mother."

"Well, I never had a sister, so that does feel right."

The front door banged open and Glister gave a single bark. Shane momentarily stared at them before closing the door.

"Grave's ready." He didn't sound drunk, but Jill had seen that glassy-eyed look on Rob more than a few times. "Sounds like you were having a wake without me."

Rob accepted gravy from Keri.

"You can join us. Pa would love that we are all together here today."

Shane laughed, but it wasn't funny.

"Yeah, we're all together. You have no idea what that means to me. My bed been given away?"

"We offered. She wouldn't take it."

"It's warmer in the basement." Alicia's smooth forehead creased with worry. "He wouldn't want you to go off the deep end."

Jill didn't know what that meant. Jacob wouldn't want that, but how would Alicia know since she had never met Jacob?

"He had the flu." Shane stared at Alicia with anguish in his eyes. "There was no way I could talk him into getting on the plane and he knew you wouldn't leave if you knew, so he made me lie and leave him there to die."

Instead of going up the stairs, he turned and slammed out the front door again. Alex shot out of his chair and followed him out the door. Alicia heaved an enormous sigh and put a hand on her belly.

"And, they don't think I knew that?" She spoke to no one in particular.

"Men always think they need to protect us." Jill felt ancient enough to make that evaluation. "Should we do something about that?"

Rob set down his fork and caught up her hand.

"We all grieve differently, and we knew he'd have a hard time. He was already having a hard time." He blew out his cheeks. "We can only pray. Pa foresaw this and that was his advice."

Jill tried to spoon up some green bean casserole, but she started to cry.

"And he's still sucking up all the oxygen in the room." Marnie spoke to Cai, who stared at the door Alex had gone through.

"I don't know what to tell you, Marn. He'll get through it."

"And, if he doesn't?"

Jazz and Michael held hands, heads bowed, lips moving. They were the only ones who seemed to know the right treatment for what ailed Shane. Alex came back inside.

"I took his keys away from him." He hung them up on the hook behind the door. "He'll come home when he gets cold."

"And we might leave a plate for him," Rob said. "Sit down. Let's eat this great meal and be grateful that we grieve reasonably."

"Is there anything we can do to help?" Mark asked Alex.

"No. He's just always been – I don't have a word for it in English." Alex made a flashy sign that probably only Poppy knew the meaning of and couldn't share.

"Brilliant and passionate." Alicia might call Shane by another name, but she clearly knew him well.

The meal continued and soon they were drinking coffee with pie while Lisa used Glister as a Stratolounger. The yellow Lab seemed ecstatic. The little schnauzer growled from his carrier in the corner.

When they cleared the table, Jazz and Michael offered to wash and Alicia pulled Jill into the mudroom to draw the rinse water.

"You should know – Ric lost someone he loved in Miristan and – he seemed okay after that, but then when he got back to the States...." She considered her thoughts a moment. "He tried to commit suicide." Jill's heart began to race as the bottom fell out of her stomach. "Mike was there and stopped him, but – the reason he came home was because he knew he needed to rest. He didn't need more grief and -- and, losing Jacob and maybe Mike – that's not good."

Tears poured down her dusky cheeks. Instinctually, Jill hugged this woman she'd met scarcely 24 hours before and they wept together.

A Time to Choose

Shane leaned over the bonfire as Rob came up on him. He blinked into the darkness like he expected wraiths to appear any moment. Maybe he had already been visited by wraiths. Had those dreams been dreams or visitations?

Rob removed his baseball cap as he approached.

"Who's with Grandpa?" Shane turned a log over.

"Ed Greyeyes showed up. I figured I'd give him and his boys some time."

Shane cranked off the cup on the thermos and poured himself three-quarters of a cup. He topped it off with bourbon.

"The Rez and some Army guys stormed the Wyandot Lake facility day before yesterday. They lost one Army guy and John Swaim broke his hand somehow, but they got all the supplies that were left. There was just one guy guarding, so that was quite a bit." Shane muttered swear words under his breath. "So, Ed was headed this way with the Army guys because Cai made a deal with them and then he learned about Pa's passing. He wanted to send Uncle Israel off with an Indian flair. I'm never comfortable with that."

"Why do we have to bring God into this fucking mess?"

"When was the last time you slept?"

"Through the night? Never. Your point?"

"You're not a mystery to me. I haven't had a good night's sleep since this whole mess started. Pa understood that you never really leave the suck behind. You get better, but there's always something going to happen that'll trigger it. Yours was already close to the surface and Pa's death has triggered it."

Shane swallowed the hot coffee, wincing from the pain.

"Did you get a letter from him too?"

Rob frowned at him, then shrugged.

"Hell, I got a whole binder." Shane frowned with confusion. "I'll tell you about it later. That's a nice bottle of booze – not the one that's been kicking around in your closet the last few weeks."

How Rob knew about the contents of his closet might have mattered any other day.

"Jason."

"Oh, that man! I will never see what Pa saw in him."

Shane poured more bourbon into the cup and moved to put the cap on. Rob's gaze flickered.

"You want some?"

Rob snorted, shook his head.

"Every day, all day, especially on days like today."

"Toast Grandpa with me."

Shane held the cup out toward him. The desire for oblivion roaring through him, Rob sighed and took it, staring deep into the amber depths. This was the fastest way he knew to not feeling.

"He was the best person I ever knew." Shane nodded agreement. "Always up for a challenge and wise – oh, so wise."

"Passionate and consistent." Shane gestured with the bottle.

"Matter-of-fact and to the point, but never bossy. I wish I'd learned that trick from him."

"There's a lot of stuff I wish I'd learned from him." Something dark and scary moved behind Shane's eyes as his gaze flickered toward a gravestone to Rob's left. He looked. Shadows – moving, swirling, taking shape. He'd seen the photo. He expected an Indian woman in a gingham dress, wielding a long buck knife. He blinked at the Vietnamese woman in an ao dai of dark blue over light grey. Her long black hair moved in a breeze he couldn't feel, and she carried an SKS in her hands. "You see her too, don't you?" Shane asked.

Rob turned his gaze back to his son and raised the cup in toast.

"We became Death and there's a price for that. Here's to Pa understanding that for the both of us."

Shane wiped tears away and raised the bottle to his lips, the expression in his eyes daring Rob to choose.

The End

###

A Taste of "Winter's Reckoning"

Dell Conopher squatted in front of the coal stove, working the bellows, watching the glow slowly build. His hands ached with the cold and his view out the side window tightened his stomach.

Snow had drifted up against the barn door overnight and he had a bit of shoveling to do before he could get in to collect the eggs and milk the goats. Winter had come early, and most days flakes fell from the sky. When the wind picked up that snow piled up in inconvenient places. Without mechanical devices to clear the snow away, it meant time taken from vital chores just to access vital chores. He closed the stove and headed upstairs, wondering where Abigail had gotten herself to. When he'd woke up at the first blush of light and found her not in bed, he'd expected to find her making breakfast, but the kitchen had been cold and empty, no food pulled out on the counter. He'd concentrated on building up the fire before going to look for her.

When he reached the top of the stairs, he paused to listen. Abigail's low voice filtered out from Kix's room. Dell pushed open the half-closed door to see Abigail checking their oldest boy's temperature.

"I thought he'd gotten over the flu. I wouldn't have had him working this week if he were still sick."

She looked over her shoulder at him. A small woman with a braid that fell almost to her knees, she still looked nice in jeans after five children.

"Can you close the blinds?" She pointed to the window. "He's complaining of a headache and he's running a fever."

Dell stepped over to the window, meaning to pull down the blinds, but then staring down the front driveway as 20 people came struggling through the snow toward his house.

"Abby, go get a gun and get the kids up and armed. We've got company."

Dell grabbed his AR15 from the hook above the coatrack and stepped out on to the porch. He heard the window above his head open. Kix might be sick, but the kid knew the stakes. A mob had stripped the church's refugee center of every scrape of food a week ago and beat Brad Snow when he and some of the refugees tried to resist.

"What can I do for you?" Mace Kettridge led the vanguard, but others struggled along behind. Dell figured Mace was the instigator of this train of trouble headed his way.

"We've come for your stores."

Dell's rifle had been across his back, but now he brought it forward. People recoiled.

"I don't want to shoot my neighbors, but I've got nothing for you. I've got seven mouths to feed and just enough calories to make it to spring."

"And we're already out of food, so you need to share."

"Get off my land." Dell thumbed off the safety. "You and I have known each other a long time and I don't want to kill anyone, but I'm not given up my kids' food, so get going."

Mace leveled his own rifle at Dell. A shot rang out, a round splatted the snow beside Mace's foot. Dell heard Abigail chamber the next round in her Remington.

"You lower that gun, Mace, or the next one goes through your head." Abigail sounded certain of her aim. She *was* a better shot than Dell.

Dell heard two more windows open above the porch. That had to be Kix and Geneva, his oldest daughter. He'd told them after the raid at the church that they needed to be ready to defend the property and the all-important food stores.

"You can't keep food from starving people," someone shouted. Before Dell could say anything in response, a bullet tore through the siding beside where Dell stood. He dropped behind the porch wall and sent a round in Mace's direction. He heard more weapons fire from above his head and several rounds punctured the siding he was hiding behind.

His father's wisdom in lining the inside of the porch with wood dawned on him as he ducked for safety.

Other Lela Markham Titles

Other Great
Breakwater Harbor Books

Meet Lela Markham

Hi. I was raised in a house made of books in Alaska and told tales from the time I could talk. A teacher eventually made me write one of them down. I hated the exercise, but it was the spark that ignited a fire that has never gone out.

My daring husband, two fearless offspring and I live the adventure of a lifetime here on the Last Frontier where the midnight sun encourages wandering the wilderness and the long dark winters favor reading, writing and staring at the northern lights ... hence the moniker Aurorawatcher.

It's all about the aurora watching!

www.ingramcontent.com/pod-product-compliance
Lightning Source LLC
Chambersburg PA
CBHW031942260626
47157CB00017B/2024